I0833134

SPLINTERED VIGIL

THE NEW PROTECTORATE FRACTURE:
BOOK ONE

ABIGAIL KELLY

AUTHOR'S NOTE

Splintered Vigil is a novel set within the wider *New Protectorate Series* and can be enjoyed without reading the other books in the series, but it's best read as a companion to *Grim's Delight.* A full character directory can be found at abigailkkelly.com. Content warnings can also be found there, as well as in the backmatter of this book, alongside a glossary.

~Abigail

FULL SERIES LIST

The New Protectorate:

Glow - novella

Astray - novella

Weathering - novella

Consort's Glory - novel

Empire - novella

Courtship's Conquest - novel

Strike - novella

Vital - novella

Burden's Bonds - novel

Kohl - holiday novella

Faraway - novella

Sanguine - novella

Devotion's Covenant - novel

Valor's Flight - novel

Burden's Moon - short story collection

Captive's Sentinel - novel

The New Protectorate Syndicate:

Grim's Delight - novel

Grim Games - novel

The New Protectorate Fracture:

Splintered Vigil - novel

The United Territories and Allies

ESTABLISHED 1917

The United Territories and Allies
Current borders (2044) established
in the 1917 Peace Charter.

Member territories share a common currency and many laws, but maintain individual sovereignty. Each territory holds representation in the UTA Congress and Court, found in the United Neutral Zone.

CHAPTER
ONE

CONFIDENTIAL

18 January 2041

An assessment on the psychological state and recommendations for the members of Fracture from Dr. M. Starsbury, M.D. submitted by request to the Sovereign's Office:

On 2 June 2040, I was given the assignment to assess the mental and emotional wellbeing of the members of the special Patrol unit known as Fracture by General Valen Yadav. These members were Vesta Kincaid, Sloane Fortuner, Arjun Donovan, Lucien Prince, Johanna Titus, Arlo Downing, and Cesare Runeare. My assessment took place over the course of six months, during which time I conducted interviews, inspected their living quarters, examined their backgrounds, and shadowed them when their assignments allowed.

This brief should be considered an overview of my findings. A report on each member, as well as much more thorough recommendations, can be found in the attached report.

The objectives of the assignment were split into two parts. The first was to determine whether the members of Fracture (hereafter referred to as "subjects") could be adequately rehabilitated and reintroduced to independent life amongst the civilian population. The second objective depended on the findings of the first. Should the subject(s) be found unfit to return to the general populace, I was asked to recommend the best and most humane course of action for their future.

OVERVIEW:

Under proper supervision and with intensive support, the subjects are not a danger to themselves or others. Without supervision or support, the subjects represent a viable threat to the health and safety of the population of the Elvish Protectorate.

OBJECTIVE ONE:

After six months of intensive study and deliberation, it is my professional opinion that none of the subjects can or should be allowed to live unsupervised amongst the civilian population. This is not only for their own mental and emotional stability, but for the safety of the populace.

All of the subjects have endured horrors and conditioning the likes of which most people would not survive. As elves taken from their families, some as young as three, and raised by a rotating squad of Thaddeus II's most brutal and war-damaged hitmen, they lack the fundamentals of basic communication skills, emotional intelligence, and compassion. It is my belief that many of these things can be taught, but given their many years of conditioning and service, they will never achieve what most would consider "normal" behaviors.

When asked what they would do should they be released from their service, none of the subjects had an answer. Even the suggestion of living an independent life seemed to unsettle them, and in a few it even sparked outright aggression.

Socially, they appear to have developed a unique pack-like structure with two "alphas" at the top: Vesta Kincaid and Sloane

Fortuner, who seem to split authority evenly and defer ultimately to their Captain, Kazimier Rione. These bonds are not built on what most people would view as warm, familial relationships, but a mutual understanding and codependence. In my time with them, I observed many instances of what I can only label as silent communication between the subjects. Their understanding of each other is so complete that it is rare that they truly need to speak, and when they do, they tend to express themselves through clipped speech and strategic bursts of violence.

OBJECTIVE TWO:

After determining that the subjects cannot at this time or in the foreseeable future be released from supervision, I turned my focus to finding the healthiest path forward for the team. While my list of recommendations is long and involved, the most important point can be boiled down to one vital conclusion: If the government wishes to see the subjects live semi-independent lives, the members of Fracture CANNOT and SHOULD NOT be split up for any reason.

Although nearly all of the subjects (notable exceptions being Downing and Prince, see p. 57, subtitle CODEPENDENCE) are extremely independent and exhibit striking anti-social behaviors, they heavily rely on the pack structure of the team to regulate their emotions and validate their experiences. Although they may often seek solitude, they would never under normal circumstances wish to completely cut themselves off from the pack.

It is my belief that should a subject do so, it would represent a dire mental and emotional state in need of immediate intervention. At the time of my assessment, I saw no indication that any members of the team wished to live on their own. They appear to be aware that their stability depends on their coexistence.

However, I have grave concerns over how that dynamic will change when any of the subjects find their mates. Not only will it cause immense emotional and psychological upheaval — as it does in all elves — it may threaten the fragile support system that keeps every member of the team regulated. Broadly speaking, the subjects have no capacity to handle the emotional turmoil, arousal, possessiveness, jealousy, or territorial urges that come with the critical period of bonding.

It is my expert opinion that the members of Fracture should be shielded from any possibility of finding their consorts until such a time that they are deemed capable of handling the changes both on an individual level and as a group. All necessary precautions should be taken and a plan put in place for the dangerous possibility that those precautions might prove inadequate.

It is well known that all elves go through a period of dangerous instability when they find their consorts. For the members of Fracture, it would be more than dangerous. It would be catastrophic.

OCTOBER 2047 — San Francisco, The Elvish Protectorate

Killing wasn't the point, but it was always a pleasure.

Sloane enjoyed hunting. Whether it was for an assignment or for his extracurriculars, he never tired of it. He had no memories of what it was like to play as a child, and only a bare bones understanding of what civilians found pleasure in, but a lifetime of training had wired the idea of a successful hunt to satisfaction. The pounce and the kill — they were as close as he came to knowing happiness.

He got a lot less of that these days.

After she beheaded her father and took over the territory, Delilah's changes took a long time to reach them. The rest of the territory needed immediate stabilization, and they'd served her faithfully in the shadows. But when the dust cleared and it became obvious that a bloody civil war had been avoided, it was their turn.

They'd been called Thaddeus's attack dogs. The terror in the dark. The shadow squad who could find anyone, anywhere, and leave a bloody message for all the world to see.

Now they were a liability.

What did one do with attack dogs when they were no longer needed? Put them down.

So it came as something of a surprise when instead of taking them out, a wave of psychiatrists, mind healers, and specialists were brought in to "make reforms." New luxuries were brought into the Fracture barracks. New doctors were assigned to each member. New rules were strictly enforced.

They weren't expected to maim, torture, or kill anymore. Not unless their lives or those of civilians were directly threatened. For the first time since Thaddeus snatched them from their families, they were given the gift of mercy.

They had no fucking idea what to do with it.

The team wasn't fit for domestication. They couldn't be assimilated or softened. They certainly couldn't be expected to know what to do with *kindness*.

Each of them had adapted to the unsettling change in circumstances in their own ways. They found hobbies, *extracurriculars*, that scratched the itch their assignments no longer did. For Sloane, the team's premier assassin, it was hunting.

He left the barracks without a word. Consistent good behavior had gotten him the privilege of freedom when off duty. It was another new luxury he and the rest of Fracture exploited to the fullest extent.

Sloane rarely had a plan for his hunts. He didn't need one. The Elvish Protectorate was one of the most strictly controlled territories on the continent, but even it had its seedy underbelly, injustices, and violence behind closed doors. He rarely had to search long to find someone the world was better off without.

On this particular foggy October night, however, he wasn't having a lot of luck.

Tension bunched the powerful muscles between his shoulder blades as he vaulted over the top of a chain link fence blocking off an alleyway. Elves valued cleanliness above just about anything, since their heightened senses made them particularly affected by powerful smells. That meant that their streets were cleaned nightly by automated bots. The same couldn't be said for alleyways, where elves rarely ventured.

Luckily for Sloane, his full-face helmet filtered out scent. Cutting off one of an elf's most powerful senses seemed counter-intuitive for a group raised to be hunters, but the loss was worth it. Their sense of smell was a powerful tool, yes, but it was also their greatest weakness. One whiff of the right person at the wrong time…

Of course, not smelling the rot of trash, piss, and discarded food behind a bar was nice, too.

Sloane had to rely on all his other senses to find his prey. His breath whispered out through the helmet's filter as he landed in a crouch on the other side of the fence. His boots, steel-toed and laced high up the shin, flexed comfortably as he stabilized on the balls of his feet. He scanned the alleyway.

Besides the thump of bad music inside the bar to his right and the flash of headlights from passing cars at the exit of the alley, there was little of interest.

Fuck, he thought, gloved hands curling into tight fists. He hated going back to the barracks without a catch. It was the only thing that kept him going through the mind-numbing monotony of their new, sanitized assignments. Getting a good kill in, wiping one more stain off the face of Burden's Earth, stopped him from losing what little of his mind he still possessed — and taking out all the pent-up aggression on his teammates.

The last time he failed, he and Arlo sparred so intensely they'd both ended up in Joanna's clinic with half their bones broken. The repairs to the gym were *still* coming out of their pay.

But it was more than just a need for release. It was about a tangled knot of purpose and thwarted instinct, a result of all that malicious rewiring Thaddeus and his trainers had labored so intensely over. Without the hunt, he was useless. Purposeless. A weapon with no edge and no enemy.

To return to the barracks unsuccessful was, in his mind, worse than failure. It meant that he'd failed his only purpose in life.

The bar was his last hope. The sun would rise soon, and that meant that the Haight district would be flooded with vampires headed home for the day. Not all of them, just like not all of the business that was conducted within the confines of The Lush, were criminal in nature. But he'd had luck there in the past, so he figured it was a good final stop of the night.

A low metal groan drew his attention to the bar's back door. The thumping beat of the music grew louder as it opened. A small yellow light flickered to life above the frame with the motion, casting a watery glow over the figure that slipped out.

"…next week! I'll let you know if my schedule changes!" A chipper, feminine voice was the last thing he expected in the dank filth of the alley.

Sloane didn't move a muscle as he waited for her to step out from behind the door. A chorus of voices called out to her, wishing her goodnight before she let the door swing closed behind her.

She was willowy, with lithe limbs and a head of long raven hair. Her skin was a deep olive tone that looked silky to the touch. When she stood there for a moment, her focus on digging in the glittery purse slung over her shoulder, he had what felt like all the time in the world to observe the soft curve of her nose and sooty fan of her lashes against the tops of her cheeks.

She was arrant. He knew it at a glance, something inside of him flinching instinctively away from the devastating vulnerability of her. To someone like him, everything about her was almost perverse in its softness.

One painfully delicate hand rummaged in that ridiculous purse, the bones of her wrist flashing beneath the sleeve of her pale pink sweater with every movement. So much smaller than his. So easy to snap.

Elves had eaten humans, once. They'd eaten pretty much anyone weaker than them, and no one was weaker than arrants — those poor humans born without even the flimsy protection of magic.

To Sloane, this pitiful little creature looked like a doe, blissfully unaware of the wolf hiding just out of sight.

Something pulled inside him; a deep, sucking sort of feeling he couldn't easily identify. It wasn't anticipation and it wasn't quite hunger. It was some foreign mix of both and neither — a need that had no name, no predecessor, and no equal.

She wasn't prey. Not the kind he sought, anyway. And yet she was something he needed to possess.

The woman stood in that dim light for several long moments, tapping away at her phone. Her lips, shiny with some sort of makeup, were set in a soft pout. The cool light from her phone's screen reflected in them like a beacon.

The more he stared at them, the worse that nameless need became.

A wild kind of anger sparked to life as he watched her, like her helplessness and ignorance were a personal slight. How could she not sense him there, crouched mere feet away? Had she even bothered to look around the alley before she stepped out? Didn't she realize what an elf could do to her with barely any thought at all?

Their bones were harder than concrete. Their claws had a molecular structure similar to diamonds. Their upper and lower fangs were self-sharpening and could come together with a bite force great enough to bend steel. He was a predator unlike anything else on the planet and she was…

Beautiful.

Sloane blinked, taken off-guard by the thought. As far as he could remember, he'd never used the word in his life. There hadn't been any reason.

But when she tucked her phone back in her bag with a soft sigh and brushed her hair back behind her ear, it was the only word that made sense. She was beautiful. Something in the way her features were put together and the softness that radiated out of her like heat off blacktop made her that way.

Sloane reared back, sinking further into the shadows as he examined the strange creature. To him, she seemed like something that came from another world. The reasons why wouldn't come to him no matter how hard he tried to drag them out.

She wasn't any different from the thousands of people he'd encountered — and hundreds he'd killed — in his lifetime. A human was a human. An elf was an elf. Everyone could be killed, so no one was special.

She wasn't even doing anything interesting. He doubted she was on her way to commit a crime. Going by the short black dress under the pink sweater and the fact that she used the employee exit told him she was likely a server just getting off work for the night. There was nothing, *nothing,* noteworthy about her at all.

But he followed her.

When she walked out of the alley in her tennis shoes, a hum in her elegant throat, he was right behind her. The reasons why continued to evade him but they mattered less and less with every step.

It took him a block to realize what he was doing, and only after a man passed a little too close to her for his comfort.

Protection duty.

His boot nearly hit a discarded can as he quickly dipped into the shadows between buildings, his gaze locked on the slim shape of her back and swaying hair. He'd never been allowed on a protection assignment before. Those were given to Vesta and Cesare, who liked people best, or Arlo and Lucien, who were inseparable and required unique assignments. No one, not even their new, progressive captain, would consider Sloane fit for a job that didn't require killing.

But he followed her. And he was pretty sure he didn't want to kill her.

Sloane's vision narrowed until all he could see was the shape of his prey. The sense that something terrible was going to happen to her, that if he looked away for even a moment she'd be taken from him, was overwhelming.

His blood rushed in his ears, nearly blocking out the sounds of the street that filtered in through his helmet's speakers. It felt hotter than normal. Brighter. Like he'd been injected with something that made him feel… more. Bigger.

So when she turned a corner into another dark alley, clearly intending to cut time on her walk, it was a shock to feel something in his chest lurch. The fine hair on the back of his neck prickled with unease.

She clearly didn't hear the shuffling footsteps at the other end of the alley or have the honed instinct to detect threats that he did. Something was wrong. Something was waiting. For the first time in his life, the urge to reveal himself not to kill but to protect nearly overwhelmed him.

Sloane abandoned his cover just in time to hear a high, nervous laugh.

"Oh, Cole! I didn't see you," she exclaimed, too far away.

When Sloane entered the long, narrow alley, he found a reedy man standing over the doe, one hand clasped on the softest part of her upper arm. Neither appeared to notice their audience when the man replied, "Your blonde friend wasn't working tonight. I figured you'd need some company walking home, so I caught up with you."

"That's really nice of you, but I don't think Roxanna would be too happy if she knew you were walking other girls home, Cole. Best you should get along, huh?" The cadence of her voice changed. It slowed and sweetened, reminding him of the way he'd heard some people speak to their pets or bawling young.

Sloane walked slowly, the tread of his boots silent on the cracked concrete. That needy, aching thing in him began to beat at the underside of his sternum — a steady *thump, thump, thump* to match his footsteps.

"C'mon, Cece," Cole whined, "she won't know. She's been too busy for me, anyway."

"I'm sorry to hear that, but I really need to get home." The woman, *Cece* — such an odd, pretty name for an odd, pretty woman — moved to step around Cole.

Several things happened at once: the man grabbed her arm to yank her back toward the dingy brick wall, Cece yelped, and Sloane moved.

Fighting and killing were muscle memory. Blinded, bleeding, and impaired by a severe head wound — it wouldn't make a difference. He'd fight entirely on autopilot and win, because losing hadn't been an option since he was six years old.

His reaction to the sight of a man grabbing *her,* however, was something altogether different.

It wasn't autopilot. It wasn't even instinct. It was a sudden and explosive severing of a nerve, that essential mechanism that kept him so tenuously tethered to basic decency.

One moment he was standing in the shadows, watching a hand close around her pink-swathed arm, and the next his own hand held the back of Cole's head against the gritty brick and mortar. A watery scream escaped the man's throat as the delicate bones and cartilage of his face gave way under the pressure.

Sloane didn't hear any of it. Flames engulfed his senses. His fury was the kind that could only be described as *scorched earth,* a feeling so all-consuming that it destroyed everything it touched.

Until someone touched *him.*

CHAPTER **TWO**

A HAND, SMALL AND GENTLE, SETTLED ON HIS CHEST. IT PRESSED down just over that severed nerve like it belonged there.

Sloane blinked rapidly, the veil of fire clearing only enough to reveal that perfect face. She was alarmingly close. A sick feeling squirmed in his gut at the realization that she'd slipped under his arm and put herself chest to chest with him all without him even noticing.

She could've slit my throat, he realized.

Instead, she'd put both hands on him. Gently. Not even pushing. Sloane couldn't remember the last time someone had touched him like that. He couldn't even imagine allowing it.

Stepping between an elf and his prey for any reason was brave. It was also so reckless it left him stunned. He stared at her like she wasn't just a doe but a creature from another world, baffled by how easily she disregarded her own safety.

"...easy, okay? I think he got the message. Let's just back up a bit." Her voice bubbled up through the roiling flames, as cool and calming as fresh water.

His body moved without his permission again. Sloane took one large step back, releasing Cole with a shove toward the wall.

The man slid to the ground with a gurgling sound, leaving a streak of red and a smattering of broken teeth on the brick.

Instead of staying put, Cece matched Sloane's steps. Her gaze never left his face, hidden by the smokey black glass of his helmet's visor, as she called out, "Cole, are you okay?"

"What the *fuck!*" He stumbled to his feet, one hand pawing at the wall and the other frantically smearing the blood that gushed from his smashed nose and bleeding gums. There were oozing black holes between the cracked teeth, which matched the scabbed vampire bites on his neck. *"The fuck!* I didn't— didn't *do* anything!"

Sloane's upper lip lifted, revealing razor-sharp fangs no one could see. The only thing that stopped him from lunging for Cole again was the fact that Cece put herself firmly between the men, like she knew that his instinct was to protect her at all costs.

"I think this… officer believes you were accosting me," she explained. Gaze searching his visor, she hazarded, "You were protecting me, right? Or are you a friend of Roxanna's?"

Sloane's voice came out flat and modulated by the programming in his helmet when he said to Cece, "You required assistance."

Her wide eyes flicked down, taking in his black, standard Patrol-issue kit and the gloves all elves wore. The long line of her throat bobbed with a hard swallow when she returned her attention to his visor. "You are a Patrol officer, right?"

No, he wanted to tell her. *I'm worse.*

Instead, he inclined his head. Fear was written in the tense lines around her eyes and mouth. For the first time in his life, the sight bothered him. He didn't want to tell her that he was a member of Thaddeus's hit squad, his team of pet assassins everyone feared.

He wanted her to be… something. Something softer.

She didn't immediately relax, but she did let out a breath.

"Cole, get out of here before he arrests you. We both know you can't take another strike on your record."

"Cece—"

Her head snapped in the bloodied man's direction. "Glory give me strength, Cole! Shut the fuck up and *go* before I tell this guy to finish what he started. And if you *ever* follow me or another server home again, I'm telling Roxanna. You think this was bad? Wait until your vampire hears you've been following other women!"

That seemed to light a fire under him that the beating to his face hadn't. Cole wheezed as he scuttled away, his shoulders hunched and his t-shirt bloody. Sloane turned his head sharply to keep him in his sight until he left the alley altogether. Everything in him screamed to follow, to finish the job and get the kill he'd hunted all night for, but that pulsing severed nerve in his chest stopped him. It refused to let him move even an inch away from the woman who stared up at him with eyes as big and brown as a doe's.

Flexing his claws, he demanded, "Why did you protect him? He attacked you."

"And you smashed his face in so bad it actually *flattened,*" she replied, shockingly frank. "I think he learned his lesson."

Doubtful.

Scum like Cole, who followed women down dark alleys and didn't like the word *no,* rarely learned anything besides how to not get caught. That was why Sloane did what he did. If Patrol and the laws that governed the Elvish Protectorate let monsters slip through the cracks, it was his job to pick up the slack.

He said none of this to Cece. Instead, he watched her intently through the glass of his visor, his claw-tipped fists curling and uncurling. The nerves in the tips of his fingers tingled with an urgent feeling he couldn't place. "I'll escort you to your home," he informed her.

Her lips parted with surprise. It became difficult, suddenly, to look anywhere besides that tiny, glossy opening into the warm well of her mouth.

"Thanks for the help but you really don't need to," she protested, palms up.

It would've been the easiest thing in the world to sling her over his shoulder and deliver her to a safer location. That was what a real protector would do. If he were on assignment, he wouldn't have thought twice about it.

But he wasn't, and something about the wary look on her face made him second-guess his impulse to use force to get what he wanted.

Sloane did a rapid calculation in his mind, weighing the risks versus the possible benefits of a new approach. If he used force, she would be more afraid of him. If he tried the hitherto untested tactic of coercion, she might… not be.

He reeled with the possibilities. At the forefront of them all was the foreign longing for the return of her hands to his chest. He wanted to know if it felt good a second time, too.

The modulator in his helmet scrubbed all inflection and identifying features from his voice, so she couldn't hear the cautiousness in his tone when he said, "It's late. You were attacked. You are alone. It's my duty to get you home safely."

She shifted her feet nervously in the grit and dust of the passageway. "No offense, but you're, like, really scary."

"Correct." He nodded toward the alley's exit.

A soft sound escaped her. It wasn't quite a laugh but it was close. A new light entered her eyes when she peered up at him then. It looked something like curiosity. "Most people would try to deny it or maybe put the other person at ease."

Sloane couldn't readily recall a time when he'd willingly spoken this much, let alone put someone at ease. "I have no reason to do that. Your observation was correct. I am scary. It's an advantage."

There was a long moment of silence. With a twist of her full lips, she appeared to accept the fact that he wouldn't be swayed. Still eyeing him, she turned toward the exit.

Sloane tucked his hands behind his back and shortened his strides to match her much shorter legs as he followed her out onto the street.

"Is it always?" she asked, running her fingers through her hair with a nervous flick of her wrist.

He had to think hard about his answer. Not because it was a difficult question, but because he found himself distracted by the curve of her jaw when she tilted her head just-so.

"Usually," he amended.

Truthfully, it was very rare that he encountered a situation that couldn't be turned in his favor with a large dose of terror. Fear made prey stupid. Stupid prey made for easy killing. Killing gave him meaning.

Everything had its place.

But he didn't want to see fear in this woman's eyes. It served no purpose. If he didn't want to kill her or extract information from her, then it was a useless tool. He'd have to find a better one to get what he wanted, which was, at that precise moment, to get her to safety.

And to be touched by her again.

His blood still rushed in his veins, too hot, as they walked down the quiet street. The few people out in the hour before sunrise gave him a wide berth, which suited him just fine. He didn't like the idea of anyone getting too close to his charge. The thought filled him with a deep and dangerous sort of discontent. It was the same way he felt about his few possessions.

No one was allowed to touch his things. No one was allowed to even look at them. What was his was *his.* End of story.

"Have you been a Patrol officer long?"

Sloane's gaze moved from examining the street for threats to tracing the contours of her profile in an instant. "Yes," he answered, surprising himself.

Her dark brows furrowed. "Do you like it?"

"That is irrelevant."

"How? Shouldn't everyone like what they do? Even just a little?"

He watched her closely, more curious about the inner workings of her mind than anything else. He'd never thought to talk to prey before and had no idea what truly motivated them. "Do you?"

"Not really," she admitted, rubbing her shoulders. Only then did he notice that her sweater was gone. Lost, he realized, sometime during the scuffle with Cole. A sharp need struck him when he imagined that soft garment lost in the filth of the alley.

Oblivious, she continued, "But there are good parts about working in a vampire bar. It pays the bills and works with my school schedule. I get to be with my best friend, usually, and it can be… exciting. I swear I don't have creeps following me home on a regular basis."

Sloane found himself grinding his fangs, unconsciously sharpening them as he imagined what it must be like for a creature as soft and vulnerable as her to work in a vampire bar. "That's too dangerous. You should find a new job."

She snorted. "Now you sound like my mother. If you *must* know, I'm working on becoming a teacher."

He grimaced. Caring for young was an esteemed position worthy of respect, but it wasn't a job he enjoyed. That was why their captain used work in the Solbourne Nursery Center as punishment for misbehavior.

If he had to choose, he'd pick having his claws pulled out one by one over caring for a fleet of slavering, sociopathic young every time.

Mind churning through the problems she'd presented him, he demanded, "Do you walk this route at this hour regularly?"

She gave him a wary look. "I don't know if I should tell you that."

That's a yes.

They turned a corner. He glanced around critically, judging

the distance from her work, the sparse street lights in the slightly run-down area. It wasn't far from the glittering Haight district, with all its vice and blood vendettas, but in San Francisco, moving even one street over was like crossing into another universe. The street was all sleepy old homes with caged windows — a remnant of the war years — and apartment buildings that hadn't seen upgrades since the 60s.

"You shouldn't walk by yourself," he firmly instructed her.

"I don't, usually. My friend works in the same bar, but she has the flu." She shrugged. "I can handle myself."

Sloane took in her fragile frame, her blunt nails, and the sheer softness of her. "You cannot."

"Okay, this was a bad night, but I—"

"You are soft and small and defenseless," he bluntly explained. "Your senses are dull and your reflexes non-existent. In a confrontation, your best bet is to run as fast as you can. That is unacceptable. You may be weak, but you deserve to be safe at all times. It's my job to make sure you are."

She shook her head. "You know, for a job that doesn't seem to bring you joy, you seem to take it pretty seriously."

Already making plans, he replied, "I take protection duty very seriously."

Cece slowed to a stop in front of an apartment building. Sunlight had just begun to color the horizon. It touched the long black strands of her hair, turning them a deep, bloody red. She faced him with a nervous smile. "Well, um, thank—"

"What is Cece short for?" The words tumbled out of him in a way they never had before, as if each one was a link in a chain he desperately wanted to wrap around her, holding her there with him in the soft glow of dawn.

She blinked rapidly, that nervous quirk of her lips softening into an expression he'd never been on the receiving end of before: one of gentle delight.

"Cecilia," she answered, walking backward up the short flight of steps to the door. She placed her hand on the knob, but she didn't flee his company immediately. Not like she should've. Not like any sane creature who valued their life ought to.

Her big brown eyes, liquid gold in the new sunlight, gazed intently at his visor. "What's your name, Officer?"

Fire crackled in his belly and licked up his throat, making it hard to speak. "Classified," he finally answered, forcing himself to take a step back, away from the doe.

"Oh," she breathed, smile falling. "Well… thank you. For the assistance."

He nodded once. It was the only thing he could think to do as he watched her turn away and enter the building. The flames spread beneath his skin, tracing the fine webbing of his nerves until every part of him burned with the desire to follow her up the stairs. To make sure she was safe. To listen to her voice. To watch a doe in her natural habitat and maybe get a glimpse into a world he could barely imagine.

But Sloane was well trained in the fine art of self-deprivation. Besides, he had a hunt to finish.

He forced himself away from his doe, but he didn't bother depriving himself of a smaller consolation prize. It was an easy thing, retracing his steps back to the alley. It was even easier to pick up her discarded sweater from where it lay in a heap on the ground.

And after he'd stored it in a cache to be retrieved later, it was his pleasure to finish his night exactly as he envisioned: hunting down a man who thought he'd gotten off with only a few missing teeth.

CHAPTER THREE

SEPTEMBER 2048 — SAN FRANCISCO, THE ELVISH PROTECTORATE

Cecilia tucked her serving tray beneath her arm and leaned her hip against the edge of the bar as she waited for the bartender to hand over two cheap bottles of alcoholic synth-blood. The Lush was hot and humid as bodies crammed together between high tables and the dance floor.

She'd thought that perhaps the recent high profile murder that happened on the premises might deter business, not increase it. She was wrong. They'd been packed nearly every night since management and the authorities had given them the all-clear to reopen.

The old adage that all publicity was good publicity was true, she supposed, especially when it came to bloodshed in a vampire bar.

The upside for her was that the tips were great. The downside was that her best friend and fellow server had abandoned her to marry a vampire across the continent, which sucked out what little fun the job still possessed.

Without Dahlia, working in The Lush was an endless grind of

abysmal dance music, grasping hands, spilled synth, and grueling late nights.

It was also a lot more dangerous. In theory, anyway.

Cecilia brushed a sweaty lock of hair away from her forehead with her gloved forearm. She had to be careful to keep her hands clean, which wasn't easy on the best of nights. It was especially difficult when they were way past capacity and she had to dodge guests sloshing synth and regular alcohol every which way.

She offered the bartender a chipper grin when he plunked two warmed bottles on the bar in front of her. He looked as miserable as she felt, but there was no time to commiserate. Even if they could've heard each other over the thumping bass, it was her personal philosophy that a bright attitude could solve most of life's problems.

Except, perhaps, the one she had with upper management.

Duke, the new sole owner of The Lush, watched her from his seat at the opposite end of the bar. Once, he'd been the handsome, aloof older brother of Devon, the vampire who ran the bar — terribly — but with his death, Duke had returned to San Francisco to take over.

And, according to rumor, to find out what happened to his brother. She didn't know the man well enough to say whether he was motivated by sentimentality. With Duke it was hard to tell what mattered more: making money or solving his brother's disappearance.

Either way, it was best to avoid him.

Dahlia had warned her that he might come sniffing around her old apartment, and since everyone knew they were best friends, there was a very real possibility he'd ask Cecilia questions. Dahlia made her swear to tell her if he made any threats or she felt unsafe. Of course, Cecilia promised she would.

She wouldn't, obviously, but a white lie was a small price to pay to give Dahlia peace of mind.

Cecilia wasn't scared of Duke. If she was, they'd have a

bigger problem than any potential threats. Knowing her, she'd probably want to sleep with him.

She'd never told Dahlia that was the main reason she'd insisted they apply to work at the bar in the first place. They shared almost everything, but there were some things not even childhood best friends needed to know — like how Cecilia, notorious scaredy-cat, liked fear a little too much.

For a while, the thrill of working in a dangerous vampire bar had set her blood on fire. Five years in and now without her best friend, the shine had come off the proverbial apple in a major way.

Cecilia's feet, pinched by the narrow toe and diabolical heel of the shoes all the female servers were forced to wear, screamed with discomfort as she made her final rounds for the night. She deposited warm bottles with a smile, demurred when a vampire casually asked how much a sip of *her* would cost, and did her best to skirt Duke's seat at the bar without looking too obvious.

By the time her shift ended, she was sweaty and exhausted. Knowing how different the temperature was outside, she shrugged on her pale pink coat over her skimpy black dress and slung her bag over her shoulder. A long shower and a microwave dinner were in her future, and just about the only things that could motivate her to make the trek home.

Pausing by the back door, she checked her phone. A message from Dahlia lit up the screen. It was a picture of her brand new car, courtesy of her cousin Tomas. Blood red and way too fast for her best friend's less than stellar driving skills, it was a sight to behold.

Needs a bumper sticker, she replied. *Maybe 'honk if you bite'?*

Dahlia replied almost instantly. *I was thinking 'My husband is my passenger princess.'*

Shouldering open the door, Cecilia snorted. San Francisco's cool night air kissed her damp skin as she stepped into the dark alley behind the bar. She'd switched her heels out for a glittery pair of sneakers, which were essential when one never knew what was in the ever-present puddles and piles of detritus found there.

Good choice, she typed out. *I'm sure Felix will enjoy that. Probably too much, actually.*

Dahlia sent an evil-looking emoji before she asked, *Are you headed home?*

Just left the bar. Can't wait for my feast of frozen mac n' cheese. I might even get real wild and break out the fudge bar I've been saving. The squeaky hinges of the old door alerted her to someone else exiting, prompting her to begin walking as she typed.

Dahlia's response popped up just as the sound of someone clearing their throat made her turn.

Duke stood in the dull glow cast by the *employee entrance* sign above the door. Blond, ruggedly handsome, and dead-eyed, he watched her with a flat, calculating look that made the hair on the back of her neck stand up.

"Oh, hi," she greeted, fingers flexing around her phone. "Did you need something?"

She doubted he was there to ask her about next weekend's schedule, but a girl could hope.

Duke watched her for a moment, a muscle in his jaw twitching. "You headed home?"

It occurred to her that she ought to lie. The smart thing would be to say she was headed to her boyfriend's house, or maybe to her second job. Letting him think she would be missed if she suddenly didn't turn up was the best survival strategy when dealing with vampires on the hunt.

But Cecilia had never been a good liar, and she was even worse at keeping her mouth shut.

"Yep!" she chirped. "I'm gonna make some dinner and hit the sack. My feet are killing me after tonight's rush."

Her boss stepped away from the door. She'd never been particularly intimidated by him before. Sure, he was a little scary, but he'd always been so uninterested in the staff that he seemed… safe certainly wasn't the right word. Unlikely to care enough to hurt her was probably closer to the truth.

But he wasn't uninterested now.

Cecilia edged toward the opening of the alleyway in what she hoped was a natural-looking movement. Her heart rate jumped as she ran the numbers on how likely she was to survive if he got his hands on her, as she always did when a vampire stalked her down a dark alley. It was a depressingly frequent occurrence.

Well, it used to be, anyway.

She'd known for a long time that there was something wrong with her. Some crossed wire or misaligned axle that linked up arousal to fear. Even at that moment, when Duke began advancing on her, she felt the rush of it down her spine and between her thighs.

Gods knew she wasn't attracted to *Duke,* of all people, but the threat of him… Yeah, that was enough to get her fucked up engine going.

"You live close by, right?" Duke offered her a stilted smile full of fang. "We haven't gotten a chance to talk yet. How about I walk you home?"

Cecilia knew the interrogation was coming, but she expected it to be contained within the relative safety of the bar, not whatever *this* was.

"Dawn's pretty close," she informed him, chuckling nervously. "We should just schedule a chat for my next shift."

And that'll give me more time to think of what to say besides 'I'm glad your brother's dead and he's been turned into goo.'

She didn't know for *sure* that Devon was goo, but she'd seen enough true crime documentaries to think it was a fair possibility. Another likely scenario was he'd been tucked into a barrel and chucked into the Bay. She preferred the goo, though.

Dust to dust, slime to slime, shithead. You shouldn't have fucked with my best friend.

"There's plenty of time," he replied, laying his hand on the small of her back. Her spine stiffened one vertebrae at a time as he guided her out of the alley and onto the sidewalk.

San Francisco was a daytime city, to be sure, with a population that leaned more toward arrants and elves than nocturnal folk. Despite that, the streets were never completely empty even in the wee hours of the morning.

People passed by them on the narrow sidewalk, their heads down and their steps quick — a necessity when traversing San Francisco's notoriously bouncy streets. The rumor was that they'd been saturated with magic during the catastrophic event that razed the city in 1906, and it'd taken her and Dahlia a full month to stop looking like fools whenever they stepped outside.

Now city life and all its quirks came naturally to them. The only thing Cecilia had never quite gotten used to was the way strangers pretended like they couldn't see each other. No one waved or nodded or said good morning. Everyone existed in their own little bubble as they walked as quickly as they could down the street. A sub-ideal quirk for a woman being walked to her doom.

"So, uh," she began, "what did you want to talk about?"

"You're friends with Dahlia, right?"

Cecilia tensed. She knew it was coming and she still couldn't stop the instinctive response to freeze up when her best friend was mentioned.

It took a smooth movement around a woman walking in the opposite direction to break Duke's contact with her back. "Yeah. We've been friends since we were little."

"I haven't been able to get a hold of her since she quit." Duke didn't take his eyes off her as they turned a corner onto her street. The gold shimmer of the street lights reflected in his flat gaze like oil on water. "No one has. And I've heard some really interesting rumors about what she's been up to since she left."

"You mean since someone threw a grenade at the rooftop lounge," Cecilia corrected, her normally cheerful tone edged with more bite than was probably smart.

Duke's lips thinned. "Since then, yes."

Keeping her eyes ahead, she said, "Dahlia nearly *died.* I can't blame her for wanting to quit and run as far from here as possible."

"Is that the only reason she left?"

They slowed to a stop in front of her rundown apartment building. The light above the entrance had been broken for weeks. The harsh lines of Duke's face, so different from the boyish, pretty-boy looks his brother once sported, were cast in deep shadows as he loomed over her.

Sucking in a deep breath, Cecilia drew her shoulders back and faced the vampire head-on. "Duke, I know you're looking for your brother. I can tell you with absolute certainty that Dahlia did *not* leave the city because of him. She needed a new start and moved in with her boyfriend of *three years.* I'm sorry if that disappoints you, but it's the truth."

Was it the *whole* truth? Of course not. It wasn't a lie, though, and that made it a lot easier to sell.

Dahlia *did* abandon Cecilia to live with Felix in United Washington. After she was accidentally turned into a vampire. And also after Felix goo-ified Devon.

She wasn't a monster. Cecilia did feel a twinge of sympathy for Duke for the loss of his brother — even if Devon was a first-class prick who thought preying on his employees was a perk of the job. And if she were being *completely* honest, she would say that Dahlia wasn't the only person she was protecting.

A handful of Amauris had come to pack up Dahlia's apartment less than twenty-four hours after she left. Even if she hadn't warned Cecilia that they were dangerous, she would've known instantly. That special sixth sense she possessed pinged off the charts the instant she laid eyes on them.

Whoever the Amauris were and whatever they did, they were bigger predators than someone like Duke could handle.

He'd never done anything to her or anyone else she knew. If he was really just trying to find out what happened to his brother, she wanted to at least do what she could to keep him away from certain death.

Daring to lay a hand on Duke's corded bicep, she gentled her tone. "I really am sorry you can't find your brother. I wish I could help, but I don't know anything — and neither does Dahlia."

The sound of something crashing in the alley beside her apartment building made her jump back a step. Cecilia pressed her hand to her thundering heart and let out a nervous laugh, but Duke didn't seem to notice the disturbance.

"He was last seen headed here," he grunted, apparently unmoved by her sympathy. "The night he disappeared, he went to see *her.* Are you telling me that you didn't see or hear anything? That she didn't mention it?"

"I definitely never heard or saw Devon come around after the explosion," she confirmed. "And to be honest, Duke, no. Dahlia probably wouldn't have mentioned it. You know why? Because your brother showed up a lot. He was always doing creepy shit like that. It would've been normal to both of us."

For a long, taut moment, it looked like Duke wasn't going to let it go. He took a small step toward her but stopped short before she even had time to tense up. His head whipped to one side and his shoulders hiked defensively.

Cecilia's heart jackknifed in her chest as a familiar feeling registered along the back of her neck: the certainty that she was being watched.

Her breath shortened. She *knew* that if she peered into the darkness between the street lamps there wouldn't be anything to find. There never was. No matter how hard she looked in reflective surfaces or from behind her curtains, she couldn't spot the phantom that'd followed her nearly every night since she'd been accosted in the alley.

But he was there — and this time, he'd fixed on Duke.

She wasn't sure how she knew. She just *did.*

"You should go," she warned, even more serious than before.

Cecilia stepped backward, toward the short flight of concrete stairs that led to her apartment building's entrance.

Duke's head swung around, no doubt searching for the phantom. She doubted he'd have any more luck finding him than her. Even accounting for a vampire's keen night vision, she didn't think he'd see anything more than shadows.

Her phantom was very, very good. *Mostly.*

"Seriously, Duke," she pressed, jogging up the steps. Her hand found its way into her purse and plucked out the old fashioned set of keys the landlord had given her when he promised to update the security system five years ago. They jingled when she added, "You should head home. It'll be dangerous to be out here soon."

It suited her just fine if he thought she meant the rapidly approaching sunrise.

Duke's upper lip curled over his fangs, but he didn't follow her up the stairs or stop her from unlocking the door. Backing away from the entrance, he told her, "We're not done."

Summoning her tried and true defense, Cecilia's lips pulled up into a wide, air-headed smile. "Of course not! I'll see you at work. Have a good rest of your night, huh?"

She made her escape as quickly as possible, but she had no real hope that something as flimsy as the apartment building's old locks would keep someone like Duke out if he really wanted to get in.

A sick feeling settled into the pit of her stomach as she power-walked up the four flights of stairs and down the musty hallway that led to her door.

She slipped into her unit and pressed her back against the door with a relieved sigh. Her studio stretched out before in all its dim glory. Trying to liven the place up with soft yellow curtains, verdant plants, and funky acrylic art pieces hadn't been able to entirely eliminate the air of neglect that permeated the entire building.

It hadn't bothered her when Dahlia was around, but it wasn't quite so easy to ignore after a night like the one she'd had.

Peeling herself away from the door, Cecilia forced herself to take a deep breath. Not bothering to turn on any lights, she shucked her shoes and jacket as she made her way to the tiny kitchenette. She set her phone down on the counter without looking at Dahlia's last message.

Worry churned in her gut as she watched her frozen dinner spin in the microwave.

Telling Dahlia about Duke's questions was the smart thing to do. It was what her friend had asked her to do. It was the reasonable, mature course of action.

But Dahlia was so happy, and her relationship was complicated enough without adding worry for Cecilia into the mix. It smacked of the abandonment issues she totally, super *didn't* have for her to run screaming to her friend the second things got a little hinky.

Duke had no reason to hurt her other than an association with the person he suspected *might* have been involved in his brother's disappearance. That hardly seemed like a good enough reason to disrupt Dahlia and Felix's honeymoon period.

Besides… if she was being honest, she wasn't really worried. Not because Duke *wasn't* a real threat, but because something in her gut told her he wouldn't get the chance to make good on it.

That honed awareness tightened her belly. Cecilia turned away from the microwave to lean against the two square feet of countertop her kitchen boasted. She slowly brought a can of strawberry soda to her lips as her gaze settled on a window.

There was no evidence to prove her theory. Nothing but her gut feeling and fleeting glimpses out of the corner of her eye. Sometimes she laid in bed and stared out her window, straining to catch a glimpse of a broad-shouldered silhouette on the rooftop across the alley.

She knew he was there. He was *always* there.

Cecilia took a slow sip, savoring the cool, crisp sweetness of her favorite drink. It helped ease a little bit of the familiar disappointment. There was nothing to see outside the window. It was too dark outside and too bright inside. Even during the day, there wasn't anything of note beyond the brick wall of the building next door.

Her own miniaturized reflection gazed back at her, exhausted from a long night, still wearing her ridiculous, low-cut uniform, and searching for someone she'd never see.

CHAPTER **FOUR**

The microwave's cheerful ding made her jump. Shaking herself, Cecilia set her soda aside. Her fingers just grazed the button when the front door of her apartment burst open.

It slammed against the wall with teeth-rattling force. She yelped and jumped away from the counter as two large vampires she vaguely recognized as bouncers from the bar stormed into the apartment.

"Whoa, what—" Whatever she might've been about to say was cut off when one of the vampires lunged for her.

Huge hands closed around her arms and lifted her off her flailing, kicking feet as Duke strode through the broken door. It'd only been a few minutes since she saw him last, but somehow he looked more haggard and cruel than he had when she left him.

"Sorry about this, Cece," he sighed, kicking the door shut with the heel of his boot. It shook the thin wall as it jammed into the frame at an odd angle. His gaze swept across her little apartment apathetically before it settled on her cell phone, which lay uselessly on the counter.

Duke strode away from the door to pocket it. Nodding to the man holding her, he ordered, "Put her in a chair."

"Duke, what the *fuck* are you doing?" she cried. Her sneakers bounced off the hulking vampire's shins as she thrashed.

He barely seemed to notice. The vampire had no trouble hauling her across the studio to drop her into the antique armchair she and Dahlia had spent a memorable weekend learning how to reupholster.

Her ass had barely hit the cushion when Duke's other lackey dropped his heavy hands onto her shoulders, pinning her to the chair. Fear sluiced through her veins when Duke crouched in front of her, a sleek black bolt gun in his hand.

"I really hoped you'd tell me on your own," he muttered. His free hand scrubbed across his face, briefly muffling his low voice. "You were always such a fucking chatterbox at the bar, but now you don't want to talk. Figures."

She'd done a lot of risky things — even things she didn't tell Dahlia about — to chase that fleeting, dangerous high, but staring into the Duke's flat eyes was a step beyond even her.

She recoiled as far as the hands on her shoulders would allow. Her bones had turned into something she could only compare to jelly, and her skin flashed between being too hot and too cold when she glanced at the weapon in his hand.

"Duke," she squeaked, pressing her heels into the scuffed wood floor, "I really don't know what you're talking about. Please, just— just let me go."

"Can't do that until I find out what the Amauris did with my brother."

Cecilia shook her head vigorously. "I don't know where Devon went. I *don't.*"

"Of course you don't," he replied, sounding incongruously reasonable. "But you and I both know who *does.*"

Cold fear turned into fiery protectiveness in an instant.

"You want Dahlia," she surmised. An incredulous laugh escaped her. "You want me to… what? Help you get to my best friend so you can get to Felix? What?"

The vampire's lips thinned. "I don't need your help."

"Then why are you doing this, huh?" She looked up at the man holding her captive with scathing disdain. "If you're stooping to terrorizing women who haven't done anything to you, seems to me like you're pretty desperate."

"Oh, you haven't seen terror yet, Cece." Digging her glittery pink phone out of his pocket, Duke continued, "I'd really rather not hurt you, but I will if I have to. We both know that Dahlia was turned. *I* know that my brother went to her apartment the night she got released from the hospital. *You* know that she's now living the high life in United Washington with Felix Amauri."

His thumb tapped the phone's screen. It lit up, casting the harsh lines of his face into even more unsettling angles. "What I don't know," he continued, "is what happened to my brother after he went to see her. We're going to find that out together."

Cecilia stared at him, shocked into silence by the layers of his audacity. Firstly, at the implication that Devon had gone to see Dahlia out of some concern for her wellbeing and not because he intended to coerce her into the vampire equivalent of marriage. Secondly, the fact that he knew as much as he did and had *any* belief that his brother might still be alive.

She didn't know much about Felix, but what little Dahlia dared to share with her gave her a pretty good idea that he wasn't the kind of man you lived to cross twice.

"Why?" she breathed. "You can't get revenge on someone like—"

He rolled his eyes. "Don't be fucking dramatic. I don't want revenge. I want *restitution.* I'm owed a lot of fucking money from the Amauris if they killed my brother *and* destroyed half my bar. I'm gonna collect."

Duke didn't notice her incredulous stare. He was too busy fiddling with her phone. He didn't bother looking at her until he held the device out to her. "Now, you're going to be a good girl and give Dahlia a call."

A breath exploded out of her — not quite a laugh, but close. "What do you want me to say to her?"

"You're going to tell her that if she doesn't give me what I want, I'm going to shoot you."

Her throat spasmed. "And what if she says yes?"

Duke clicked his tongue. Laying his hand on her knee, he gave her a pitying look. "Then I'm still going to shoot you. He was my brother, you know? Fair's fair."

Her stomach dropped. Either way she was fucked. The only choice she had was how badly she and her best friend would suffer.

Cecilia wouldn't have classified herself as particularly brave or selfless. She was soft and hadn't experienced much hardship in life besides being caught between two parents who despised each other. She was not hero material.

But she was a damn good friend, and she'd sooner throw herself off the rusty fire escape than put Dahlia in harm's way — or leave her with the lasting trauma of hearing her friend's murder over the phone. That need to protect the only family that meant anything to her burned as hot and deadly as the power in the battery pack of Duke's gun.

Ignoring the phone, she leaned forward as much as her captor would allow. Her lips pulled back in a mockery of her normally sunny grin. "Duke, I say this with absolutely zero due respect: go *fuck* yourself."

The butt of Duke's gun cracked against the soft rise of her cheekbone. The skin split as Cecilia's head whipped to one side hard enough to make her neck crack.

She'd fallen off a bike once when she was seven and smacked her chin on a curb. Dahlia had run as fast as her scrawny legs could carry her to find an adult, leaving a dazed Cecilia to sit beside her abandoned bike, blood trickling down her neck.

Until the moment Duke struck her, falling off her bike was the most painful injury she'd ever sustained.

Stars exploded in front of her eyes, but it took what felt like a long time for any pain to register. White noise filled her ears as her nerves struggled to catch up with the brutal strike. Her brain didn't seem to know what to do with the information it'd received.

Her vision went wobbly as reflexive tears filled her eyes. She stared out the window, blinking hard several times, and tried to get her bearings again. Her pulse throbbed in her cheek like the beat of the awful music the DJ played in the bar.

Movement beyond her warped reflection in the window made her squint. It took her a second to realize what she saw wasn't some pain-induced hallucination.

There really *was* a man pulling himself up the rickety old fire escape.

Or at least, she thought that's what it was. It was hard to tell with a dark, glossy visor covering his face and the way he swung his massive body up over the railing, straightened his arms without letting go, and smoothly rocked his legs forward.

A year had passed since she saw more than a glimpse of him, but something in her recognized him instantly.

My phantom.

She didn't have time to consider what his end goal was. The animal part of her brain understood. It compelled her to turn away from the window and squeeze her eyes shut half a second before a pair of black combat boots shattered the glass.

Shards rained down on her as the vampires reached for their guns. She lurched forward, throwing herself off the chair and onto her hands and knees just in time to avoid losing part of her head to a plasma bolt.

The acrid scent of it seared the inside of her nose as she crawled away. Glass sliced her palms and bare knees but she didn't feel it.

Pressing her back against the kitchen cabinet, she swallowed a scream as a massacre played out before her.

The man in black didn't appear to have a gun. He didn't even have a knife. While the three vampires each had bolt guns, he fought with nothing more than his gloved hands.

Matte black claws slashed at the vampire who'd held her in the chair. His gun clattered to the ground as a dark smile spread across his throat. In the span of a heartbeat, his mouth opened and his head flopped back, almost completely separated from his neck. Blood erupted in a geyser across that lovingly upholstered chair and window as he collapsed onto the floor.

I'm going to have to reupholster that chair again, she thought, too stunned to do much else.

An involuntary sound of alarm escaped her as she caught sight of Duke, the vampire closest to her, raising his gun to fire at her phantom. The newcomer's head swiveled toward her just in time to avoid a point-blank shot to his helmet.

The plasma bolt just grazed one side. It was more than enough contact to do devastating damage to most material, but apparently not whatever the helmet was made of. The white-hot plasma merely scorched the strange glass.

The bolt seared a hole in the wall behind him. It hardly had the chance to smoke before the phantom swooped down on Duke like a gods-sent calamity.

Cecilia watched in horrified fascination as he went for the vampire's extended arm. She'd never seen anyone or anything move the way he did. It was faster than fast and so graceful that she had trouble tracking him.

And he said nothing. Not when the vampires hollered at him, demanding to know who he was and warning him to leave or they'd shoot again. Not even when Duke frantically tried to bargain with him.

In one smooth movement, he'd grasped Duke's arm, raised his knee, and brought the arm down across it — once, twice, and a third time.

Bone burst through flesh with a sickening crack. A sickening yowl of agony escaped Duke's throat. His gun fell to the floor and slid into the widening pool of blood made by his nearly decapitated lackey.

Cecilia drew her scratched legs up to her chest as if they might shield her from the horror. She wanted to cover her eyes, but she couldn't lift her arms to do it. She couldn't even close her eyelids. Her gaze was locked on the phantom as he tore off the lower half of Duke's arm and casually tossed it aside.

Blood gushed from the wound, but it was the least of the vampire's worries when the phantom grasped both sides of his head. She couldn't quite figure out what he intended to do until he began to squeeze.

The heels of his gloved hands pressed inward, into the delicate indents of Duke's temples. With one ruthless shove, the sides of the vampire's head caved in. His mouth opened in a silent scream as the capillaries in his eyes burst. Blood streamed from his nose and the corners of his eyes as they popped like cherry tomatoes in their crushed sockets.

It was over in a matter of seconds but it felt like it took hours for Duke to stop struggling. The man in black dropped him to the floor. Duke lay twitching and gurgling, the shape of his head reminiscent of some crooked neck gourds that sold for too much money at the grocery store around the fall equinox.

She couldn't stop staring at him. Even when the last vampire standing made an unsuccessful run for the door, she couldn't tear her gaze away from her dying boss. He stared sightlessly back at her through the pulped gelatin of his eyes, blood oozing from his mouth and pearly fangs gleaming in the dull yellow light streaming through her shattered window. His last breath was a thready, pathetic wheeze.

The only thing that managed to pull her attention away from him was the steady tread of combat boots across the old wood floor.

She swallowed hard, shaking from head to toe, as they came

to stand between her and Duke's body. They were completely black, but she could make out the gleam of blood splatter on the matte material and heavy rubber tread.

His slow crouch was so smooth that she didn't even hear the rustle of his clothing. He rested his wrists on his knees and cocked his helmeted head.

The pose was so casual that she nearly let out a burst of hysterical laughter, but managed to swallow it back just in time.

The fingers of his deadly right hand flexed and curled. From somewhere deep within that blacked out helmet, a familiar robotic voice intoned, "You require assistance."

"I don't," she rasped. The words were nearly inaudible, as if her throat had been scraped raw by a scream she never got to release.

She flinched when the hand that had so casually split a throat raised. The very tips of those metal-covered claws touched a spot below her wounded cheek.

In that same toneless voice, he insisted, "You do."

Her mouth opened to protest, but she didn't get a chance to. Instead, a yelp burst from her lips as something sharp struck her bare thigh.

Cecilia looked down in horror. While she'd been distracted, he'd apparently retrieved what looked like a very small, unlabeled pen injector. The tiny needle was stuck in her leg while his thumb depressed the plunger at the top.

"What is that?" she screeched, trying to kick him and his needle away. "Whatever that is, just—"

"You require assistance," he repeated. A gloved hand dropped to pin her leg down, holding her still. Fear surged as she vividly recalled what those hands had so easily done to Duke's arm. And other parts of him.

A pathetic whimper slipped past her lips. "Please just let me go."

The shape of him began to waver. Even his robotic voice seemed to come from farther away when he replied, "No."

Tongue growing worryingly heavy, she slurred, “Why?”

She listed to one side, but she didn’t make it far. The phantom caught her head and eased her down onto the floor. The scent of his gloves — blood-saturated leather and something indefinable — permeated her lungs as her vision darkened.

“Because,” he answered simply, “you need me.”

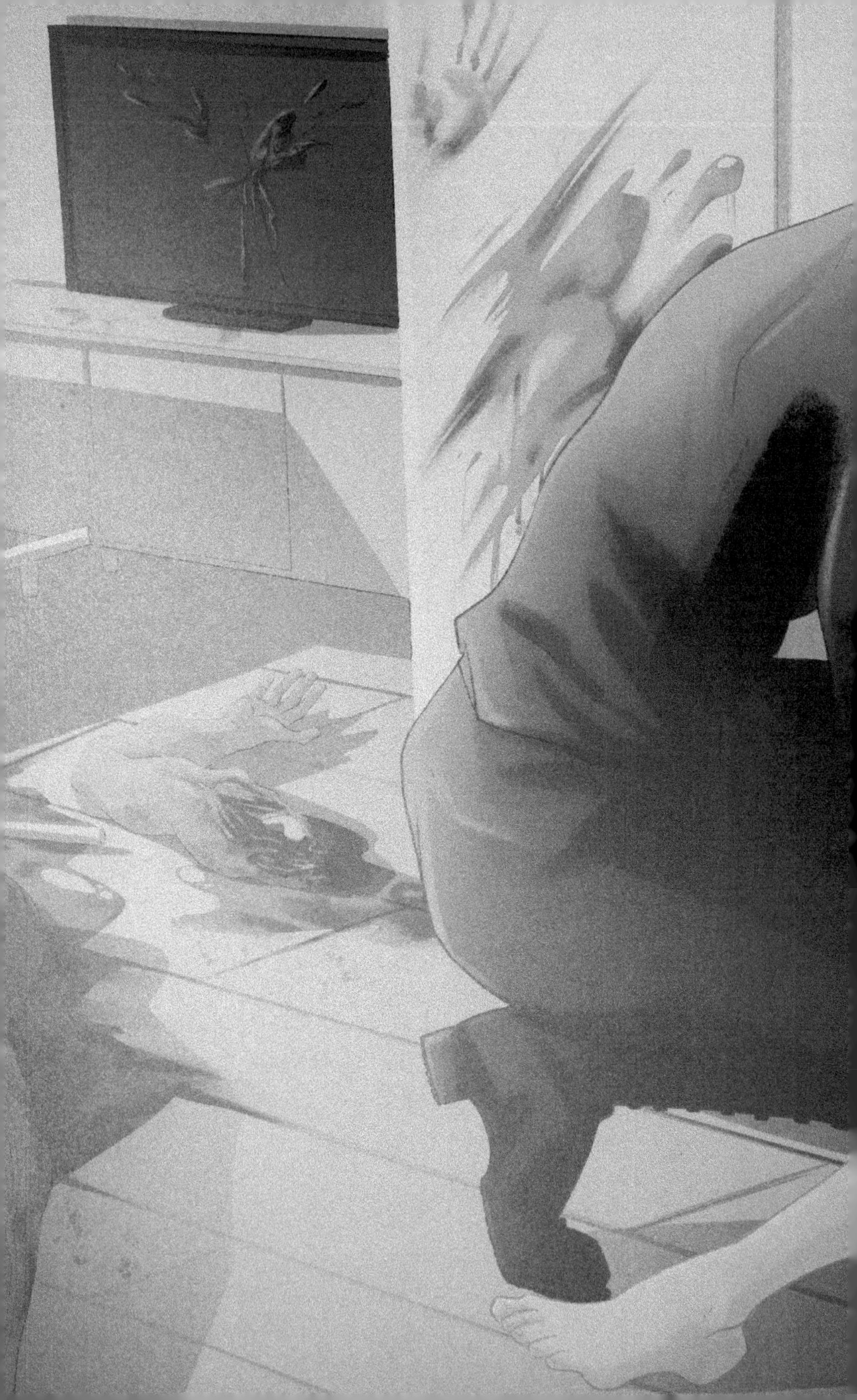

CHAPTER FIVE

SLOANE PICKED HER UP, SLUNG HER OVER HIS SHOULDER, AND strode across the apartment. Her long black hair swayed against the thin armor covering his back as he navigated the tiny home he'd watched for so many months. He didn't bother stepping around puddles of viscera or the twitching limb he'd torn off the dumb fuck who pistol-whipped his doe but stomped right through them both.

His breath rasped through his helmet's filter. He couldn't remember the last time he'd been breathless, let alone… whatever it was he was experiencing now, but he didn't have time to think about what that meant.

The soft weight of his target, held so carefully over his armored shoulder, was his sole focus.

Sloane held her tightly with one arm as he reared back to kick out the remaining glass that clung to the window frame. It wouldn't puncture his armor or even his skin, but Cecilia was far more delicate. She'd sustained enough damage due to his negligence. He refused to add any more.

When he had her secured, he'd return to the apartment to clean up the mess he'd made.

Carefully ducking through the empty window frame, he

stepped onto the old fire escape. It groaned pitifully under his considerable weight. Silently cursing, he hurried to pull the curtains shut over the window, hopefully disguising the carnage for a little while, before he began the treacherous one-handed climb down the ladder.

Normally he wouldn't have bothered, preferring to simply jump to the ground, but he was painfully aware of how brittle Cecilia's bones were. Instead of the fastest route, he gripped the backs of her thighs and climbed down with one hand. His uniform absorbed the artificial light in the alley, keeping him hidden, but it wouldn't do much good in the coming sunrise.

Even Fracture had to do their best to stay out of sight during the day.

His boots hit the cracked pavement of the alley with a solid *thwump.* Sloane adjusted his grip on his target and stepped confidently toward the curb. He'd left his bike at the barracks, just as he always did when he took up his post outside her home. To give the captain peace of mind, it was equipped with a tracker that Sloane wasn't supposed to know about. Of course, they all knew they were constantly monitored, so it wasn't a particularly effective deterrent of bad behavior.

When he wanted to be seen, he took the bike at the barracks. When he didn't, he took one of the several other identical bikes he stashed around the city. Unfortunately, none of them were suitable for the situation at hand.

The vampires had come in a flashy vehicle that would work far better.

Sloane fished a small metal device from his pocket and held it up to the shiny red door. It worked by hacking the m-enhanced chip that connected all modern vehicles to the street grid and acted as something like a universal key fob. A handy tool to have for someone like him, especially because the scum of Burden's Earth never seemed smart enough — or have the taste — to buy vintage cars.

The car's security disengaged with a quick flash of the

narrow headlights. Streaks of dawn were beginning to lighten the sky above the street when he opened the back passenger door and laid Cecilia across the shiny black seats. He didn't stop to admire her. He couldn't, or else he'd never get her to safety. Sloane barely allowed his gaze to skim over the vast expanse of her exposed legs before he firmly shut the door.

Evacuation, he thought, leaping over the hood of the car. *Get her safe. Get her patched up.*

After that… well, he didn't have a plan, but he'd never been much for them anyway. Sloane acted first and figured out the rest later. It was why he was such a good assassin, and also why he'd never been able to stop himself from stalking her after that first night. Just because he'd given himself the assignment of her protection duty didn't mean he'd changed his tactics.

His heart hammered as he slid into the driver's seat. Sloane pulled away from the curb smoothly, his gloved fingers curled around the steering wheel. That raw, pulsing nerve in his chest screamed with feeling as he navigated the tangled knot of San Francisco's streets. The m-grid kept him from the screeching speed he would've preferred, but it also helped to not draw any attention to them.

Sweat dripped down the back of his neck, soaking the folds of armored fabric that attached to the underside of his helmet. The words *I have her, I have her, I have her* pounded the inside of his skull like dozens of fists. The fists hit harder when they drove through the Presidio, where the sprawling Patrol barracks and officer quarters were. There was no way any of them would know what he'd done or that he had a civilian in the back of the stolen car, but the threat they represented raised his hackles anyway. There were hundreds of trained people who'd know immediately that they should be separated. They'd try to take her away, and he'd never see her again.

Never, never, never.

He had to grit his fangs to ease the tension until they crossed the border onto the bridge. The world was a blur as he crossed the Golden Gate with his precious cargo. The sunrise splashed reds and oranges across the sky, as vivid as the mess he left in her apartment.

He couldn't leave it there. Once he had her secured in his bolthole, he'd return and dispose of the bodies in his usual way.

No one would know.

Paranoia blended seamlessly with determination. Sloane hadn't planned this, but that didn't mean he was unprepared. He'd been doing nothing but prepare for something like this moment for a year, just in case.

In case someone hurt her. In case she ran. In case they tried to take her from him.

For all scenarios, the response was the same.

Sloane drove for an extra hour, far beyond his bolthole, to a rundown storage facility off the freeway, where he quickly and efficiently moved his cargo into an unmarked vehicle he kept there, alongside a cache of money, fake identification, and weapons. Everything, including Cecilia, went into the trunk. Sloane carefully pillowed her head on a bag of clothing before he shut the door.

That done, he moved the vampire's car into the storage unit and made a plan to dispose of it, too. He doubted anyone would report it missing, knowing the circles the owners most likely ran in, but he hadn't survived this long by being sloppy.

With everything loaded up, he climbed back into the nondescript SUV and drove back the way he came. Just before he crossed the bridge again, he turned right. The property he'd purchased twenty years ago was deep in the heart of what was then about to become a Territory Recreation Area, meaning only the local wolf shifter pack could be his neighbors. It'd been a tip from Delilah that helped him secure the perfect bolthole, and he'd been as grateful as a man like Sloane could be ever since.

Located on the edge of a sea cliff overlooking the Bay and San Francisco beyond it, Battery 129 was built as a solid concrete watchtower at the height of the Great War. When the war ended, the massive guns had been removed and the soldiers stationed there reassigned. Abandoned, it fell into disrepair.

He purchased it under a series of shell companies and false identities just before the news broke that the area around it would never be developed. It was the perfect hideout — one of three he had scattered across the continent — and he'd spent the two decades since secretly turning it into more than a concrete shell.

The security perimeter disengaged as his biometric signature registered, allowing them to pass safely over the border into his territory. Sloane pulled up to the disguised entrance and idled there for a handful of seconds to wait for the sensors to confirm his identity. The ground rumbled faintly beneath the SUV's tires as the entrance in front of him, draped in vines and partially obscured by scrub, pulled to one side. A long concrete tunnel leading to a garage appeared behind it.

Sloane pulled inside, cool overhead lights flickering on as he passed beneath them, and parked the vehicle next to several unmarked motorcycles and another, smaller car. There was a small amount of relief at being in his territory at last, but it vanished as soon as he opened the trunk.

Cecilia lay on her side, her dark hair draped over her face and her long-limbed body lax. The sedative he'd given her would last several hours, but he still handled her gingerly as he pulled her out, afraid that even small movements would disturb her.

His breath wheezed through the helmet's filter as he stared down at her in his arms. He'd watched her sleep countless times. The shape of her lips and the fan of her lashes were intimately familiar to him. But he'd never *held* her. He never touched her at all.

Holding her in his arms while she slept was… different.

Sloane tucked her into his chest, mindful of her head, and hurried up the spiral staircase that ran up through the cliff and connected the garage to the watchtower. Most of the small fort was built within the cliffside, making it extremely defensible. It would take a small army to get through all the security he painstakingly laid down, and another one to actually break through the three foot thick concrete walls. Despite its closeness to the city, it was by far the most secure hideout he possessed — and therefore the only one he felt comfortable bringing Cecilia to.

The living quarters were undecorated, but he'd done his best to make them comfortable in the ways he understood. The bed he deposited Cecilia on was plush, and he'd gotten her favorite brands of body wash and shampoo for the shower. He'd even found her exact toothbrush and placed it by the sink. It sat there, unwrapped and ready for her, since he bought it six months prior.

There were no windows in the bedroom, but he'd placed string lights like the ones he observed in her apartment over the doorway, and a soft pink rug in the center of the floor. It was a weak imitation of her colorful world, but he was proud of what he'd managed to cobble together, all things considered.

And she looked damn good in his bed.

Sloane's chest rose and fell with increasingly labored breaths as he slid his arms out from beneath her. Her head tilted to one side, revealing the perfect shapes of her profile and the nasty bruise left by the prick who pistol-whipped her.

A rumbling growl passed through the modulator. "Fucker," he hissed, daring to curve his gloved fingers below her chin. "I'd kill him for you twice if I could."

Cecilia didn't respond. Her breathing remained even, undisturbed by his voice or his touch. The temptation to indulge his curiosity about the texture of her skin and hair, the scent of her and the feeling of her breath on his face was almost too much.

Sloane pulled himself back immediately.

Protecting her was his priority. It was the only thing that mattered. That included protecting her from himself.

Hissing at his own lack of self-control, he strode to the bathroom, where he kept an advanced med kit. He'd patch her up first, then see to everything else. Sloane ran through how much time they'd have before he was missed as he expertly extracted and organized the medical supplies he'd need.

It was a lucky thing that he'd just gotten off a week of local assignments. The members of Fracture had recently been forced into taking *weekends,* something none of them knew what to do with at first. That meant he had two days before anyone reported his disappearance to the captain.

Sloane grimaced. He wasn't afraid of Kazimier. Realistically, he knew they were evenly matched. But he didn't like his odds if the rest of Fracture hunted him, too.

And they would, if they thought he'd gone AWOL. They hadn't just been trained to be threats to the populace. They were trained to kill each other, too.

Doesn't matter, he decided as he began the painstaking process of plucking glass from the cuts in her knees, hands, and feet. Each shard reminded him of just how fragile she was, and every one of them was a recrimination of his failure.

If something as simple as *glass* could hurt her, how could he expect her to survive in the world without his protection? Even a momentary lapse had put her at the mercy of three vampires. Only the gods knew what could happen if he left on an extended assignment. The thought of leaving her alone for months at a time sent chills down his spine.

Keeping her locked away in the Battery was the only choice.

Sloane used only the tips of his metal claw-caps to grip the rubbery bandages as he carefully placed them on her body. By the time he was done, she appeared to have more bandages than skin, but he wasn't about to be too cautious with her.

Easing the blankets out from under and then over her sleeping form, he sat on the edge of the bed for a moment, his hands braced on his knees.

Sloane had gone days without sleep. He'd run hundreds of miles and scaled buildings with his bare hands. Nothing, in his extensive experience, left him as out of breath as tending to his doe.

His gaze was drawn back to her magnetically as he tried to find his normal rhythm. *Beautiful* was the word to describe her. *Perfect* was another.

The only beautiful, perfect thing in his entire fucked up existence. The only person who looked at him with doe eyes. The only person who asked him for his name. The only person who *smiled.*

The only person he'd die to protect.

Sloane's exhale shook as he surrendered to the urge to strip off one glove. Her right hand lay on top of the sheets, fingers curled loosely in sleep. Unsuspecting and breakable and *there.*

His skin was a purple so pale it could be mistaken for white. It seemed like a painfully alien color against the warmth of her skin tone when he hovered his fingers over her knuckles. The tips of his real claws, diamond-hard and razor-sharp, touched the back of her hand first.

A flashing warning appeared in his peripheral vision. It was the heart rate alarm wired into the screen of his visor.

Sloane swallowed hard. His fingers trembled as he slowly pressed their pads against the silken skin of her knuckles.

She *burned.*

Like he'd stuck his fingers into the heart of a plasma charge, the smallest contact seared him to the bone. Sloane gasped, shocked by the instant pleasure-pain that came with the touch. He panted as he followed the lines of her tendons beneath her paper-thin skin and fine webbing of veins.

A flush of heat suffused his body, starting from his fingertips and traveling up his arm to infect every cell. A popping, tingling sensation came with it, like there was some sort of chemical agent in her flesh that was rapidly spreading through his system.

Alerts continued to pop on his visor's screen. A warning about his heart rate. Abnormal vital signs. Blood oxygen exceeding normal levels. Perspiration increasing. None of it made him pull away.

He couldn't. Not even the concrete ceiling and cliff caving in on top of them would've made him move from that spot, or stopped him from tracing his way up her wrist toward the soft curve of her inner elbow.

"Cecilia," he mouthed, daring to draw the tip of his tingling claw over a dark freckle.

Her arm jerked. Sloane reared back and leapt away from the bed as she drew her limb in toward her chest, her head turning restlessly on the plain white pillowcase.

Away from him.

A flash of shame burned almost as hot as the feeling that came when he touched her. Snatching his glove from where he'd discarded it on the bed, Sloane swallowed the bitter taste of want and fled, locking the door behind him.

CHAPTER
SIX

THE BODIES WERE EASY ENOUGH TO DISPOSE OF. THE CAR WAS EVEN easier.

Corpses were simple to handle when one had the right tools and a strong stomach. The vampires were stuffed into three barrels of lye he kept ready, and the car was stripped of all identification before it was plunged unceremoniously into the heart of a junkyard two hundred miles from where he'd stolen it.

The most difficult part of the day was, unfortunately, returning to the barracks.

Unlike the rest of Patrol, Fracture's headquarters was located in Stern Grove, a small, forested corner of the city blocked by a tall gate. Towering Blue Gum eucalyptus and native redwoods ringed the barracks and trapped a nearly perpetual ghostly fog. The area was chosen by Thaddeus II himself, who wanted them isolated in every possible way — even from their fellow soldiers.

Normally, Sloane was good at acting like he hadn't done anything wrong when he walked through the barracks. That was mostly because he never felt any guilt when he did. This time was different.

Tension was a live wire between his powerful shoulders as he strode through the door. He rapidly ran through everyone he knew to be on an assignment and those who might be off-duty. They'd all been relatively local since they'd been "benched for deliberate, if creative, disobedience" by the sovereign, which made things trickier than usual.

He wasn't normally in the mood to socialize, if one could even call what the members of Fracture did such a thing, but he was even less so knowing that his charge was back in his bed. If any of them knew, they'd try and take her away from him. They might even try and steal her for themselves.

Who wouldn't? Sloane's breathing deepened as he passed into the mess hall, his focus on the entrance to their private quarters. *She's perfect. And they'd all be better at keeping her safe. They'd take one look at her and snatch her away.*

"Are you all right?"

His back stiffened. A bright pop of fury erupted inside his chest. It wasn't aimed at the empath who so casually curled up on one of the arm chairs in the lounge, a tablet in her hands and a blanket thrown over her legs. It was aimed at himself for failing to notice her.

Gods, where is my fucking head?

The answer was simple enough, he supposed. His head was back at the Battery, in bed with the woman he'd vowed to protect.

Sloane flexed his claws when he flatly replied, "Yes."

"Are you sure… Sorry, I still have trouble figuring out which of you is which with your helmets on."

He forced himself to turn slightly toward his captain's mate. Not that getting a better look at his visor would help her. They were designed to keep team members anonymous. If no one ever saw their faces, it helped Thaddeus perpetuate the myth that he had a secret army of hundreds of shadow soldiers rather than a handful of broken elves too good at killing.

But Atria had other ways of figuring out their identities.

The instant the air began to buzz around him, full of the strange kind of static all witches seemed to carry with them, Sloane's skin crawled.

"Ah, Sloane." A smile stretched across Atria's face. It wasn't the same as Cecilia's smile. Atria's was… patient. Like she did it to manage him rather than because she felt any true warmth toward him. Which didn't really make any sense, because Atria had known him longer and Cecilia had only smiled at him that one time.

It was the truth, though. He felt it in that raw, aching thing in his chest.

Oblivious to his growing impatience, Atria continued, "I should've guessed. Kaz told me you'd be around. You've got a couple days off, right?"

Sloane doubted he'd ever get used to how much the captain shared with his mate. He knew she was good friends with the sovereign's consort, Margot Goode, and a wildly intelligent scientist in her own right, but he didn't think it was wise to give her access to so much confidential information.

And he'd never, *ever* be comfortable with her ability to read his emotions.

Fighting the urge to simply ignore her and walk away, he replied, "Yes."

Job done, he turned to leave. He didn't make it far.

The sound of blankets rustling heralded further delays. "Wait, Sloane!"

Fighting back a snarl that would've gotten him a brutal ass-kicking from her mate, he turned his head to look over his shoulder at the witch. She'd sat up and slung her arms over the back of the couch. The marks of her previous order, Burden's Bonded, ringed her slim wrists, but it was the tattoo around her neck that marked her as Kazimier's mate.

Her brow furrowed deeply as she stared at him with those penetrating brown eyes that saw too much. Speaking slowly as if she was trying not to spook him, she asked, "Are you sure you're okay? You feel… off."

His mind went quiet. In the span of a heartbeat, all paranoia and anxiety over the state of his charge vanished. In its place was the perfect, empty stillness of the predator.

As Sloane silently watched her, letting her question hang unanswered in the air, he wondered if she knew how easily he could kill her. Even having seen her impressive range of abilities used in combat, it wouldn't take him more than a minute to dispatch her. Witches were just as weak as arrants if you got to them fast enough.

He had no desire to kill her. She was his captain's consort, and that meant she was one of them. But he'd kill any one of his team members to protect his doe.

And he'd do far worse to keep her.

Sloane stared at her blankly from behind his visor, his breathing slow and even. For a long moment, she ceased to be a person. She was no longer his captain's mate. She wasn't an honorary member of Fracture. She was an obstacle and a threat to the only thing that mattered to him.

Atria had no idea how narrowly she avoided danger when she added, "I don't mean to pry. I just… If there's ever anything I can do to help you — something that you can't go to Kaz or the rest of the team for — just know that you can come to me, okay? Not to put you on the spot or anything, but you've got plasma streaks on your helmet."

Passing his hand over the damaged side of his helmet, which would need to be replaced if he didn't want a single hit to shatter the new weak spot, he muttered, "A weapon misfire."

Atria blew out an incredulous breath. "Oh come *on,* Sloane. I won't snitch."

His eyes narrowed. "You'd tell your mate."

"Only if whatever it was posed a risk to yourself or someone else," she replied, somehow managing to hold his gaze steadily despite the visor. When she dipped her chin, her long, dark hair slid against her cheek. For just a moment, the similarities between his doe and his captain's mate were uncanny.

All at once, the familiar predatory emptiness left him. She was once again a woman, a team member, and a witch whose features echoed those he'd become so very fond of.

She firmed her jaw before announcing, "Otherwise, no. I wouldn't tell Kaz. And I would expect the same from him. You're his family, Sloane, which means you're my family, too. We keep each other's secrets."

A strange frisson of something passed through him. A feeling, maybe, but one he didn't care to acknowledge, let alone identify.

"It's a bad idea to be my family," he warned her. "They usually end up dead."

He didn't stick around to hear her reply. Sloane strode out of the mess hall and down the corridor to his room, intent on accomplishing his task.

It was good, he reasoned, that he ran into Atria. He'd been seen, which would hopefully give him just a little more time before anyone reported him as missing. There was no reason to kill her when a witness might actually make things a little easier.

It had absolutely nothing at all to do with the new, uneasy stirring in his gut at the thought, or how similar she looked to his doe.

Taking a bag wasn't unusual for any of them, so he didn't bother trying to hide it as he walked out of his room with a black backpack slung over his shoulder. It had everything he needed — the scant few possessions that meant anything at all to him.

When he walked back out into the mess hall, he wasn't surprised to find Atria still in her spot. This time, he wasn't determined to ignore her.

Passing the couch, he asked, "Where do you get the strawberry soda?"

"Huh?" She blinked up at him, dark eyebrows arched with surprise.

"The strawberry soda you keep in the fridge," he clarified. "Where do I get it?"

Atria shook her head slightly. "Oh, um… You can get it at pretty much any grocery store. You've been to one, right?"

"Yes," he lied.

Information obtained, he crossed the room. When he reached the door, Atria called out, "I thought you hated sweet things!"

He pushed open the door. "Not all sweet things."

Sloane switched vehicles one more time before he finally made it back to the Battery, a six pack of strawberry soda dangling from the tips of his claw. He released a slow breath as he reverently laid out Cecilia's soft pink sweater. Mother of pearl buttons winked in the golden light of sunset that streamed through the large windows overlooking the cliffside.

The urge to take off his helmet was strong, but he knew it was useless. The scent he was so addicted to had faded only a few weeks after he brought it back to the barracks. And yet he continued to press his nose into it at every opportunity, some desperate animal in him whining as it searched for the essence of her.

He'd never smelled anything like her before. He'd never *felt* anything like how he did when he breathed her in. It'd rattled something loose in him. Like the first falling stones heralding an avalanche, it unlocked an uncontrollable need to be near her, to watch over her, to pin her down and *bite*—

Sloane pushed himself away from the counter. There weren't many hours left in the sedative dose he'd given her, and it was ridiculous to sit there pining after a sweater when his doe was safe in his room.

Compulsively straightening his kit, he followed the stark concrete hallway to the primary suite. A lock blinked red beside the door knob, awaiting his code. Sloane's heart rate picked up again as he swiped the complex pattern on the screen.

The door unlocked with a hydraulic hiss. Throat tightening with anticipation, he stepped inside the bedroom.

Immediately, his gaze landed on the bed. The *empty* bed.

Senses screaming to high alert in the span of a heartbeat, he twisted to the side just in time to catch the full force of a metal lamp to the plasma-damaged side of his helmet. The blow shattered one side of his visor and, with a single breath of her scent, what was left of his control.

CHAPTER SEVEN

CECILIA FROZE, THE REMNANTS OF THE BENT LAMP CLUTCHED IN HER sweaty fingers.

She knew she should move. Just standing there, arms raised, and gawking at the monster she struck was the stupidest possible thing she could do. Every true crime show host screamed in the back of her mind, urging her to take her opportunity and sprint out the door.

Except she was still seeing double, so she couldn't quite make out exactly where the door was, and he hadn't actually *moved.*

Cecilia blinked rapidly in an attempt to clear her head. It wasn't easy. She'd only just managed to stand without tipping over when she heard his footsteps outside the door. Her balance was off, she wasn't one hundred percent sure that she wasn't stuck in a nightmare, and if she tried too hard to recall how she got to the concrete room, all that came to her was spraying blood and dismembered bodies.

It took a lot of work to sort out what was real and what was the drugs.

When she squinted at him, she found that her first impression was correct. He really was just standing there, blocking the doorway with his enormous body, his helmeted head turned away from her. He didn't even look like he was breathing.

Knees wobbling, she forced words out of lips that still didn't feel quite like they belonged to her face. "Did… I kill you?"

The room was dark without the lamp. She'd woken up to tomb-like blackness only broken up by the soft twinkle of fairy lights strung over the door. Even in her drugged state, she immediately noticed that the walls were concrete and starkly windowless. Now the twinkling lights looked downright sinister as they illuminated the jagged, broken glass of his helmet as it turned in slow motion to face her.

Cecilia had seen some scary stuff in her time at The Lush. She'd scrubbed blood from booths, seen brawls that ended with guns drawn, and, most recently, watched three grown men be torn apart by the monster standing in front of her.

Her phantom.

Nothing came close to the terror he inspired in her when he turned to fix her with a single burning eye. She couldn't see much more than that through the cracked glass of his helmet, but she didn't need to.

Cecilia's fingers went numb. The lamp fell to the floor with a crash, but the monster didn't even flinch. He stared at her with that dark, burning eye. His diamond-shaped pupil was blown so large it swallowed his iris, giving him a look of fathomless, empty blackness.

An alarm beeped faintly, but she had no idea where it came from. Cecilia stumbled backward on her bandaged feet as a primordial fear took over her body. It piloted her backward like she had any hope of escape in the windowless cell he'd put her.

The fear *burned*. Slowly, at first, then with a steadily building roar in the pit of her stomach.

Cecilia's breath hitched as she pushed herself into the corner farthest away from him. Her thighs pressed together reflexively when a pulse of desire echoed between them. Her vision swam when she flattened her sweaty palms against the cool concrete walls, briefly turning the monster into two.

He didn't chase her across the room. He didn't yell or throw the lamp at her. He didn't even growl.

What he did was much, much worse.

He *walked.* Slowly. Each step a perfectly measured and executed movement that pulled him farther out of the glow of the fairy lights. His heavy boots crunched in the chunks of glass on the stark floor, then went silent as he passed over the fluffy rug. He walked and he didn't say a word.

Cecilia began to hyperventilate. She looked around for more weapons, but unless she could summon some serious adrenaline super strength, she didn't think she could chuck the bedside table at his head with any sort of effectiveness.

Besides, without the element of surprise, what chance was there? She'd seen him rip Duke's arm off like it was nothing. That kind of strength and brutality was beyond her comprehension.

"You should know," she warbled, flattening her spine against the wall as he officially entered her personal space, "my best friend is a stone-cold crazy bitch. If you kill me, she'll spend the rest of her life hunting you down and destroying everything you hold dear. And then she'll shove something down your throat and watch you die. I know because she's told me she would, word for word."

Dahlia would never forgive her if she died like this. The woman could hold a grudge like no one Cecilia had ever known, and it'd just been the two of them against the world for so long that she was absolutely certain she'd see her furious best friend in the afterlife.

She warned me to be careful, Cecilia silently bemoaned. *She told me to call her if Duke came asking questions. Why didn't I call her?*

Her breathing was little more than shallow pants as the monster pressed his palms flat against the wall on either side of her head. Heat blazed off of him, scorching her despite the fact that he hadn't touched her. The alarm grew louder as his head dipped. For a wild moment, she thought it might be a manifestation of her panic, but she quickly realized it was coming from within his shattered helmet.

There was another sound, too: a deep, rattling purr so powerful it seemed to shake the very air between them.

Cecilia shuddered as he dropped his head onto her shoulder. The sharp bite of glass against the tender skin of her neck made her jump, but she had nowhere to go and no room to move. Despite being slightly taller than the average arrant woman, he completely towered over her.

The burning in the pit of her stomach intensified with every deep, audible breath he drew in, muddling the very real terror with the same fucked up desire that she'd never been able to explain.

How humiliating. I'm gonna die turned on and not even in cute underwear.

The monster sucked in another deep breath. The pitch of his purr changed as his gloved hands slid slowly down the gritty wall with an ominous rasping sound.

"My doe," he whispered. His voice was distorted and double-layered. One was the robotic monotone she remembered from all those months ago, while the other came from within the shattered edges of the helmet. *That* voice was… different.

Rough. Deep. Breathless.

Lust scorched a path down her spine, aimed straight for the juncture between her thighs. Trying to force it down, Cecilia sucked in a deep, shuddering breath. "What…"

She wasn't even sure what she intended to ask. *What do you want? What is happening right now? What can I do to get you to let me go?*

Whatever might've come out of her mouth was irrelevant because he cut her off with a very elvish hiss.

Her phantom drew one hand away from the wall. She tensed,

waiting for those claws to do… whatever it was he intended to do to her, but nothing happened.

Instead of touching her, he reached toward his own neck. There was a quiet click, then a rustling noise as he lifted the bottom of his broken helmet up. Her eyes darted down reflexively, but there was little to see. He hadn't taken the helmet all the way off. It'd been lifted just enough to reveal a sturdy chin and finely sculpted lips. Pearly fangs, an upper and lower pair, were starkly white against the dark shape of the tongue that snaked out to drag against the curve of her jaw.

Electricity sparked along every nerve-ending. Cecilia gasped, her fingers curling against the concrete, desperate to find purchase as her knees wobbled.

She knew he was an elf. Most elite members of Patrol were, and he was clearly that. But she'd never really been close to one before. They didn't socialize with arrants — or anyone besides their kind, really. Things had been changing since the sovereign took a witch as his wife, but she wagered it'd take at least a century for those changes to trickle down to her lowly social rung.

To her and people like her, the elves were not just indestructible predators who'd once cracked open their bones to suck out the juicy marrow. They were the lawmakers. The protectors. The monsters in the dark. They kept the streets clean and the universal income flowing, but they were ruthless in their pursuit of order.

To them, she was nothing.

So it really didn't make any sense to her why she'd been thrown in what could only be described as the world's strangest cell. She wasn't important enough to ever make herself known to *any* elf, let alone a member of Patrol. Aside from that one incident in the alley, she didn't think she'd ever been worthy of even a glance from one of them.

The few times she'd been near an elf, her instincts had

screamed from an ancient place in her mind that still remembered when they'd served her people on dinner plates.

But when *this* elf ran the flat of his tongue over the hammering pulse in her throat…

Cecilia bit her lower lip until it stung. A sound caught in the base of her throat. It was a strangled, involuntary moan that made her face flame with embarrassment.

One moment the elf was drawing a line down her throat with his tongue and the next he was across the room, one massive hand pushing the shattered mask back into place.

Cecilia lost her balance and sank onto the cold floor. Flabbergasted, she stared at her captor as he pressed his own spine against the opposite wall. Like *he* was the one desperate to get away from *her*.

The elf's single visible eye was so wide she could make out a white ring around that fathomless black center. His deep chest rose and fell with labored breaths that rasped loudly through his helmet. Those deadly claws, capped in what looked like black metal, sank into the concrete and gouged deep grooves. The sight of them made goosebumps rise all over her body.

She brought a shaking hand up to her neck. Cool, damp flesh met her fingertips. Her voice trembled when she demanded, "What is this? I thought— I thought you were protecting me. Why are you *doing* this?"

The elf's eye darted left and right. "I am," he croaked in that unsettling mix of voices. "I— I—"

Feeling emboldened for reasons that most likely related to the drugs in her system, Cecilia lurched away from the wall. It was intensely gratifying to see *him* flinch backward, like she was the one who posed the threat.

Pointing an accusatory finger at him, she said, "You saved me from Duke, sure. I'm grateful for that. But what the *fuck* is this? You drugged me, put me in a cell, and now you— you *lick* me?"

"You required assistance." There was something like a whine

in his bass voice, like he needed her to believe it not for her sake, but for his.

Cecilia stumbled forward, jabbing her glossy, pink-tipped finger at the closed door. "I *require* you let me go!"

"Stop," he barked, looking like he wanted the wall to swallow him whole. "Stop walking."

"Why?" She bared her flat, useless teeth at him. "You afraid of me now? Well, you should be!"

It was an astonishing thing, seeing the moment he decided to run. Him, the terrifying elf who could break her spine with two fingers and half a thought, turned his attention to the door a moment before he made a break for it.

Cecilia let out a screech of outrage as he dove for the door. She wasn't far from him or it, but he was so much faster than her. Even when she wasn't fighting off whatever sedative he'd given her, he would've beat her to it.

The door slammed shut in her face. Furious at him and her missed chance, she banged on it with all her strength.

"No! Let me out!" Cecilia grabbed the knob and twisted it with both hands, but it wouldn't budge. A series of clicks along the doorframe told her that whatever lock he had installed, it wasn't the kind she could pick with a bobby pin or bash open with her shoulder.

A guttural scream tore from her throat. "Don't you dare do this to me, asshole! Don't you *dare!"*

Slapping a hand on the door, she sank into a crouch. She'd been too key-up to notice the ache in her head or the throbbing pain in her cheekbone, but it came to her with a vengeance as she tried to catch her breath.

Gods, she thought, dropping her forehead onto the door, *Dahlia is going to be so pissed.*

CHAPTER **EIGHT**

In some small, withered part of him that still remembered what it was like to be normal, he knew what she was and why he was so drawn to her. He'd always known.

But it was an unmitigated disaster to have it confirmed.

Sloane threw himself away from the door. Clawing at his helmet, he released the latches and hurled it down the empty hallway. It landed somewhere far away with a crash, the compromised glass shattering, but he didn't care. It was useless anyway.

He'd never fully appreciated how the helmet and its filters protected him. It'd always seemed like over-cautiousness on the part of their handlers, this terror that they'd be slaves to their pheromones one day. He'd had his visor broken before and it'd never been an issue in combat or any other situation.

But of course, everything was different with Cecilia.

Sloane dug his claws into his sweaty hair and sank into a crouch against the wall opposite the bedroom. His chest heaved with every desperate breath as his body rebelled.

Every cell popped and bubbled. The fine strands of his muscles seized one by one. His fingertips burned with exquisite pleasure-pain as his claws retracted for the first time. Every sense sharpened as his brain rewired itself.

In a single breath, he'd gone from her protector to her greatest threat.

My consort, he thought, fighting the urge to crawl back to the door, to her. *My mate.*

Sloane didn't think he'd ever been hysterical before. Not since he was five, anyway, and taken from his parents. But the panic that eclipsed him as he realized what he'd done was close to it.

All elves knew the Pull. They knew what it meant when their claws slid back into their fingertips and their insides burned with need. It was the singular bond born in an inescapable chemical reaction, one that tied consorts together for life. Constant contact and pheromone exposure was a necessity. Without it, an elf would gradually die or become insane. Both were common.

It was their greatest weakness, and one they'd gone to great lengths to hide from the other beings of the world. Fracture's handlers had always warned them about the signs, and what they should do if they suspected they'd had contact with their consorts: *run.*

They were too dangerous for mates. They couldn't be trusted. They could offer nothing — not affection, not family, not stability. And the risk of what the hormone imbalance might do to the members of Fracture were too high for anyone with a brain to accept.

But he'd ignored all the signs. He'd stalked her. He'd brought her to his home. And now he'd sucked in lungfuls of her potent scent and tasted her skin and—

Sloane didn't even realize he'd crawled on his hands and knees to the door until he got there. The urge to be near her was a wild, roaring thing in him. Hearing her screaming and banging on the door, knowing he was the cause of her distress, made him want to claw his own flesh in recompense.

I'm sorry, he silently moaned. Sweat dripped down the slope of his forehead to fall from the tip of his nose as he battled every ancient instinct demanding he soothe her.

What did he know about soothing anyone, anyway? Nothing. The most he could offer her was isolation.

Sloane pulled himself away from the door. Putting distance between them was as unnatural as yanking out his own fangs, but he did it. For her.

Protecting her had been his obsession and perhaps the only worthwhile thing he'd ever done. He wasn't going to give that up now.

His skin crawled as he climbed to his feet at the end of the hall. His broken helmet lay against the wall, the shattered glass visor staring up at him impassively. The steady beep of the internal alarm was an accusatory rhythm.

He couldn't recall a time in his adult life when he'd made so many mistakes that could've got him killed. Any plasma damage to a helmet meant immediate replacement. That was standard protocol. He *knew* better. But he'd gone in there anyway, risking not just his own safety, but hers.

Can't protect her. Can't be a good mate. Fuck. Fuck!

Unable to stand the sound of the alarm a moment longer, Sloane kicked the helmet as hard as he could. It crumpled under the force of his steel-toed boot, its sleek form crushed like one of the Pink Pop soda cans that sat so innocently on the kitchen counter.

The alarm guttered out.

It was a lucky thing he kept a spare in his armory. Gods only knew what he'd do if he smelled her again, or if he had to face her without the protective barrier of the smoky glass visor.

Sloane stalked toward what was once a soldier's sleeping quarters. Another lock guarded the door. He hadn't thought much of it when he installed it, other than the fact that it was standard protocol to lock up unused weaponry, but now he was grateful for his foresight. Cecilia had proven herself shockingly resourceful, so he had no desire to see what she'd do with unfettered access to plasma weapons.

His neck heated at the memory of how his doe had gotten the drop on him. It was a small mercy that he'd likely never see another Fracture member again. If any of them found out he'd been clocked by an arrant woman with a *lamp…*

Letting himself into the armory, Sloane slammed the door shut behind him with a vicious growl. Heat crackled under his skin as his body urged him to go back.

He'd always heard that the Pull could be escaped if one removed themselves quickly enough, but no one had an answer for how much exposure it really took to make the bond permanent.

It *felt* permanent. Nothing in his body felt as it had just an hour ago. He wasn't Sloane, Thaddeus II's rabid attack dog. He was something infinitely more dangerous.

Hers.

But it had to be reversible. One moment of contact couldn't be all it took to seal her fate. He could not and *would not* allow it.

Sometime later, he didn't feel any better or more normal, but he couldn't hide from her forever. The plan, if it could really be called that, was simple: he'd never breathe her in again, and he'd never, under any circumstances, allow skin to skin contact.

He didn't bother thinking about small details like how that would work if he had to keep her under his protection for an extended period of time, or what it meant that a part of him couldn't imagine letting her go. He certainly couldn't give up his duty to protect her. Not *now,* knowing what she was to him.

Sloane was a man of action. He handled the problems set before him and chose not to worry about the ones rushing over the horizon.

Currently, the problem in front of him was the bedroom door.

A scowl grooved his mouth behind his new visor. The colorful cardboard box he held in one hand felt incongruously heavy as he stared at the smooth gray door.

It wasn't fear that stopped him from entering the bedroom. It was the opposite. Sloane had never wanted anything more than to see his doe again, which was the problem. A lifetime of brutal training had refined the instinct to reject his wants. The more he craved seeing her again, even after only a couple hours of separation, the sharper the instinctive recoil.

But he couldn't avoid her. He didn't want to — even if she tried to hit him with the lamp again.

Sloane sucked in a deep breath of filtered air and swiped his finger over the keypad. When he cautiously pushed the door open, he found his doe sitting stiffly on the floor across the room, her legs tucked against her chest and her long hair disheveled.

The sight of her hit him like a truck.

Instinct roared, demanding he rip his helmet off and run to her — to crawl, if necessary. The Pull popped like bubbles in his veins, a shot of pure need that nearly overwhelmed him.

It was dark with only the twinkle lights to illuminate the windowless room, but his predator eyes had no trouble making sense of the shadows. Even with the blood splatter on her dress and the bruises that decorated her face, Cecilia was the most beautiful creature he'd ever seen.

He even liked the venomous glare she aimed his way.

Desperately locking down his instinct, Sloane slowly closed the door behind him. His heart hammered as he stood there, box in hand. There was a compulsion to stand at attention for her, like he'd been trained to do for all his superiors, but he reined it in.

The silence in the room was oppressive. Sloane had taken an icy shower in a fruitless effort to cleanse himself of her pheromones and his sweat, but it proved pointless. Cold sweat beaded on the back of his neck as he locked eyes with her.

He'd never been more grateful for the modulator in his helmet than when he croaked, "Do you require more medical attention?"

Cecilia's dark brows shot up. "Are you asking if I feel okay?"

"Yes."

This time, he didn't have any trouble dodging the projectile she sent his way. The pink toothbrush bounced harmlessly off the door as he stepped smoothly to one side. "No, I *don't,*" she seethed, "because I'm being held captive by a maniac who knows what fucking *toothbrush* I use!"

Sloane blinked. After a considerable pause, he replied, "That doesn't seem relevant to my question."

For a second, Cecilia appeared genuinely baffled by his response. "Are you kidding me?"

"No." He glanced at the bed. Frowning, he asked, "Why are you on the floor?"

"You answer my questions and maybe I'll tell you why I'm on the floor," she growled, arms crossing.

Sloane clicked his tongue against the back of his fangs. "You didn't ask a question."

"Are you— Good gods, are you *new* or something?" Cecilia pushed herself off the floor. Standing with her hands on her hips and bare feet spread, she began ticking off questions on her fingers. "Let's start with the standard kidnapee rundown, huh? Where am I? Who are you? Why am I here? Are you going to kill me or otherwise hurt me? You know, all the questions one might ask when they've been drugged and locked away in a concrete cell."

Non-plussed, he answered, "You're not in a cell. You're locked in my bedroom."

Cecilia's lips parted. After a handful of seconds, she deadpanned, "You understand that's worse, right? I need to know you understand that."

He really didn't see how that could be possible. As someone who'd spent much of his life in Thaddeus II's dungeon below Solbourne Tower, he'd seen exactly what a true jail cell was. Sure, his bedroom had certain similarities, but he'd tried his best to provide some comforts for her.

"There's a rug," he pointed out, in case she'd missed it. "And lights. And a bed."

"Your bed." Cecilia eyed the piece of furniture like it would suddenly rise up and bite her.

Not understanding what the issue was but sensing that pursuing the topic further would only cause more problems, Sloane executed a tactical pivot. "You're in my home. You're here because it's safe. I don't plan on killing you or hurting you. I want to protect you."

Drawing on all of Cesare's ramblings about gifts and food and how to make friends, Sloane carefully approached the center of the room. He placed the box on the floor, the colorful label facing her, and then retreated back to the door.

"You must be hungry," he said, tucking his hands behind his straight back.

Cecilia gawked at the box. Pushing strands of dark hair out of her eyes, she wheezed, "Cereal?"

Behind the shield of his visor, Sloane nervously licked his lips. "It's food."

"What kind of drugs did you give me?"

Confused by the abrupt change in topic, he answered, "A mild sedative."

Cecilia rubbed her eyes. "And how *much* did you give me?"

"Enough." *But clearly the dosage was miscalculated.* "It should be completely metabolized by now. There are no documented side effects for arrants besides grogginess, mild headache, and potential nausea." Feeling oddly defensive, he added, "It was necessary for your safety and an expedient exfiltration."

"So I'm not hallucinating this," she grimly noted. "You really brought me a box of Fruit Crunchums."

"It's what you like."

"So you've definitely been watching me." Cecilia let out a laugh, but it didn't sound particularly happy. Pressing the heel of her palm to her forehead, she breathed, "I mean, I *knew* it, but this is— And the *toothbrush—"*

Sloane had no idea what to do when she quickly turned and

walked into a corner, where she crouched low and covered her face. In a muffled voice, she said, "Glory save me, I've been kidnapped by my stalker. It finally happened. It really, actually happened. Cece, you finally got what was always coming to you. Fuck. Gods, fuck you, honestly. I don't deserve this."

Concerned, he warned her, "You should never turn your back on a predator, Cecilia."

"Well, what're you gonna do?" The demand came from behind her hands. "You've already got me. And you could kill me with your pinky toe if you wanted to, whether I was facing you or not. So who even cares?"

Sloane glanced down at his boots. "I don't want to kill you with my pinky toe."

"No, of course not, because you brought me Fruit Crunchums! You clearly want me to live!"

"I do." *You're my consort. Your health, your safety — it means everything to me.*

Twisting her neck, Cecilia peered at him through her spread fingers. "Why? Why do *any* of this? You don't even know me!"

It was on the tip of his tongue to tell her he'd spent every spare moment over the past year studying her, but even with his limited social skills, he understood that probably wasn't wise. Instead, he insisted, "It's my job."

Dropping her hands, she gave him an incredulous look. "To stalk and kidnap women?"

"To keep you safe." He reluctantly moved away from the wall to nudge the box with the toe of his boot. "Eat."

Her gaze darted between him and the box of vile-looking food product. Speaking slowly, she asked, "You really want me to eat?"

"Yes. You need food to live." There was a brief pause as some strange, foreign entity battled for control over his tongue. "And… you like it. You should have things you like."

She swallowed. Eyeing him speculatively, she said, "I'll eat — under two conditions."

Sloane's back straightened. "Name them."

"Tell me your name."

A spasm of discomfort wracked his insides. Mouth dry, he informed her, "That's only one."

"Tell me first and then I'll give you the second one."

Ruthless, he thought, impressed despite his unease. Even after a year of observing her, he'd never witnessed this shrewd side of his doe. But then again, he'd never seen her brain a man with a lamp, either.

He liked it.

Figuring he was in for a penny in regards to breaking every protocol he lived by already, he answered, "…Sloane. Sloane Fortuner."

"Sloane," she muttered, sending a shockwave of desire through his very bones. Those big brown eyes, liquid black in the shadows, stared up at him when she demanded, "Sloane, get me a bowl, spoon, and milk."

CHAPTER NINE

For a long time, the only sound in the cell was the *tink tink* of Cecilia's spoon hitting the bottom of her bowl.

She sat against the wall, her bandaged legs crossed in front of her and the plain white cereal bowl in hand. Her captor, *Sloane,* stood rigidly by the door until she snapped at him to sit down. Cecilia didn't actually expect him to listen, but she wasn't altogether surprised when he immediately sank to the ground to mimic her pose.

She'd never excelled at much. School didn't come easily to her, and she had no natural talents to speak of. The only skill Cecilia had ever reliably called upon was reading people.

And Sloane, despite his facelessness and voice modulator, was becoming increasingly easy to read.

Eyeing him as she crunched on the cereal he'd placed at her feet like a cat drops a mouse, Cecilia tilted her head slightly to get a better look at him. One eye had begun to swell, thanks to Duke's handiwork, but it didn't impair her sight too much as she took him in.

"So… what's the plan here, champ?" She lifted the bowl for a long sip of artificial fruit-flavored milk.

"To keep you safe." That flat, modulated voice grated against her nerves almost as much as his answer did.

Lowering her now empty bowl to the floor, Cecilia crossed her arms. "You said that already, but that's not a plan. Try again."

There was a long pause. She could almost feel his gaze searching her face, trying to determine exactly what kind of response she wanted. It was almost as vivid as the sensation of his flat, raspy tongue sliding along her throat that just wouldn't leave her.

"You will stay here until it's safe to leave," he amended.

"What or who are you protecting me from, exactly?"

He had an answer to that question immediately. "Everything."

Cecilia took a deep breath. "Okay. Right. So let's just… start from the top. You've been stalking me for at least a year, right?"

"Guarding you," he corrected.

"Right," she dragged out. "Following me to and from work. Watching me through my windows. Other creepy shit, I'm sure." Cecilia looked at her hands, which rested in the folds of her bunched up mini dress. Picking at her sparkly pink nail polish, she muttered, "I noticed."

His helmet seemed to scrub his voice of all inflection, but she still thought there was an edge of disbelief in it when he said, "Impossible. I'm very good."

"At killing things, maybe, but not hiding from a woman's intuition. We *know* when we're being followed, champ."

The faint sound of creaking leather drew her gaze to his fist curling against the concrete floor. "If you knew I was following you, why did you continue to meet up with strangers in secluded places?"

Cecilia slapped her thigh and let out a crow of satisfaction. "I *knew* it! I knew you were messing with my dates!"

Ever since her last disastrous attempt to satisfy that danger-loving desire that seemed to want to destroy her life — in this instance, a brief and toxic relationship with an orcish biker named *Crash,* of all things — she'd vowed to find a good, normal man. She wanted to be a teacher in the cut-throat world of San Francisco's education system, then to have a home and kids. Chasing the worst man in the room at every opportunity was incompatible with those dreams.

But the dates stopped calling her back. Then they began to reschedule. And then they stopped showing up altogether.

It felt like paranoia to suspect her phantom, but after the third man stood her up, Cecilia couldn't think of what else it could possibly be. She was a dyed in the wool charmer and bon vivant.

It certainly wasn't *her.*

So it was deeply satisfying to have her theory validated when Sloane leaned forward and replied with absolutely zero shame, "Men are threats. I eliminated them."

The dizzying high of getting an answer to a question that had plagued her for months was quickly squashed. Blood draining from her cheeks, she whispered, "Oh gods, you didn't kill them, did you?"

She really, really didn't like how long it took him to answer.

"No. There was no need. It was easy to convince them it was in their best interests to leave you alone."

I bet it was, she thought with a shudder. Her last potential date was with a math teacher, of all things. She couldn't imagine what it must've been like for someone like him to be confronted with *Sloane.*

Rubbing her eyes, Cecilia muttered, "I'm a normal person, Sloane. I'm not under constant threat. Those guys were just *guys.* Ones I specifically picked because of how nonthreatening they were, I might add. I don't need whatever protective duty you've decided to slap on me."

"You were attacked in your home," he replied, so fast it seemed like the modulator momentarily struggled to keep up with him. Those powerful shoulders bunched around his ears, pulled up by an invisible string of tension. "You were beaten and threatened by three vampires. If I hadn't resumed my post, you could've been killed or worse — therefore making your statements are untrue."

Cecilia ran her fingers through her hair. They still trembled faintly, though she couldn't tell whether that was a result of an adrenaline crash or a side effect of Sloane's handy sedative.

She hadn't exactly had a minute to really digest everything that'd happened with Duke and his gang of bullies. It seemed a lot less immediate than the fact that she'd been drugged and kidnapped by the man who'd ripped them to pieces. But when Sloane said it like that, she was taken back to that moment in the chair when Duke raised the pistol, and the crack of it when he struck her cheek.

He would've done worse to her. Whatever was necessary, in his mind, to get what he believed he was owed. And then when he got it, he would've killed her to get revenge on Dahlia.

A wave of nausea forced her to draw up her legs and place her head between her knees.

He would've made it an awful death, she realized, swallowing bile.

The thought of what that would've done to Dahlia was worse than any ephemeral pain. Death would put an end to that quick enough, but Dahlia's wounds would never heal.

They'd been inseparable for nearly their entire lives. They'd been family when their blood relatives weren't. To know that bond had been so close to being weaponized made her want to throw up every Fruity Crunchum she'd spooned into her gullet.

Blowing out a calming breath, she said, "Okay, fair. I can see why you think the exception proves the rule in this one instance. It doesn't, to be clear, but I see how it looks. And I… I mean, I'm *grateful,* obviously. Thank you for saving my life. But you can see why everything you did after that has been a little distressing, right?"

"I could see that you were distressed," he answered in a very non-answer kind of way.

She sighed. "Yeah, I guess that was expecting a bit too much."

"Why were you attacked? I need more information to accurately assess the present threat."

Cecilia looked up from between her knees. His dark visor revealed nothing, but she imagined she could still see that burning eye beneath the plasma-proof glass. She could *certainly* still feel his tongue.

"There is no threat anymore. And it's a really long story," she croaked.

Sloane didn't miss a beat. "I only require pertinent details. Proceed."

She wasn't sure why that was so funny or why that felt so very *Sloane,* a man she only knew from shadows in the corner of her eye or a gleam of something that shouldn't be there on the rooftop across from her apartment. And yet she snorted with laughter anyway.

The bizarre reality of the entire situation was finally catching up to her, she thought. The attack, the grisly murder, the kidnapping, the cell… Now a bowl of cereal and a stilted conversation had finally pushed her straight over the edge.

Getting the words out from between huffs of laughter, she explained, "My boss— my old boss, Devon — wanted to get with my best friend Dah—"

"Dahlia McKnight, arrant, blonde, white, under six foot, apartment 4F, server at The Lush and student enrolled in a business program. Visited your apartment one to four times a week, recent witness of the assassination of Yvanna Amauri. Approved for visitation based on your apparent familiarity, lack of criminal record, and established routines. Recently absent. I marked that as a concern to follow up on." Sloane inclined his head. The fairy lights glittered in the shiny glass dome that kept him hidden. "Continue."

Trying very hard not to be derailed by that deeply unsettling string of accurate information about her friend, Cecilia muttered, "She got turned into— uh, you probably know that, I guess. Anyway, she's with this super scary vampire named Felix, who caught Devon hassling her and..."

Sloane made a sound that might've been a hum if not for the modulator. "He eliminated the threat."

There was no way to tell if there was real approval in his voice or if that was just her imagination. The chances were good that it was real, though.

"Exactly," she continued, resting her chin on her knees. "But then Devon's big brother came looking for him. Dahlia isn't around because she moved in with her husband — which is really rude, by the way. His cousins packed up all her stuff so I don't even get to steal her clothes anymore.

"Did I like looking at them while they packed it all up? Yes, of course. I have two eyes, a heart, and a deeply unsatisfying sex life. Is it still messed up that she abandoned me with no notice? I think so. Not that I'm not happy for her, obviously, because I really, really am. But you know we had a plan, right? How are we gonna raise our kids together if she's across the continent with her new vampire family and I'm here single and alone and fucking *miserable—"*

Cecilia cleared her throat. *Good gods, I think I need more of that sedative.*

Embarrassed by her little outburst of vulnerability, she tried to get back on track. "Anyway... You met Duke. He thought a good way to get Dahlia and Felix to tell him what happened to his brother was to— Well, you saw."

It took her a second to place a faint ticking sound. It came from the steady beat of Sloane drumming his metal claw-caps against the concrete floor.

Speaking slowly, he confirmed, "So this was not tied to any outstanding debts that might've been owed to the vampire syndicate?"

Cecilia shook her head. She'd done some reckless stuff in her day, for sure, but she'd never been desperate — or foolish — enough to borrow *money* from the brothers who owned the bar.

"The attack wasn't motivated by any criminal activity or wider interest by other parties?"

"Not that I know of," she replied, grimacing. "Duke and Devon weren't exactly well-connected. And to be honest, I think even the criminals they associated with would be relieved that at least Devon is gone, if not both of them."

"So you don't believe there are any outstanding threats against you now. What about retribution for Duke's elimination?"

Eyeing him, she muttered, "You know, I really don't enjoy how you use that word."

Sloane's head tilted slightly to one side. "Heard. I will try to use the word *threats* less in the future."

"Why is that the word you think— Actually, no. Not important." A little chilled after sitting for so long on the heat-sucking concrete, Cecilia gave herself something to do and ran her palms briskly up and down her bandaged legs. "No, I don't *anticipate retribution.* I guess it's not out of the question, considering I know virtually nothing about Duke or Devon's personal lives, but it seems unlikely. They both kinda sucked."

"What about Felix?"

She narrowed her eyes. "What about him?"

"He's clearly dangerous."

Cecilia sat completely upright. Alarmed by the turn in conversation, she exclaimed, "Not to *me.* Felix would probably jump in front of a train for me — and I haven't even officially met the guy. But he'd do it for Dahlia, no questions asked. Good gods, the man keeps trying to give me a new apartment and sometimes even money when he thinks I won't notice. He's not a threat!"

"You're arrant," Sloane replied, claws stilling their restless motion. "Everyone is a threat to you."

"Newsflash, champ, but of the two of you, I'm pretty sure *you're* the one with the higher body count. So if anyone's a threat to me, it's you." Cecilia gestured wildly toward the room, her gaze roving around the bare gray walls. "When Felix kidnapped Dahlia, at least he didn't throw her in a cell!"

She half-expected him to deny it, or at least play the *I'm your protector* card again, but he didn't. Instead, Sloane rose up from the floor. His shoulders were stiff and his arms held perfectly straight by his sides when he announced, "Correct. I am the bigger predator. That's why you need me. There's no one more qualified to keep you safe."

He turned away from her. In that lifeless robotic voice, he finished, "I'd burn this territory to the ground for you, Cece."

Heart racing, Cecilia watched him move toward the door with wide eyes. "Where are you going? Are you locking me in again? Wait—"

"You're cold," he said, back to her. "You require more appropriate clothing. I'll return shortly."

Before she could argue — or worse, beg her captor to stay — he slipped out of the room. Cecilia fell back onto her butt with a shaky exhale.

"Damn it," she hissed, dropping her head into her hands. "I really hope it doesn't take him as long as it did to get the milk."

CHAPTER **TEN**

He was gone just long enough to give her ample time to think.

Cecilia sat gingerly on the edge of the large bed, her tailbone smarting after so much time on the hard floor. Lost in thought, she stared blankly at the crisply folded corner of the sheets. Even after she'd spent gods only knew how long sleeping on top of them, they still looked like they'd been folded with a laser level and secured with a staple gun.

Her toes curled in the ridiculous pink shag rug. It wasn't identical to the one she had beneath her bed in her apartment, but it was close. The toothbrush she found in the attached bathroom, however, *was* the exact same color and brand she used.

Objectively, that was a bad sign.

Even Cecilia, who loved the sweet taste of danger on her tongue, couldn't be okay with the series of events that had led her to this concrete bunker. Sloane, her phantom protector, had become her kidnapper. He was also a down-bad stalker.

Bad, bad combo you've got there, champ.

She'd *known* she was being stalked, of course, but there was something romantic about having a protective shadow making sure she got home all right after work or peeking through her window when she took her top off. Confronted with the reality of having a dangerous man watching her every move, however, was a different beast.

But Cecilia was a practical sort of optimist. Growing up in a home held together by nothing more than appearances, there'd yet to be a situation she couldn't turn around with a little elbow grease and sunny delusion.

Every bad situation had its benefits. She just had to figure out what they were and exploit them.

Sloane is obsessed with me, she thought, lips twisting from one side to the other. *Obviously, that's unhealthy. But I'd probably be dead if he wasn't, so let's call it a wash.*

As scary as he was, she didn't get the feeling that he wanted to hurt her. That didn't mean he wouldn't, but it seemed less likely that she'd end up dumped in an unmarked grave, so she'd take it. And going by the way he kept jumping to get things for her, Sloane appeared desperate to please her. She could use that.

Obsession meant he liked her. Liking her meant he'd want her approval. Wanting her approval meant he'd try to get her what she wanted, up until those wants crossed an invisible line. If she could find that line, she could gradually push it further and further back, opening up more chances to escape.

As part of her extensive post-graduate education to become a teacher, Cecilia had taken several psychology and behavioral courses. She'd once spent an entire semester learning the best ways to communicate and defuse conflict. At the time, she'd found that particular class mostly asinine and condescending, but the lessons rushed back to her as she tried to puzzle out the best way to deal with her captor.

Separate yourself from the conflict. Hear what they're saying. Confirm what was communicated. Clearly state your position without blame. Suggest possible solutions and request feedback. Rinse, repeat.

Cecilia lifted her head to look at the door. She couldn't hear him out there, but she swore she could sense him. Her heart rate picked up whenever he got close. Goosebumps prickled her arms and legs not from the cool temperature but from an elemental sort of awareness. When the locks disengaged, it wasn't fear that made her body flush from head to toe.

She held her breath as the door opened, letting in a shaft of sunlight. It vanished almost as soon as it appeared.

Sloane slipped into the room, his large body swathed in black. His shoulders alone could've eclipsed the sun.

Kicking the door shut with a bootheel, he carefully placed two bags on the floor. They were huge canvas rucksacks apparently stuffed to the brim and cinched shut with a draw string at one end.

A little uncomfortable with how oddly… body-like the bags looked, she cautiously inquired, "Whatcha got there, champ?"

"Your possessions," he answered, tucking his hands behind his back in that rigid stance he favored.

Cecilia's eyes widened. Lurching off the bed, she momentarily forgot to be wary of getting too close to him as she hurried toward the bags. "You got my things?"

"Correct. While you were sedated, I returned to your apartment. The bodies have been disposed of and your valuable possessions collected." He didn't move away when she knelt at his feet, her hands already scrambling to loosen the drawstring on one bag.

She'd done her best to clean the blood off her skin-tight mini dress in the bathroom, but the possibility of changing into *clean,* warm clothing made her acutely aware of the fact that it hadn't done much good. She never wanted to see her work uniform again, let alone wear it.

Which shouldn't be a problem, she realized, suddenly a little queasy, *since my boss is dead.*

Shunting that thought aside as something she would have to deal with later, Cecilia thrust her arm into the bag's opening and began tearing out every neatly folded article of clothing he'd stolen from her home. He made an odd sort of grunting noise as she carelessly flung her things around her.

An explosion of comfort rained down around her — a sea of pinks, pastel purples, precious vintage finds, and things she'd stolen from Dahlia over the years. When one bag emptied, she moved onto the other one.

The moment she shoved her arm into it, her fingers met a hard pebbled surface. Cecilia's heart stopped.

She knew what it was by feel alone, but she still couldn't believe her eyes when she extracted the small bedazzled urn.

"You… grabbed my cat?" she choked out.

She barely registered the way he slid into a slow, predatory crouch beside her. His wrists balanced on his knees in a deceptively casual pose when he answered, "That is not a cat."

Holding the ugly urn she'd tearfully bedazzled in a reverent grip, she carefully turned it so he could read the name she'd spelled out in clear crystals. "Yes, it is," she insisted. "This is Oyster. I found him as a kitten when I was fifteen. He died a couple years ago and I… Why did you— I mean, how did you even—"

Sloane cocked his head to one side. "You sleep with it beside your bed. It appeared to hold sentimental value to you."

She didn't mean to laugh. The sound that came out of her wasn't even true laughter. Instead, it was a kind of disbelieving huff crossed with baffled delight. Sloane was so strange, so unreadable, and their situation so outrageous that hearing him talk about any sort of emotion was deeply bizarre.

Only half-joking, she said, "So you understand sentimental value, huh?"

He nodded slowly. "I do."

Taken off-guard, she searched the smoky reflective glass of his visor. He was close. Very close. Her own image was stretched and distorted in the surface, but she swore she could just make out the dark shape of his face beneath it.

In a softer voice, she asked, "What holds sentimental value for you, Sloane?"

"Anything you touch."

Oh, he's a disaster, she thought, facing flushing. "That's not an answer. That's a pick-up line."

Those terrifying claws curled and uncurled, seemingly unconsciously, between his bent knees. "Are you requesting specifics?"

Gently setting Oyster aside, she gave herself an excuse to look away from him and began pulling out the rest of what he'd brought. Her makeup kit and several pairs of shoes tumbled out when she replied, "Sure. I want to understand you."

"Why?"

"Because you are currently holding me captive," she answered bluntly, "and you seem to know everything about me. Also, you licked my neck. It only seems fair."

If she expected an apology for the neck incident, she didn't get one. Sloane replied, "I have a sweater."

Cecilia paused. Looking at him dubiously, she noted, "You don't really seem like a sweater kind of guy."

There was a beat of silence before he asked, "What kind of guy do I seem like?"

She really didn't know how to answer that. Not because she *didn't* have an answer, but because she wasn't sure it was smart to say aloud.

Grabbing a bundle of comfortable clothing from the mess around them, she stood up and dumped it on the bed. Keeping her eyes down, she reached behind her for the invisible zipper of her dress.

"What are you doing?"

"Changing," she answered, struggling to get a grip with her bandaged hands.

Sloane's voice came from a different position behind her when he pointed out, "There's a bathroom."

"Oh, please. Like you haven't seen it all already, roof boy." When she finally grasped the zipper, only to immediately hit a snag, Cecilia cast him a look over her shoulder. "I require assistance."

It seemed to take a minute for him to grasp what she was asking for. When he did, Sloane confirmed, "You… want me to unzip your dress."

Keeping her gaze level with his visor, she said with more bravado than she felt, "You say you only want to keep me safe. Prove it. Give me a hand and don't be a creep about it."

When he took a cautious step closer, she turned her head to face the wall and held her breath. She wasn't sure why she did it. It was a bad idea, and she hadn't thought it through at all. But that reckless, desperate thing in her that craved danger took over her body in a flash. Asking him to prove himself was a clumsy excuse to cover up the fact that it was a different, more shameful sort of test.

Cecilia held the bodice close to her chest with sweaty palms. His warmth radiated through her back as he stepped behind her. She could faintly hear his breath whispering through what sounded like a filter as his fingertips closed around the tiny metal zipper.

Heat licked down her spine as he traced its path downward, revealing her naked back to the cool air of the room. Even as the tension of the garment released, it became harder and harder for her to breathe.

Words tumbled out of her mouth, soft and a little panicked. "Am I your prisoner, Sloane?"

The zipper's painfully slow descent slowed to a stop at her mid-back. "No."

She swallowed. "So you'll let me go?"

"No."

"So I *am* your prisoner."

A heavy, gloved hand settled on her hip. She felt him bend over her as the zipper continued down its little track. Sloane's robotic voice came out quieter when he replied, "No."

Her breath came out in tiny little puffs as the dress loosened completely. She held it to her naked chest and felt her heart pounding beneath it. "You don't know what you're doing, do you?"

Despite the fact that his job was done, he didn't move away. His left hand remained on her hip, and she felt the other hovering at the base of her spine, like he didn't want to let go of the zipper. "The world is unsafe for you. You claim the vampires wouldn't want retribution, but you don't know that. I can protect you here. I have to."

"I get lying low, but I have a life," she protested, staring at the wall. Cecilia thought about stepping away, knowing that he would likely allow it, but she didn't. She couldn't. "There are people who'll miss me, Sloane. People who'll do anything to find me. Even if I wanted to stay here—"

The fingers on her hip tightened. "What would make you want to stay?"

"I'm hearing that pleasing me is important to you," she said, cautiously tapping into all those condescending communication lessons. "But protecting me is the *most* important priority."

"Correct."

Found the line.

Cecilia nodded. "Not being held prisoner is a priority for me. Being trapped in a bunker with my stalker makes me feel afraid. Do you understand that?"

"Heard," he replied. "Tell me what you require."

"Not being locked inside, for one."

"I appreciate your intel, but I believe you have a limited view of the potential fallout from your attack. Until I can confirm that you aren't in any danger, the best course of action is for you to remain here under guard."

"I could go to Dahlia and Felix's house," she offered. "They have, um, intense security. And if they knew what happened, they—"

"No," he interjected, flat and abrupt. "I don't trust anyone else to keep you safe."

Cecilia licked her lips. Taking a shot in the dark, she murmured, "You don't trust anyone, do you?"

"Not with what matters to me," he answered. There was no hesitation with his honesty, which somehow made it sadder.

Cecilia sucked in a deep breath. No matter how she did it, it never felt like enough air got into her lungs when he was near. Her voice came out whispery when she said, "And… I matter to you."

"You are all the good in my world."

He didn't say she was the only good thing in his life. He didn't say she mattered. He said she was *all* the good. Everything.

Cecilia had to brace her knee against the edge of the bed to keep herself upright. For someone who spoke through a modulator and clearly had no solid grasp on healthy relationships, Sloane had a wicked way with words.

She turned her head, but he was close enough that it was hard to see him. Not that there would've been much to see anyway, what with the mask and all.

Lying to herself that he'd made a good point about Duke's murder, she said, "If… *if* I stayed, it couldn't be forever. A few weeks, tops, to let things cool down. *And* I'd have to be able to call Dahlia. If she wakes up at dusk and doesn't see a text from me, she'll freak out. Trust me, you do *not* want Felix hunting me down for her. He's almost as crazy as she is."

A kiss of metal on the overheated skin of her spine made her shiver. It was the very tips of his claws, she realized, thighs clenching hard beneath the short skirt of her dress.

Sloane slowly lowered his head. The hard curve of his helmet touched her temple when he warned, "I would strongly advise her against sending anyone to hunt you down."

Breathless, she asked, "Why?"

"Because they won't survive it, doe."

CHAPTER **ELEVEN**

"WHAT KIND OF PLACE *IS* THIS, ANYWAY?"

Despite the fact that Cecilia's voice was piped directly into his ears through his helmet's speakers, it sounded like it came from underwater. Sloane breathed heavily through his mouth as he watched her approach the wall of windows that overlooked the ocean. The lights of San Francisco's skyline glittered across the navy stretch of the bay, giving the edges of her figure an uncanny, gleaming quality.

Being near her was torture.

Every muscle quivered as he stood stiffly a few feet behind her, his hands tucked behind his back not only because it was the proper position but so he could stop himself from reaching for her.

The shape of her naked back was burned into his mind. The fragile line of her spine, the smooth expanse of her skin…

Sloane bit his lip hard. His fang pierced it smoothly, sending a much-needed prickle of pain through his system.

"It's a decommissioned battery," he finally replied. The rough edges of his voice were smoothed by the modulator, but he still wondered if she could hear his desperation.

Cecilia turned away from the window to look at him. She'd

put on a soft pink shirt and matching sweatpants after he'd been instructed to turn his back. After decades of brutal training and psychological assessments, he knew tests when he saw them. So he'd turned, even though it went against every instinct he possessed.

Not that she was any less desirable in her sweats than she was half-naked. Sloane couldn't take his eyes off her as she stood there, one hand propped on her hip and the length of her hair a dark wave down her back.

"Battery?" Her brows drew together with confusion. "Like… electricity?"

"Like defenses," he corrected. "This is Battery 129, a strategic defense bunker built during the war."

Cecilia turned on her bare heel to prowl around the open living quarters. He eyed her warily, half-wishing he'd stuck to keeping her locked in the bedroom. Not because he worried she'd escape — she wouldn't — but because she was altogether too active now that she was free.

"How are your injuries?" He followed her into the kitchen, which she appeared intent on examining.

Ignoring him, she asked, "Is this a Patrol bunker or something now?"

"No."

He stood to one side of the kitchen island and tracked her movements intently, fascinated by how loud she was even when she wasn't saying anything. The rustle of her clothing, the taps of her feet on the floor, and the soft little sounds she made in her throat when she opened one empty cabinet after another were alien to him.

Perched on the roof of the building beside hers, he'd only ever gotten to watch as she went about her strange rituals. It satisfied a deep, unnamed craving to be so close to her as she did something as mundane as check the fridge.

Her nose wrinkled when she opened a drawer and peered inside. "So this is your place?"

Wondering what she was seeing at that could possibly put that look on her face, he stepped around her to look over her shoulder. Seeing nothing out of the ordinary in the containers of raw meat, he replied, "This is one of my places."

She slid the drawer back into place. "But it's so empty. You don't actually live here, do you?"

"I typically live in the barracks." When it didn't appear she minded his proximity, he shadowed her as she moved to another set of cabinets, where he'd stored the foods he believed she'd enjoy.

Grabbing a bag of chips out of the cabinet — a flavor he'd seen her eat with Dahlia once — she surprised him by hopping up onto the island. Even with the boost, she was quite a bit shorter than him. Cecilia swung her legs back and forth as she expertly ripped open the bag. Popping a chip into her mouth, she eyed him intently.

"So what's the deal here?" she asked, sticking one arm halfway into the bag.

Sloane stood awkwardly by the refrigerator, unsure whether he was allowed to approach or what he should be doing with his arms. She looked so at ease perched on the countertop that it disarmed him. He'd never had to deal with captives before — outside of an interrogation room, anyway — and certainly not one who appeared determined to assert her dominance through sheer confidence.

Seeing her in his space eating the strange human food he'd gotten for her filled him with a satisfaction he normally associated with a successful hunt. His chest expanded with a deep breath that rattled with a purr on the way out.

My consort in my home, he thought, marveling at the strangeness of her. The longing he felt, the pure pleasure of her presence, created an urgency in him that he could only describe as similar to panic.

Watching her blunt little teeth snap a section off a ruffled chip, he demanded, "Elaborate."

"You're a Patrol officer. Are you gonna go to work while I stay locked in here or what? Also, isn't it, like, super against the law for you to spy on civilians?" She pointed one bandaged foot at him, her delicate toes arched. "Going by how you killed Duke, I'm gonna guess that you're used to working outside of the law, but I'm wondering how you thought this whole thing would play out."

Sloane was silent for a beat. He didn't want to lie to her. It went against something ancient and important in his DNA to deceive his consort. She was his. He was hers. Even if he could never allow himself to truly be with her, he knew enough about mates to understand that lying to them was taboo.

But he also flinched away from the thought of telling her who he really was.

She was too young to have experienced the terror of Thaddeus's reign, but she'd know about the infamous shadows squads. She'd know about the masked soldiers he used to kidnap, torture, and kill. She'd know and she'd hate him for it.

Throat working hard around a jagged lump, he forced himself to say, "Protecting civilians is our job." *Now.*

Cecilia snorted. "Nice workaround you've got there, champ."

"I'm not going back to the barracks," he added. "You won't be alone here."

"But don't you have to work?" She gestured to his clothing and mask with a chip. "Or is there some sort of special leave for officers who kidnap women?"

Technically speaking, there was a mandatory three month leave for any elf who found their consort. It was more for the sake of everyone around them than the elf in question, since they became irrationally territorial, possessive, and prone to lash out at any perceived threats to their mates. The first three months were also essential to the bonding period. Skin to skin contact was vital to establishing the chemical connections that lay at the heart of a mated pair.

But none of that applied to Fracture.

Sloane's heart rate sped up. He knew what he was supposed to do if he found his consort.

Fracture didn't get the luxury of three months to indulge in their new relationships. They didn't get to indulge in anything.

If they found their consorts, they were required to follow the Starsbury Protocol: separation, evacuation, isolation.

Immediate separation upon recognition, then evacuation from the area, and isolation from the consort until the pull lessened its grip. Of course, they were also required to report any incident to their captain, who would then be in charge of keeping them from their consort — with force, if necessary.

Arguably, Sloane *had* followed the protocol. Just not in the way the good doctor and his superiors intended. He'd separated himself from the team, evacuated with his consort to a safe location, and isolated them together.

Theoretically, he *could* return to the barracks and continue with his duties, but that would require leaving Cecilia alone. Not to mention the fact that the risks of discovery increased dramatically if he continued to go back and forth regularly. Eventually, one of his nosy teammates would try to follow him, and if they discovered he'd found his consort…

They'd take her away.

That hot, snapped nerve in his chest pulsed with fury at the very idea.

Sloane had no idea what he was going to do now, but he was certain about one thing: no one would take Cecilia away from him.

"I'm on leave," he explained. It was technically not a lie, since his weekend was still active.

Cecilia made a thoughtful sound. Giving him a narrow-eyed look, she asked, "You suspended or something? No offense, but going by what I've seen, you don't exactly scream *rule follower.*"

The corners of his mouth twitched. "I'm not."

It was a fun little game Fracture played. Already alienated from elvish society and the hierarchy of Patrol, they liked to see just how far they could push limits. They also got a lot of pleasure out of literal interpretation. That was why they'd been on what was essentially house arrest since they tracked down the captain and his mate. The sovereign had given them strict orders to *find* his brother, not *bring him home.*

Of course, the sovereign hadn't taken that well.

"So you're gonna stay here." She paused to eat another chip. "With me. For how long?"

"However long it takes."

What *it* was... Well, she could interpret that however she pleased, because he had no answer for her.

Cecilia set aside the bag of chips and dusted off her hands. Her head tilted as she peered into his visor. "Are you gonna wear that thing all the time?"

Licking his lips, he rasped, "I only take it off within the barracks."

"Why?"

"Protocol."

"But why is it protocol?"

"You ask a lot of questions," he observed.

Those dark brows arched. "Can't blame a girl for wanting clarity when she's considering spending an undeclared amount of time with the stalker who kidnapped her."

"I saved you," he insisted.

"And I'm, like, wicked grateful for that," she replied, nodding. "But you've also been stalking me for a year *and* you took me to a secondary location against my will. It's a big ask, demanding I trust you. It's an even bigger one to want me to stay."

Sloane flexed his claws behind his back. "I thought you'd decided already."

"I'm *deciding,*" she clarified. "It's a process."

"You required freedom. I let you out of the bedroom. What more do you require?"

Cecilia gave him a long, patient look he'd often seen caregivers at the nursery give to misbehaving young. "Okay, well, first of all, being *let out* of the bedroom has a bad ring to it. You hear the implication, right? I need to know you hear that."

When he said nothing, she let out another sigh. "Look, Sloane, I appreciate the thought behind all of this and the, uh, trouble you've gone to, but I can't escape the reality that if I agree to stay with you for a while, I'm officially the stupidest person alive."

"Because I'm dangerous," he confirmed.

Cecilia didn't respond right away. Curling her fingers around the edge of the countertop, she leaned forward slightly as she examined him. His skin tingled wherever she looked. Despite the visor, despite the layers of his armored kit, he felt naked under those searching eyes.

In a quieter voice, she said, "Yeah, you are. I'm probably gonna have nightmares about what you did to Duke for months. I'm terrified of you."

His stomach sank.

She was right to fear him. Despite being the only person on the planet he could never harm, he was still the biggest threat to her. One inhale without his helmet and she would never be free. She'd never have the life she dreamed of. She'd be the sole obsession of a monster who'd done things even her nightmares couldn't conjure.

But is she free now?

Sloane tried to imagine letting her go. If he discovered there were no threats from the vampires and nothing else to save her from, he'd have no reason to keep her by his side. She'd go back to her life and he'd return to watching her from afar, surrounded by pigeons and dreaming of what it'd be like to simply be near her.

I can't, he realized, bile curdling in his belly. *I'd come up with some other excuse. I'd find something else to keep her here. I can't go back to watching.*

Eventually he'd be found out. Eventually she'd find another

mate. Eventually the control he'd clung to for so long would snap and he'd do it all over again.

He had to keep her. The question was *how.*

As Sloane stood there, watching her watch him, he realized that two obstacles stood in his way: Fracture and Cecilia's fear.

The first could be handled easily enough, but the second… He had no idea how to make someone care for him. No one had before.

Desperate to know where to begin, he demanded, "How do I make you unafraid?"

Cecilia didn't respond right away. She appeared to weigh something in her mind as she bit her lip.

After a long stretch of quiet, she ordered, "Come here."

He followed her command instinctively, but he didn't dare get too close. Every inch between them was vital to keeping his self-control intact. When they began to vanish, the need to rip off his helmet, to wrap his hands around her waist, to know what it would feel like to press the length of his body against the softness of her was unbearable.

But she wasn't satisfied with the distance he tried to keep between them.

Cecilia pointed to the floor directly in front of her. "Here."

Sloane could've sworn every nerve in his body came alive. Energy unlike any he'd felt before zinged through his system as he slowly crossed the distance. Suddenly the helmet that had always been a shield between him and the world felt suffocating. The urge to tear it from his head made his breath shorten into sharp pants.

And then she opened her legs.

He didn't make the choice to step between them. It was the most natural thing in the world to slot himself there.

Sloane didn't know what it was like to come home, but he imagined it was something like when Cecilia welcomed him into that sacred space.

"I'm terrified of you," she repeated, softer this time, as her hands sought out his arms.

His breath caught when she gently pulled them out from behind his back. Her fingers trailed down his forearms until they found his gloved hands. Guiding them onto the countertop beside her hips, she caged herself in with his much greater bulk.

Baffled, aroused, and desperate to understand her, he growled, "Then why do you want me closer?"

Those doe eyes stared up at him, knowing and beautiful and full of danger. "Because I'm pretty sure you'll do whatever I say. And if I say don't touch me, you won't."

It occurred to him that even if he couldn't inhale her pheromones, his skin was still exposed to them. Perhaps that was why it felt like every inch of him was screaming for her touch.

Pulled in by her gravity, his head bowed until his temple was level with hers. "Is that an order?"

Cecilia's hands hadn't left his. Her fingertips hovered over his knuckles before they slid upward over the smooth leather. "Yes," she answered, finding where the end of his gloves met the beginning of his sleeves.

Being hit with a cattle prod was less shocking than when her fingertips slid beneath his sleeves to touch his bare skin.

"Ah!" Sloane's whole body stiffened. His claws sank into the countertop as the contact ricocheted through his body and rewrote something in his very cells.

Her touch vanished. "Sorry! Was that—"

"No," he gasped, trying to regain some of his composure. "I'm not used to touch. Continue."

A peculiar note entered her voice when she asked, "Not used to touch? What does that mean?"

"Elves don't... do that," he answered, chest tightening with that nameless not-quite-panic feeling. "Not with people who aren't kin. And I don't have kin."

"Oh. I didn't know that." Cecilia turned her head away to look closely at his hand. "I've never spent any time with elves."

It wasn't a surprise. Very few non-elves had. After a thousand years of catastrophic population decline and in-fighting, they were a closed off people. But things were changing now that Theodore Solbourne had taken over for his sister and chosen a witch for his mate. They weren't confined to their own people anymore.

If he were normal, he could've taken Cecilia as his consort proudly. He would've been the envy of all, with his perfect, fragile mate who pledged herself to the revered work of teaching young.

The fact that keeping her meant he couldn't let the entire world know how lucky he was made that angry nerve throb in his chest.

Steeling himself, he rasped, "You can touch me. Continue."

"And you won't touch *me?"* There was a challenge in her voice, which was a dangerous thing. For an elf caught in the throes of the pull, a direct challenge and a chance to prove his worth were impossible to resist.

"Not until you give me the order," he answered, heart racing.

"What if I never do?"

Her fingers played with the end of sleeves again. Chest rising and falling with quick, sanitized breaths, he replied, "Then I'll never touch you."

"How can I trust that, though? You could *say* anything."

After a moment of thought, Sloane crouched down to reach into his right boot. Cecilia watched him with confusion as his fingers curled around the hilt of his favorite knife. He planned to rise up immediately, but he didn't account for the way her seat on the countertop put her at the perfect height for him to bury his head between her thighs.

Sloane stared at the juncture between her legs for what felt like an eternity, his cock stiffening behind the slash-resistant fabric of his pants. He'd never had much of a sexual drive before, but when he thought of what it'd be like to run his tongue along that tantalizing seam, it nearly obliterated the tenuous hold he still had on his control.

Biting his lip savagely beneath the visor, he forced himself back onto his feet.

"Here," he grunted, holding the knife between them hilt-first.

Cecilia's cheeks were flushed when she peered at it like she'd never seen a knife before. "You're giving me a *weapon?*"

"Yes. To kill me."

Cecilia leaned away from the knife so fast he nearly reached out to steady her. "Sloane, what the fuck?"

Breaking his own rule for just a moment, he grabbed her hand and forced her to curl her fingers around the hilt. "It's obsidian — one of the only materials sharp enough to cut elvish skin on the first try. I know it works because I've used it. If I ever disobey your orders, kill me."

He tilted his chin up, showing her the thin strip of skin exposed by the edge of his high collar. "Slice here. Don't hesitate."

Cecilia slid the knife out of its sheath. She stared at the black, shimmering blade with wide eyes.

After a moment of hesitation, she raised it to his throat.

The razor-sharp edge of the knife kissed that sliver of skin just below his helmet, but he didn't move. Every instinct in him urged him to stay still, to show her that he was at her mercy. An elvish woman would've been just as deadly with her fangs at his throat, and he would've been just as aroused to know his mate held his life in her hands.

Someday, if he was lucky, he'd put his own fangs on her throat. She'd give him that trust, and he'd show her just how much he cherished it when he pinned her down with infinite care and slid his cock into the hot well of her body, forever sealing their bond.

But in that moment, he relished in the feeling of being the center of her world. There was no fear, no worry that she'd take the chance to slit his throat and run. His Cecilia had too much mercy in her for that.

It was that softness he so coveted, and what he'd defend with his life without hesitation.

Her voice trembled when she demanded, "If I told you to let me go right now or I'll kill you, would you do it?"

"Yes," he answered, throat bobbing dangerously close to the edge of the knife. "But I'd follow you."

"And if I told you not to follow me?"

"I'd make sure you never saw me."

"That isn't obeying my orders," she challenged.

Sloane placed his palms flat on the counter beside her hips. "I'll follow them until they conflict with my duty to protect you. That has been and will always be my first priority."

Cecilia let out a sound that was something like a huff. "Why me? Why do all of this for me, Sloane? I'm just a regular woman. I'm not special. What made you..."

"You talked to me," he explained, voice rough behind the shield of his visor. "You touched me."

Her lips parted. She stared at him for what felt like a long time, her brows bunched in a look that might've been understanding or it might've been pity. In a murmur, she confirmed, "And you don't get a lot of touch."

He breathed deeply. "And no one talks to me like you do."

Her gaze dropped to his throat. The blade moved — not in a slicing motion, but downward, pushing the top of his collar until more of his skin was exposed.

"Purple," she murmured, pulling the knife away. "Your skin is purple. I wondered, but I couldn't see it properly before."

Sloane watched her slip the knife back into its sheath. Tucking it into her pocket, she sat up straight and sucked in a deep breath.

"Okay," she announced, like they'd settled something, and held her hand out. "Now give me your phone."

CHAPTER **TWELVE**

Cecilia sent her phantom off to keep himself busy while she made her call to Dahlia.

A part of her still couldn't quite believe the way he just… did what she said. Even as she watched him disappear into a heavily locked room, she half expected him to jump out again and shove her back into the bedroom.

But he didn't. Sloane slipped into what he called *his armory* without so much as a complaint, apparently unconcerned that she might take the opportunity to escape. Whether that meant he fully believed she *couldn't* escape or that he'd have no trouble tracking her down if she did remained to be seen.

Either way, Cecilia padded into the starkly decorated living space across from the nearly empty kitchen, his sleek black cell phone in hand.

Settling down on the black leather couch, she curled her legs beneath her and tapped the screen.

"Spooky," she muttered, eyeing the default wallpaper and lack of pass code suspiciously. When she poked around the apps and contact list, she found nothing. There weren't any photos in the camera roll, either — which was a relief, frankly, because she was almost one hundred percent sure she'd find pictures of herself in there.

The phone appeared entirely unused aside from a handful of calls to private numbers over the course of a few months. Knowing he'd had it that long unsettled her more.

What kind of animal owns a phone for more than a day and doesn't change the wallpaper? She shuddered at the thought.

Thanking her past self for bothering to memorize Dahlia's phone number in case of an emergency, she held the device to her ear as she waited for her friend to pick up. Picking at her chipping nail polish, she tried to sort out what she'd say. The full truth was out of the question, obviously, but lying wouldn't work, either. They knew each other too damn well to get away with it.

Before she could come up with a solid strategy, the line connected.

Dahlia's voice came through the speaker like a breath of fresh air. "Hello?"

"Hey, dork," Cecilia greeted, immediately wincing at how strained those two simple words sounded.

"Cece? What phone are you using?"

Eying the empty concrete walls of the living room, she hedged, "A friend's. I lost my phone last night and didn't want you to worry."

"Oh." There was the slightest pause before Dahlia asked, "What friend?"

"You haven't met him," she replied, trying hard for nonchalance.

There was a longer pause. In that silence, she could practically hear Dahlia's eyes narrowing. Beginning to sweat a little, Cecilia cleared her throat. "So, um—"

"What's going on?" her best friend demanded.

"Nothing!"

Dahlia had many, many talents. She possessed an incredibly sharp business mind, and her confidence could carry her through any room. Cecilia had watched her go from a child of a broken home to a fierce boss bitch of the highest rungs of the vampire syndicate with great pride.

But that also meant that Dahlia was not one to beat around the bush. If anything, she'd only gotten more blunt since she became a queen of the vampire underworld — and that was saying something, because she'd never pulled punches before.

"Bullshit. I can hear it in your voice. And what do you think you're doing, calling me from an unknown number and saying it's a *friend's* phone but not telling me his name? Cece, you're about as subtle as a brick to the head. What's going on?"

Cecilia gently probed the swollen and bruised flesh around her split cheek. "All right, all right, put the claws away, boss. First of all, I'm fine. That's the most important thing."

A sharp edge entered Dahlia's voice when she demanded, "What the fuck does *that* mean?"

"It means what I said," she insisted. "I'm, like, *so* fine. Never been better."

"I would assume so, but the fact that you're being so insistent about it implies that you're not actually fine." Dahlia made a soft sound of alarm before she snapped, "Did something happen with Duke?"

"Okay, so, first of all—"

"Grim's tits, Cece! I told you to call me if he started asking you questions!"

"Am I or am I not calling you right now?"

Dahlia's quick inhale came through the speakers. "What happened?"

"Again, I'm gonna just preface this by saying I'm *fine,*" Cecilia insisted. "But when I got off my shift the other night, Duke followed me home. I'll spare you the details but suffice it to say none of us have to worry about him looking for Devon anymore."

"Spare me the details? *Spare me the details?*" Dahlia's voice moved through an impressive range of flat, incredulous notes and hysterical peaks. "Cecilia Marcella Warren, you do *not* get to spare me the details!"

"Listen, it's fine. He's not a problem anymore. My friend took care of it and I'm safe. It's all good."

It sounded like Dahlia was moving when she hollered, "Felix! Who's on guard duty for Cece?"

"You had someone guarding me?" she muttered, disconcerted by the apparent number of people who'd been watching her. Not that it surprised her, really, but it was never comfy hearing she'd had more than one stalker, well-meaning or not.

From a distance she heard Felix's response, but she couldn't make out what he said.

"Duke followed Cece home last night," Dahlia explained to her husband. "And no one checked in? I didn't get a single alert!"

"...hard to find good fucking help in San Francisco," Felix sighed, much closer to the phone. There was a shuffling sound before he said, "Cece, you're on speaker. Are you all right?"

Even more certain now than she was before that she shouldn't mention anything about exactly how she'd been rescued, she exclaimed, "I am *so fine!*"

"What happened?" There was a snapping sound before Felix called out, "Milo, get ahold of Nash. We need Ginny to pick up Cece."

Standing up abruptly from the couch, she paced toward the wall of windows. The rapidly darkening sky was a velvety plum, and the fog that rolled in over the water between wherever the Battery was located and San Francisco was a pale lavender that reminded her of Sloane's skin. It was pretty — and completely lost on her.

Clutching a fistful of her hair, she cried, "Oh my gods, no, you do *not*. Milo, I'm canceling that order!"

As nice as it sounded on paper to stay with her best friend for an undetermined amount of time in her swanky mansion surrounded by hunky single vampires and being waited on hand and foot, Cecilia just couldn't do it. Dahlia and Felix were just starting their lives together. The thought of intruding on her best friend's hard-earned happily ever after made her stomach sink with shame.

"Cece," Dahlia dragged out, "you're staying with us. If you don't want to be in the house, we'll put you in a hotel. You can even stay with my dads! They'd love to have you. But you aren't staying there if Duke—"

"Duke is dead!"

At last, silence reigned.

It was Felix who broke it. In an impressed voice, he asked, "Did you kill him?"

Scoffing, Dahlia answered, "Of course she didn't kill him." Half a beat later, she asked Cecilia, "You didn't, did you?"

The sound of a heavy door opening down the bare gray hall prompted her to turn away from the window. Gaze immediately settling on the towering form of her masked savior, she said, "My friend took care of it."

Felix hummed. "Your friend, huh?"

"She won't tell me his name," Dahlia muttered.

"Why?"

"I don't know. Cece, what's his name?"

Before she could answer, Felix jumped in to demand, "Is he a vampire? If he's a vampire, I'm *really* gonna need his name. You know, for business reasons."

Giving Sloane's visor an exasperated look, like he was going to commiserate with her over pushy family, she answered, "His name is Sloane. He's not a vampire. He's more than equipped to keep me safe. I—am—fine."

The elf in question cocked his head as he prowled closer. That robotic voice noted, "You sound like you require assistance."

Dahlia made an interested sound on her end of the line. "Is that him? What's up with his voice?"

Unable to handle her family *and* Mr. Slit-My-Throat all at

once, Cecilia put up a hand to stall his approach. He froze at the entrance of the living room.

Relieved and a little nonplussed by his easy obedience, she said, "I'm getting off the phone now. I just wanted you to know I'm fine and that you shouldn't freak out if I don't text you back."

"Cece, don't you dare hang up—"

She ended the call without preamble. Exhausted by the circus, she padded over to the frozen elf and pressed the buzzing phone into his chest as she passed him. "I'd put that on silent if I were you," she dryly informed him. "Or maybe just throw it in the ocean."

Accepting the phone, he asked, "Where are you going?"

Sighing, she answered, "To shower and think about my life choices, Sloane."

CHAPTER **THIRTEEN**

Personnel Profile:

SLOANE FORTUNER
DOB: 21 September 1917
PARENTS: Fiona Fortuner and Benedict Oliveira

DESCRIPTION:

Elf
Pale purple skin
Pale hair
Dark purple eyes
6′9″
300 lbs

BACKGROUND:

Acquired by Thaddeus II August 1923.

RECORD:

[REDACTED] confirmed kills. [REDACTED] unconfirmed.

Recorded kills triple that of the entire unit.

DISCIPLINARY ACTION:

SF frequently deemed insubordinate and requiring intensive corrective measures by his superiors. "Good behavior" was deemed to be successful kills and heavily rewarded.

PSYCHOLOGICAL REPORT:

SF shows marked maladaptive behaviors and resentment toward the world. His experiences as the first of Thaddeus II's acquisitions and preferred member of the unit have predisposed him to view all authority figures with open suspicion and hostility. Any attempts to perform cognitive behavioral therapy or mind healing have been met with outright violence.

Similar to other members of the unit, Sloane shows marked possessive behavior tied to extreme deprivation used as disciplinary action. Showing preferences toward non-essentials is deemed an intolerable vulnerability that can be exploited to control him, and therefore require excessive protectiveness and hoarding behaviors. This falls in line with the competitive atmosphere fostered by the unit's trainers.

Interestingly, while SF claims to feel no loyalty or familial identity with his unit, he exhibits care behaviors and leadership. Other subjects often turn to him for approval and reassurance first. When questioned on this, SF chose not to respond.

After much observation, it is my opinion that SF differs from other subjects in one notable way. While he does not express or seem to understand positive emotion or social boundaries, SF is sharply cognizant of morals. He has retained an extremely rigid moral compass and appears to rely heavily on it for comfort. He believes that protecting the innocent is the only reason he should be allowed to exist. It's unclear whether it is this belief or simply his seniority that has marked him (and VK) as the leaders of the unit.

With enough time, I believe this moral compass can be used as a gateway to more social behaviors and integration. However, it also puts SF at a high risk of disobedience and self-destructive tendencies. SF is secretive, distrustful, has no emotional reaction to killing, and extremely intelligent. Black and white thinking, as well as a complete refusal to compromise what he deems the correct course of action, can be wildly dangerous in this context.

RECOMMENDATIONS:

At this time, SF cannot be released into society and should be closely monitored at all times for signs that his moral compass still aligns with the wellbeing of himself, his unit, and the citizens of the EVP. Intensive cognitive behavioral therapy encouraged but will not be entered into voluntarily. Highest level flight risk.

NOTES:

SF is, in my opinion, the single most dangerous member of the unit. It is my belief that anyone who undertakes his psychological care is putting themselves at grave personal risk. Should he go AWOL, it's unlikely that he will give authorities any other choice than to terminate.

CHAPTER **FOURTEEN**

THE FIRST ALERT WENT OUT AT SIX AM. IT DIDN'T WAKE HIM UP because he wasn't sleeping.

Sloane sat at his worktable in the armory. His helmet sat before him, partially disassembled. He'd figured out how to circumvent the tracker in it years ago, so the beeping that emitted from the speakers within the padded interior weren't from that. It was from the first of several messages sent by his unit.

He was required to report for duty at five. Since they'd been on what equated to house arrest lately, that usually meant assisting either the Sovereign's Guard or the intelligence units within Patrol.

But he didn't show up, and he never would again.

A strange feeling tugged at his chest as he listened to the increasingly urgent alerts come in. He could disable them, too. That was why he'd taken out his tools. But for some reason he hesitated. It wasn't because he was unsure about choosing Cecilia — he'd never been more certain about anything in his life — but because cutting off the final tether to his unit felt… wrong.

They were all he'd ever known.

No one understood what they'd gone through or how their

minds worked. Only *they* knew. If they were shifters, they'd be pack.

But they weren't. Shifters would never make him choose between pack and mate.

Lips thinning, he reached for his tools. It was pointless to feel anything about leaving Fracture. There was no other choice. She needed him.

Gods knew he needed her.

So he disabled the alert system built into his helmet. If it made his stomach go sour, that was simply another cruel fact of life.

Sloane left his helmet on the worktable. Luckily he'd built the armory to double as a training room, so he had something to do while he locked himself away. Instinct screamed at him to run to the bedroom and guard his consort, but he had a feeling she wouldn't like it if he watched her sleep, so he forced himself to stay in the only room her scent hadn't penetrated.

Stripping off his shirt, Sloane approached the elf-made punching bag hung in the corner. Tension rippled through his muscles as he sized up the punching bag.

Normally he was a man of complete focus. He acted without doubt or uncertainty. But things had never been so… complicated before.

He didn't miss the days of Thaddeus II's reign. No one liked being treated like a rabid dog on a short leash, and he'd never agreed with terrorizing harmless citizens. It'd been decades of endless nightmares and torture for the entire unit.

And yet they'd been programmed a certain way during that time. The desire for rules, orders, and strict black and white thinking had been carved into their bones with relentless malice. They weren't supposed to have to *choose* anything. They weren't supposed to be *conflicted* or to *want.*

Those were the consequences of the humane new policies that had been introduced with Thaddeus's death, and in some ways they felt like a worse punishment than any torture.

Sloane slammed his right fist into the punching bag. It hit with a percussive *bang* as the bag swung on the thick chain that suspended it from the ceiling.

He didn't *want* to leave Fracture. He didn't *want* to give up Cecilia. He couldn't have both.

Keeping her meant he had to abandon his unit, and it also meant they couldn't stay at the Battery for long. They were too close to the city. Once word got out that he'd gone AWOL — if it hadn't happened already — they'd have to leave the territory altogether.

The Neutral Zone was the only smart choice for them, as it was for most of the criminals, deserters, and lost.

Another punch, this time with his left fist. The heavy bag swung in a wide arc.

Some part of him had always known it would end up this way, especially once he settled on protecting his doe. There were only two ways that story ended, and he wasn't about to abandon her, so taking her was the logical conclusion. It still came as something of a shock, though, and he couldn't help but wonder if it was because there was a part of him that still couldn't believe a good thing would happen to him.

He'd planned to take Cecilia, but he never could've imagined she'd *want* to stay.

The thought of her in his bed, safe and warm, sent a surge of adrenaline through him. Sloane attacked the bag with a snarl. His fists blurred as he came at it hard, imagining it was the vampire who'd struck her.

He couldn't seem to focus on one issue at a time. While his gut churned at the thought of leaving his unit, his mind couldn't stop spinning around the thought of Cecilia.

The idea of a woman like her *choosing* him was so patently outrageous that he struggled to imagine any scenario that would bring it about without coercion or trickery.

The bag swung back at him with considerable force. Sloane slammed his fist into it with a growl, his fangs clenched hard.

Sweat sheened his pale purple skin as he hit it again and again.

If he took off his helmet and let the Pull have him, wholly and completely, she wouldn't have a choice. It was the smart thing to do. He had the tactical advantage of a biological disadvantage. If he allowed himself to become dependent on her pheromones, she would have to stay with him or he'd succumb to madness and death. His doe was far too kind to let something like that happen.

But he didn't want to do that.

Firstly, the thought of facing her without his helmet was enough to send a shiver down his spine. It was one thing to reveal his face to his unit — and by extension Atria — but to be so vulnerable in front of *her…*

Secondly, and more importantly, he couldn't stomach taking that choice from her.

Breathing hard, Sloane grabbed the bag to stop its swinging. Leaning his sweaty forehead against it, he closed his eyes and imagined what it'd be like to have her. Not just as his charge but as his consort. His *mate.*

He couldn't say he hadn't imagined what it would be like. Every elf had — even those as broken and fucked up as him. It was built into their DNA to long for that perfect being who'd fit them like a custom-made puzzle piece. But most elves had at least some concept of what to do when they found that person. All he'd been taught was to run as far away as possible.

But he'd always known that if he did somehow manage to find her…

Something weak and needy in him keened for the kind of life he'd been denied. One that wasn't just bloodshed and orders. One that had laughter and softness and gentle touches. One that had *her.*

Taking a deep breath, he pushed off the bag. *Adapt,* he thought, striking it again. *Protect. Find a way to make her stay.*

CHAPTER **FIFTEEN**

He lost track of how long he trained. At some point it became less about letting off steam and more to empty his mind completely. It wasn't like his brain was helping him. All it did was circle around the same problems again and again.

By the time Cecilia began to stir, he'd only come to one conclusion: he had no idea what the fuck he was doing.

But none of that seemed to matter as much as it had an hour ago when he heard the telltale sounds of his consort opening the bedroom door. Swiping his forearm over his sweaty face, he sprinted toward the worktable to grab his helmet. Slamming it onto his head and locking it in place, Sloane stalked out of the armory, intent on finding his doe.

The air was cooler in the hallway. The naked skin of his torso, still slick with sweat, pebbled with the sudden change in temperature.

He paused his hunt when he remembered he hadn't put on a shirt. Sloane waffled for a moment, aware that a certain amount of pheromones could be absorbed through the skin. The smart thing would've been for him to walk back into the armory and retrieve his shirt.

But another thought occurred to him, too, when he heard the

sounds of Cecilia moving about the kitchen. His heart rate jumped when he remembered how she'd hopped up on the counter and ordered him to stand between her legs. He hadn't been allowed to touch her, but she'd touched *him.* The chance that she'd do it again, this time on his bare skin, was too tantalizing to resist.

The filter will do most of the work, he assured himself as he walked silently toward the center of his universe. *And it's not like clothes or armor are pheromone-proof. It's fine.*

Sloane turned the corner to stand at the entrance of the kitchen. He found Cecilia stretched up on her tiptoes to reach the plain white dishes he'd purchased just in case she ended up at the Battery. She was dressed in little more than an over-sized t-shirt and socks, and her dark hair was piled into a messy knot on top of her head. She'd removed most of her bandages, he noticed, leaving the long expanse of her legs visible to his greedy eyes.

She didn't appear to notice him there for a handful of seconds. Or at least, it didn't seem like she did until, she huffed, "Hey, champ, can you make yourself useful and get me a—"

Whatever she'd been about to ask for never made it past her lips. Cecilia had turned her head to give him a sleepy look, but something about seeing him there stopped her abruptly. Her mouth snapped shut and her eyes widened.

Brows furrowing, Sloane crossed the kitchen to stand in front of her. Tilting his head to one side, he asked, "What do you need?"

Cecilia's mouth opened, but nothing came out for some time. "Um... I just— Uh, could you get me a bowl, please?"

Eying her closely, he observed, "You're flushed. Are you unwell?"

Somehow, Cecilia's cheeks went an even duskier color. It would've been fascinating except for the fact that one cheek was heavily bruised, with a cut below her eye that he'd sealed with a butterfly bandage.

"Oh my gods, I'm fine," she squeaked, suddenly determined to scuttle away from him. Pressing her back against the counter, she asked, "Why are you half-naked?"

Sloane blinked. Looking down at his torso, he answered, "I was training."

"This early?"

"It's three in the afternoon."

Cecilia scraped some flyaway strands out of her eyes and looked away from him. "Right, right. Sorry, I forget that I'm on a different schedule."

He shrugged. "I don't mind. I sleep in two hour shifts."

"Two hour… Okay, no, I can't even think about that until I've had some cereal." Still not looking at him, she gestured vaguely toward the cabinet. "Can you? The bowl, I mean."

"I didn't anticipate how short you'd be when I built the kitchen," he explained, stepping around her to grab a bowl.

Cecilia's eyes flicked toward him with alarm. "Wait, you didn't build this kitchen *for* me, did you?"

Handing her the dish, he answered, "No. I built it before I met you. But I would've made changes if I'd known."

She blew out a breath. Shaking her head, she muttered, "Commitment issues have never even heard your name, have they?"

Not sure what she meant but fairly certain she wasn't actually speaking to him, Sloane silently stepped back to let her access the refrigerator. Cecilia was quiet for a while as she grabbed the milk he'd had to go out to retrieve and then the cereal he knew was her favorite. Settling onto one of the island's stools, she spooned a few mouthfuls of foul-looking wheat-derived crumbles into her mouth before she spoke again.

"You gonna eat something?" she asked, casting him an all too brief look.

"I'm not hungry," he lied.

Cecilia slowly crunched a mouthful of cereal. "So… you were working out, huh?"

"Yes."

Her spoon dipped into the bowl, stirring up cow's milk and artificial colors. "You keep your helmet on for that, too?"

"No."

There was a long pause wherein he supposed Cecilia seemed to expect him to elaborate. Unfortunately, Sloane wasn't interested in explaining the many reasons he wanted to keep his helmet on so soon. Letting her choose was important, but he needed her to like him before he told her the truth. The Cecilia he'd come to know wouldn't hesitate to run if he laid an ultimatum like that at her feet.

She wouldn't escape him, of course, but he didn't want to ruin the fragile peace they'd settled on. Yet.

Cecilia glanced his way again, but she couldn't seem to keep her eyes on him for long before she had to look away. "It's just for me, I guess," she muttered.

Seeing she clearly wanted some sort of answer, Sloane fished for a decent excuse. "It's… standard protocol to wear it in front of civilians."

"Okay, but you're not on duty," she pointed out, waving her spoon in his direction. "You could relax a little. I mean, you're already shirtless. And sweaty. And shirtless."

Curious about the strange tenor in her voice, he stepped closer to the island. "You said shirtless twice."

"Yeah, well, it's not what I was expecting to see first thing." She tilted her head toward the seat beside hers. "If you're not gonna eat, you might as well sit. Unless you want to go take a shower or something."

He probably did need a shower, but the temptation of sitting so close to her was impossible to resist.

Sloane slid onto the stool next to hers and spread his legs until his knee brushed her thigh. He held his breath, waiting for her to reprimand him or pull away. When she continued to eat her cereal like nothing happened, a roar of triumph crashed through him.

They were silent for a while, but it wasn't a bad silence. Sloane watched her with perfect focus, his forearms braced on the counter and his breathing steady. Seeing her up close was better than he imagined it would be. He supposed it was something like the difference between observing the moon from the Earth and walking on it with his own two feet.

Absolutely beautiful, he thought, tracing the curve of her cheek and the fan of her lashes with his gaze. Even bruised and recently rolled out of bed, she was the most beautiful creature he'd ever seen.

Cecilia set her spoon down inside the now empty bowl. Only a tiny puddle of hot pink milk lay at the bottom, which he found mildly revolting.

Turning to him, she crossed her arms in front of her chest. "I did some thinking after I went to bed last night."

Sloane tensed. *Does she want to leave?*

Before he could begin to panic, she declared, "You like me."

Still reeling from the instinctive fear that she intended to leave him, it took him a moment to understand what she was saying.

"...Yes?"

She shook her head. Spreading her fingers out on the island's surface, she said, "No, Sloane. I mean you *really* like me."

Failing to see her point or where she intended to take that observation, he cautiously answered, "Correct."

"Right, okay. It seems like maybe you're not understanding what I'm getting at here."

Sloane nodded. "I'm not. You've only said things that are obvious."

Cecilia let out a soft laugh and rubbed her eyes. "As weird as this is, it's actually kind of nice. Lemme just try and reframe how I approach this, okay?"

He waited quietly as she worked out whatever it was she was trying to say in her mind. It didn't bother him. If anything, it gave him more time to quietly observe her up close. Even though he couldn't smell her through the air-tight seal and filter of his mask, being next to her was intoxicating. He could feel the electricity and warmth of her radiating through the flushed skin of his chest, and when she moved even the smallest amount on her stool, the air rippled around him in gentle waves.

If he closed his eyes, it was almost like being touched.

"I don't know anything about elves, really," she admitted, looking down at her hands. "I mean, I know the *basics*. The stuff they teach in school, right? But I've never spent time with one, and I don't know how you date. So forgive me if all of this is standard protocol for your people and I'm just ignorant, but it *feels* like you have romantic intentions toward me. Is that correct?"

Pulse thumping hard in his neck, he answered, "Correct."

You're my consort, he wanted to tell her. *You're mine. I'm yours.*

Cecilia let out a slow exhale. Her cheeks had gone dark again, but she still didn't look up when she said, "All right, I'm going to make another assumption here. Tell me if I'm wrong, okay? But it sure seems like maybe you haven't done that sort of thing before. Dating, I mean."

More curious than offended by her assumption, he ordered, "Elaborate."

"Well… for starters, instead of asking me out last year, you decided to stalk me. Then kidnap me."

Sloane gave her a blank stare she couldn't see. "Ask you out of where? Your apartment?"

Cecilia gave him an equally flabbergasted look. "Ask me out of— Gods, Sloane, do you not even know what asking someone out is? It's telling someone you're interested in them romantically by inviting them to do an activity with you. Dinner. A movie. A walk in the park. Kissing at the front door after a magical night. That sort of thing."

It wasn't easy for him to process. "If I had… asked you *out,* would you have said yes?"

"Well, I know elves only just started dating outside their

people, so maybe it would've been a little complicated, and let's be honest, you're super-duper scary…" She trailed off to take a deep breath. Patting the counter, she continued in a quick, nervous voice, "But it's not like that's ever stopped me before, so yes, I probably would've."

Sloane had no idea what to make of that information. Carefully storing it away for later examination, he asked, "Will you go out with me now?"

Cecilia perked up. Pushing her shoulders back, she whirled around on her stool until she faced away from the counter. Fascinated by her energetic movements and astonishing lack of grace, Sloane pushed his boot against the railing of his stool until he faced her again.

She stood in front of him and clapped her hands once like he'd seen the nursery teachers do whenever they wanted to get the attention of rowdy children.

"I'm *so* glad you asked," she chirped, "because I can't stay cooped up in this fortress all the time, and I also happened to heavily imply to my best friend that we're dating. I don't like lying to her, so this will kill two birds with one stone."

Trying very hard to follow what she was saying, he asked, "You want me to kill birds for you?"

Cecilia's smile froze for a moment. "Um, no. That's just a saying. I meant that us going on a date solves a lot of problems at once."

He only had the vaguest ideas of what going on a date entailed. Sloane had certainly seen a number of them in progress over the years, but he'd only ever been a part of ending them prematurely with a well-placed bolt or throat-slitting in the restroom.

What he did know for certain was that they tended to take place outside the home, which would prove problematic.

"It's not safe outside the Battery," he informed her. "We can date here."

Cecilia spread her arms out wide. "No offense, champ, but

how? All you've got is a TV, a drawer of raw meat, and processed foods. I'd say we could do a movie night with dinner, but you won't take your helmet off in front of me for some reason, so that'd just be weird."

"It's not safe," he argued.

"Again, I *highly* doubt any vampires are out for my blood, but even if they were…" Cecilia padded closer. So close that she had to tilt her chin up to meet his gaze through the smoky glass of his visor.

It was a profound shock to his system to feel her palm settle on his chest.

The muscles below her palm contracted sharply, as if they'd been electrocuted by the perfect softness of her skin. Tingles raced through his nerves to tighten his abdomen in a wave that settled below his thick utility belt. His cock, never something he paid much attention to before, jerked to attention with a fierceness that made him bite back a hiss.

Thank the gods I found you when I did, he silently told her. *If Thaddeus's instructors knew how easily you could torture me, I never would've made it out alive.*

"I'm not your prisoner, right?" Cecilia trailed her fingertips down his chest. Every glancing touch left a trail of fire in its wake, and when she pressed her palm above the dip of his belly-button, he was forced to take deep breaths to control the urge to grab her.

"You want to make me happy because you like me. Making me happy means letting me out of the house. Letting me out of the house means you protect me, just like you've been doing for a year. That's not so bad, right?"

She had no idea what she was asking for. But when she touched his skin and looked up at him like that, Sloane couldn't refuse her. The urge to please his consort was a howl in his mind, as potent as any bloodlust or thrill of a successful hunt.

It was a terrible idea. He knew it. He also recognized that to some degree he was being played.

But she was his doe. Doing what she asked wasn't just a pleasure — it was essential.

Sloane dared to lift a gloved hand to her unbruised cheek. Skimming the backs of his claws down that lovely curve, he asked, "What does a date require?"

Cecilia's voice came out a little rougher than normal when she answered, "Going somewhere outside the home to spend quality time together. Sometimes there's food. Sometimes there's entertainment. But it can be whatever you want it to be, really."

I can work with that.

"Then we'll go on a date," he announced, fully aware that he was making a risky mistake.

Her dark eyes gleamed with pleasure. "Tonight?"

"Tonight."

"Because I'm not your prisoner," she confirmed.

"You're not my prisoner." Sloane slipped two fingers under her chin to delicately tilt it upward. He watched in fascination as her pupils expanded into wide black discs. Her lips, always a little rosy and so inviting, parted with a soft inhale.

Lowering his head until his visor touched her forehead, he whispered, "I'm yours."

CHAPTER
SIXTEEN

"Of *course* you have a motorcycle," Cecilia sighed.

A sleek beast of a bike sat in a vast underground garage, its black body as shiny as a beetle's shell. Her own eggplant-shaped reflection stared back at her with dismay.

Sloane handed her a shiny black helmet. In that flat robotic voice, he asked, "Is that an issue?"

Pulling the helmet onto her head, she muttered, "Not for you." *Because it makes you hotter.*

Cecilia hadn't gotten much sleep the night before, but she didn't feel even a little bit of the exhaustion that had clung to her when she peeled herself out of Sloane's bed that afternoon. It was impossible to feel tired when she was with her elf. Now that she wasn't quite as worried she'd end up chopped into little pieces and tossed into the Bay as merfolk food, it left a lot of room for feeling other things.

Like the thrill of his attention. Like how hot it was that he rode a motorcycle. Like how he made her danger sense ping off the damn charts.

She'd always known the messed up wiring in her brain would get her into trouble eventually. Now it'd gotten her onto the back of her stalker's motorcycle.

Her heart jumped when Sloane stepped into her personal space. He was never far from her, but it melted something in her whenever he approached her in that slow, predatory way only to touch her so, so gently.

Logically, she knew she should put a stop to it unless she wanted to encourage the obsession he so clearly harbored, but she just… didn't want to do that.

A part of her was pretty sure she should try to escape when they were out on their date. It was the smart thing to do, and most of the reason she suggested it in the first place. But when he stooped those stupidly broad shoulders to delicately latch the helmet's clasp beneath her chin, all the smart parts of her brain shut down.

Cecilia stared at her own flushed reflection in his visor as he tested the fit of her helmet. The scent of leather and something richer filled the air when he brushed her hair over her shoulders. "This is a tactical disadvantage," he intoned, rubbing the strands between his gloved fingers.

Tingles raced down from the top of her head to her fingertips, which was an objectively bizarre reaction to what was definitely not a compliment. "Do you think I should cut it?" she asked, a little breathless.

Sloane carefully laid the lock of hair over her shoulder. The tips of his claws lingered on the curve of her shoulder for a heartbeat before he reached up to gently pull the visor of her helmet down. "No," he answered. "I like your tactical disadvantages. I can easily compensate for them."

Gods, that shouldn't have been as romantic as it came across. Stomach swooping, she smoothed her hands down her pink leather jacket. It was a lucky thing she'd chosen to wear a cute pair of tweed shorts with thigh-high socks. If she'd been in one of her skirts or dresses, she would've ended up with only her panties and his clothing between them, which wouldn't be ideal. Not ideal at *all.*

But a shame nonetheless, she thought as she watched Sloane swing his leg over the bike.

Incredibly glad to have her face hidden by the helmet, she gingerly placed her hands on his shoulders and settled onto the seat behind him. It wasn't the first time she'd hopped on the back of a man's bike, but wrapping her arms around Sloane's waist and pressing herself against him was a new experience.

He blazed with heat. It soaked through the thick layers of his definitely-not-date-appropriate-clothing to warm her all the way to her bones.

Cecilia tightened her arms around his waist experimentally, testing how they fit together.

Resting her chin on his shoulder, she noted, "You know, I brought that knife you gave me. Aren't you afraid I could stab you in the kidney or something?"

Sloane didn't start the bike right away. He sat rigidly on the seat, his fingers wrapped so tightly around the handlebars that she swore she could hear the leather squeak. This close to him, she thought she could hear something else, too: the strange, raspy rhythm of quick breaths through a filter.

"I'm not afraid of being stabbed," he answered, knocking the kickstand back into position.

Compelled by the self-destructive idiot that was her libido, she dared to lower her arms a little, settling them right above his belt. "Why? Think I won't?"

Sloane rolled his shoulders like he was working out a kink. "No. Because I wouldn't care if you did."

The bike's engine roared to life. The sound bounced off the smooth concrete walls of the garage. It was almost as loud as the thundering beat of her heart as she attempted to process that casual declaration.

She squeezed her eyes shut as Sloane leaned forward and rocketed down the long concrete tunnel. The temperature dropped abruptly as a massive metal door pulled aside, revealing a nighttime landscape of coastal greenery.

Salty air whipped her hair back as her stomach landed somewhere in the garage and stayed there.

A wild burst of laughter escaped her when Sloane took a curve with a perfect lean. The motorcycle's headlights cast the road in a beam of warm light. It glanced off ghostly trees and thick foliage as they slipped in and out of the forest. When they weren't tucked beneath the boughs of ancient trees, they seemed to barely hang on to the edge of sandy cliffs.

Cecilia clung to him as she stared out over the ocean and the twinkling lights of the city beyond it. Her blood rushed in her veins, full of life in a way she hadn't felt in a long time. Maybe it was the near-death experience talking, but a reckless sort of joy bubbled through her with every smooth turn and shift of Sloane's body against her own.

She didn't know where they were going and that was probably a bad thing. Cecilia couldn't make herself care. Her life was already so fucked up that she wanted to soak in as much joy as she could.

Especially if I escape tonight.

She didn't want to think about that, though. Not just then.

Cecilia lost track of how long they rode. She fell into the rhythm of the bike and Sloane's confident movements. She wasn't even sure when she closed her eyes. It wasn't like the scenery was uninteresting, just that the flow of the road and Sloane's warmth lulled her into a bone-deep comfort she couldn't explain.

It came as something of a shock, then, when they slowed to a stop.

Her eyes opened to find that they'd pulled into a roadside eatery. Little more than a brightly lit shack with a window for ordering and another for pick-up, it was *exactly* the kind of place she loved.

Squeezing Sloane's middle, she gasped, "Did you bring me to a *burger joint?*"

"I understand they sell burgers, yes," he answered, pulling

into the gravel ditch that passed as a parking area. Dropping his booted feet to the ground to keep them upright, he cut the engine — which was very odd, because she was fairly certain he was still rumbling.

Pressing her palms flat against his toned middle, she asked, "Are you vibrating?"

"It's nothing." Sloane deployed the kickstand and straightened up. Craning his neck to look back at her, he asked, "Does this qualify as a date?"

Sliding her visor up, Cecilia pretended to squint critically at the restaurant. When she was unable to keep up the act any longer, she cast him a wide smile. "A romantic coastal motorcycle ride and a pit stop at a greasy spoon? I've been on worse."

"That's sufficient. For now." He nodded toward the ground, clearly encouraging her to hop off.

Her legs felt a little like jelly when she stood on her own two feet again, but she wasn't entirely convinced it was because of the bike. Popping the helmet off, she shook out her hair with a huff.

Noticing Sloane was watching her — presumably, anyway, with his helmet pointed directly at her — she teased, "How does my helmet hair look?"

"Interesting."

She snorted. "You're a very honest man, Sloane."

"I rarely have reason to lie," he explained, throwing one leg over the bike. She always seemed to forget just how monstrously tall he was until he stood next to her again, that visor hiding his face and his shoulders all… shouldery.

Using an adjustment of her jacket as an excuse to hide the fact that she was absolutely checking out her stalker, Cecilia replied, "Well, keep it up. I'm not a good liar, so it's nice to have someone who tells the truth as often as I do."

Sloane tucked his hands behind his back and spread his legs a little, assuming what she recognized as his military stance. "Understood."

Not sure if she was doing it sincerely or if she was trying to get him to let his guard down a little, she gave his chest a reassuring pat. "Relax, champ. We're on a date, not a mission."

His helmet titled to one side. "You are my mission."

"I thought you wanted me to be your girlfriend."

His shoulders straightened. "I do not."

It didn't make a damn lick of sense, but a spear of hurt pierced right through her gooey center. Cecilia flinched, her face heating with embarrassment and no small amount of confusion. Snatching her hand from his chest like he'd burned her, she breathed, "Oh. Got it."

Before she could even begin to guess what he *did* want her to be, Sloane clarified, "I intend to be your mate."

Suddenly all the heat in her face wasn't from embarrassment at all. It was from a feeling that was a lot more dangerous.

"Oh," she said again, more of a squeak this time. "That's... huh."

"I'm inexperienced," he admitted, so flat and yet so honest. "I haven't trained for this. You will have to explain the steps to me so I can properly complete them and meet your standards. But I will not fail."

It was the strangest thing, having a conversation like this one on the side of a middle-of-nowhere road, touched by the glow of a burger joint's fluorescent lights. She couldn't even see his face or hear his real voice.

And he's a killer, the tiny part of her brain that still cared about self-preservation reminded her. *And a stalker. And probably, like, way worse.*

It said something truly dire about her that even as those thoughts popped into her head, she could see the stars shining in her eyes reflecting back at her as she stared up at that dark visor.

"You sound awfully sure of yourself for a man who hasn't even finished our first date yet," she whispered.

"It's easy to be sure about you, Cece."

She rolled her lips between her teeth and bit down gently. He had no way of knowing how hard that would hit her, or how deep the words would sink into the mire of insecurities she'd carried all her life. As far as she could recall, the only person who'd ever chosen her was Dahlia.

Her parents were so wrapped up in their own misery that they never put her first. Every boyfriend she'd ever had inevitably shuttled her to the backburner sooner rather than later, believing her sunny disposition and easy to please nature meant they didn't need to *try.* And, even though it wasn't fair to be hurt by it, Dahlia had left her, too.

CHAPTER **SEVENTEEN**

Cecilia looked away from Sloane quickly, unsettled by the accuracy with which he'd hit her where she was most vulnerable. Clearing her throat, she summoned up her usual cheerful veneer and announced, "All right, champ! If you want to be my mate, then we need to get this date rolling."

He inclined his head. Holding one hand out toward the restaurant in a stiff but gentlemanly gesture, he said, "Yes, madam."

Her nose wrinkled. "Madam? I don't think I like that."

"It's the respectful form of address for an adult female in elvish society," he explained. After a brief pause, he added, "But I can call you whatever you prefer."

"Cece works," she answered, spinning on her heel to face the restaurant. "If you're feeling lovey-dovey you can call me honey or baby, but absolutely *no* sweethearts. I got way too many of those from random vampires in the bar."

Gravel crunched beneath her feet but somehow didn't seem to make a noise under his boots as they strode toward the brightly lit outdoor dining area. The only other customers were a couple of puffy jacket-clad teenagers huddled around a plastic table, their mouths glued to red and white striped straws as they sucked down what Cecilia could only assume were milkshakes.

"I..." Sloane trailed off, uncharacteristically uncertain.

"What?" She nudged his side with her elbow. "C'mon. Spit it out."

"I have a... name for you. That I use. In my mind."

Stopping in her tracks, she demanded, "What is it?"

Sloane stopped walking. His posture was always perfectly straight, but he appeared somehow stiffer than normal when he admitted, "Doe."

She blinked. "You said that before, I think. I didn't really catch it at the time but... Wait, do you mean like *doe* as in cute deer or *dough* as in pizza, because—"

"Doe as in deer," he confirmed.

Nudging him again, this time to get them walking, she asked, "What made you think of that?"

Without hesitation, he answered, "You're small, cute, and defenseless."

Squawking, she forgot who she was talking to when she slapped his arm with the back of her hand. "Hey! I know you elves are built like you were made in a lab, but arrants aren't *completely* defenseless!"

Sloane snatched her hand before it'd had the chance to bounce off his impressive bicep. Holding it with infinite care, he smoothed the pad of his thumb over the hills and valleys of her palm. "Correct. You command me. That makes you the most dangerous creature of all."

If her face got any hotter, she was fairly certain her eyebrows would catch on fire.

"You know, if you wanna hold my hand, you don't have to whip out all these smooth one-liners," she teased, hoping to distract him from the way said one-liner absolutely worked on her.

Sloane's grip tightened a fraction when he asked, "You would let me hold your hand?"

Good gods in the sky. This man really is a deadly weapon.

Aware she was probably being suckered, Cecilia hoarsely replied, "Yeah, I would."

In an entirely unsurprising turn of events, Sloane wasn't very good at the whole hand-holding business. Marveling at the fact that he apparently thought he was supposed to hold her entire appendage in his fist, she had to gently correct his grip.

"There," she announced when they were much more comfortably situated. "How does that feel?"

"This is another tactical disadvantage," he replied. "If a threat approached, my dominant hand would be compromised. My reaction time would be slowed and that would provide an opening to an enemy."

Moving to slide her hand out of his, she said, "Well, we don't *have* to—"

"No." His grip tightened, refusing to let her go. "I will compensate."

Tucking her chin to hide her ridiculous, smitten smile, Cecilia tugged her stalker toward the counter. Pretending like she didn't notice the cashier's alarmed scan of her bruises or the even more panicked look he aimed at the obviously military-affiliated elf holding her hand, she cranked up her smile to megawatt status.

"Hi!" she chirped. "Can I get a double cheeseburger with American cheese, no onions, extra ketchup, double pickles, fries with a side of mayo, *and...*" She took half a step back to quickly eyeball the menu. "A cookies and cream milkshake, please?"

The cashier started to sweat when he turned his wide eyes to her date. "A-and you, sir?"

Sloane took a beat before he asked Cecilia, "Am I required to eat to qualify this as a date?"

"Um, technically no. I don't think so, anyway." Giving him a narrow-eyed look, she asked, "But aren't you hungry? I haven't seen you eat anything."

"I can eat later."

"Or you can eat now, while we're on our date."

Sloane rolled his shoulders again. "That is unwise."

"Why? You have bad table manners or something?" She was certain that wasn't the reason. It absolutely had everything to do with him keeping that helmet on, which only made her want to push him more.

If he's going to stalk me for a year, kidnap me, coerce me into staying at his serial killer bunker, and also date me, this man has got *to show me his face.*

Unfortunately, Sloane didn't seem keen on giving her what she wanted.

Shaking his head, he promised, "Another time."

Even more curious than she already was but aware this probably wasn't the place to push the topic, Cecilia shrugged and turned back to the cashier. "I guess that's it."

When the nervous man rattled off the price for the meal, she reached out to scan her ID chip across the old scanner he pushed through the hole in the window, but Sloane intercepted her with a matte black card.

"Hey!" she complained, aware that it was probably ridiculous to want to pay for herself when *he* was the one still kinda-sorta holding her captive. "You didn't even get any food. I should pay."

"You will not," he flatly refused.

Using her hand to steer her toward a table at the far end of the less than polished dining area, he continued, "I don't know much about dating, but I do know that I get pleasure from providing you with things you enjoy. This food makes you happy. That means I pay."

Settling down on the chilly plastic seat, she muttered, "You know, for a stalker, you're pretty charming."

The chair opposite her own looked comically small when Sloane sank into it. The plastic squealed a bit in protest, but it somehow managed to hold itself together under what she could only imagine was considerable bulk.

"You're the only person in this world who could say that," he informed her.

"Don't got a lotta good reviews from ex-girlfriends, huh?"

Sloane rubbed his thumb over the line of her knuckles when he admitted, "I don't have any ex-girlfriends."

Cecilia was glad she didn't have her milkshake yet, otherwise she was pretty sure it would've ended up sprayed across his visor. "Sloane… have you never dated *anybody?*"

"No," he answered immediately. "I've never had any intimate partners."

Truly, she thought watching a man get his arm ripped off would be the most shocking thing she'd experience in a week. It turned out that finding out Sloane was apparently completely inexperienced was a pretty close second.

She wasn't even sure why, really. It wasn't like she knew anything about him. For all she knew, it could've been standard practice for elves or members of Patrol to eschew romantic relationships.

But it didn't feel that way.

Despite the fact that there was no inflection or emotion in that modulated voice, Cecilia sensed there was much more to the story than something as simple as protocol. Maybe it was madness, but she thought there was vulnerability there, hidden beneath the layers of his visor and plain black, military-style clothing.

Taking a second to process her immediate shocked reaction, Cecilia coughed into her free hand, hoping it would cover up the strange pitch in her voice. "So, you're… a virgin?"

"I have not had sex," he confirmed, as dry as her old high school med class's sex education.

Taking a breath, she worked hard to school her expression. "Are you comfortable explaining why you haven't… done that?"

Sloane nodded. "It's traditional for elves to exchange virginity with a friend or someone of a similar rank at thirty, but we were… discouraged from the practice."

"I mean, I wasn't exactly encouraged to have sex either, but I still managed to lose my virginity in the band room's supply closet when I was seventeen. Why didn't you disobey orders and just do it? It's not like anyone would know, right?"

"I had no interest," he replied.

Cecilia's stomach tightened. In a hushed voice, she asked, "Has that changed?"

Sloane's chest expanded with a deep breath. "Yes."

She really couldn't decide whether the news should make her more concerned or less. On one hand, there was something deeply endearing about knowing he was so deadly yet so innocent. On the other hand, it made him seem even more unpredictable.

The gods only knew what a super-powered virgin who'd spent the last year watching her through her bedroom window was capable of.

It was a lucky thing for both of them that the sound of a bell dinging broke the tension. Tugging her hand out of his, she nervously brushed her hair behind her ear and made to stand up. "That's my food."

Sloane waved at her to stay seated. Rising from his chair, he told her, "I'll get it. Don't move."

Cecilia watched him walk away. It didn't even occur to her to get up and run until he reached the pick-up window, and even then, she found herself paralyzed.

Go, that reasonable part of her screamed. *Go!*

Only her eyes darted toward the treeline. No doubt she'd get lost in there after only a handful of steps, and the road wasn't much better, seeing as she'd be on foot and he'd be on a bike.

Her heart raced as she battled her conflicting impulses. This was the first chance she'd really gotten. For all she knew, it'd be her *only* chance. For the first time since Dahlia called her from Felix's house all those weeks ago, she finally understood what her best friend meant when she insisted she couldn't just *stay.*

No matter how attractive the kidnapper, he was still a kidnapper. And a prison was still a prison, even if he let you out for cheeseburgers and motorcycle rides sometimes.

She blinked hard as her eyes refocused. The small crowd of teens in their puffy jackets passed between her table and the restaurant, obscuring her view of Sloane.

"You okay?"

Cecilia glanced at the girl who spoke. A girl with deep brown skin and shifter-bright eyes looked closely at her, phone in hand. Pointing at the bruises on the side of Cecilia's face, she asked in a quieter, double-timbered voice, "You need some help getting away from that elf?"

Another teenager, this one a lanky, curly-haired boy with a bad case of acne, chimed in, "Our pack's close by. You can come with us and you'll be safe. No one fucks around with wolves. Not even *elves.*"

The other teens nodded, their noses wrinkling in a distinctly canine way.

I could go, she realized, time slowing. *I could tell them to call Patrol or just hop in their car and let them drive into pack territory as fast as possible.*

They'd do it. She could see it in their eyes. These kids who couldn't have been older than seventeen were willing to risk their safety to help a strange woman in need. Because kids were fundamentally good, and *that* was why she'd worked so hard to become a teacher. When a child saw someone needed help, they helped.

...She just didn't want them to. Not this time.

All at once, the silent war of her impulses went silent. Cecilia's stomach unclenched as she slowly relaxed her posture.

Giving the sweet wolves a sincere smile, she assured them, "Thanks, kids, but I'm okay. I promise."

The girl with the bright eyes didn't move a muscle. "You sure?"

"Yeah," Cecilia answered, her gaze pulled magnetically toward the dark shape of her elf as he came up behind the teens, deadly hands laden with a tray covered in greasy food, "I think I am."

CHAPTER **EIGHTEEN**

THINGS WERE DIFFERENT WHEN THEY RETURNED TO THE BATTERY, and it wasn't just because he'd never felt happiness before now.

Cecilia's arms squeezed tightly around his middle as he guided the bike through the hidden garage door. Almost as soon as they left the restaurant, she'd placed her helmeted head on his shoulder and leaned her weight into him, trusting Sloane to keep her safe on the road. Whatever tension lingered in her seemed to have evaporated, leaving her disturbingly at ease.

He'd never been touched so much in his life. Outside of torture, of course.

Sloane hadn't been able to suck in a full breath since they left. He'd barely been able to focus on anything other than wherever their bodies brushed. A strange sort of static filled his mind whenever they touched, and when she took his hand…

Desire, he discovered, felt a lot like pain.

It was sharp and bright and relentless. It consumed him in the way pain tried to. The difference was that he'd been trained from childhood to ignore pain, to the point that even in its most severe, life-threatening forms it was hardly more than background noise.

He had no such defense against his need for Cecilia.

The rubber and metal of the bike's handlebars bent beneath his powerful grip as he fought for some tiny shred of control. It'd taken nearly everything he had to sit calmly with her pressed against him for so long, and then to deny her when she so earnestly wished to share a meal with him had almost pushed him to his breaking point.

It was unnatural to deny his consort anything. Instinct balked at the idea and outright rebelled at his continued insistence on denying himself the Pull.

His skin didn't fit right. His focus shattered. His world narrowed to the smallest points — those places where her delicate hands touched him. It was torture unlike anything he'd trained for, and it was the best he'd ever felt in his entire existence.

Sloane parked the bike beside one of his cars and dropped the kickstand. When he cut the engine, the world seemed too quiet. Only his labored breathing echoed inside his helmet. It'd never felt like a cage before, but the familiar padding and protective glass had become a slowly tightening scold's bridle.

He expected Cecilia to hop off the bike as soon as possible, but she didn't. Instead, she sat back and unwound her arms from his middle. The sound of fabric and hair rustling made his already over-taxed heart clench.

Her helmet fell to the ground with a small *thwack* of fiberglass on concrete. The blade of desire cut impossibly deeper when she slipped her arms back around his waist.

"Thanks for the ride. And the date," she whispered, pressing her soft cheek between his shoulder blades.

Within the confines of his helmet, his voice was a strangled thing. "It was satisfactory?"

"Very." Her hands wandered upward, across the flat of his stomach, until they reached his chest. It was impossible to hide the way his heart pounded. Even through his undershirt and armored outer layer, it must've hammered at her palms in a desperate rhythm: *I'm yours. I'm yours. I'm yours.*

Neither of them spoke. For a while, he only heard his own breathing and the ticking of the cooling engine. He didn't dare move a muscle, afraid that she'd change her mind about touching him or that he'd somehow scare her off. His fingers didn't unclench from the handle bars and his eyes stayed fixed on the gray wall ahead of him, unblinking.

"Why didn't you ask me out before? Or even just talk to me? I want a real answer this time."

A strange noise came from his throat — almost a whine. "I didn't know how." *And I didn't dare risk it.*

If she'd run, or if she reported him, or if she'd just… hated him, Sloane couldn't have handled it. Protecting her was his first priority, and any of those possible outcomes would've posed a threat to his duty.

Cecilia's arms tightened, not because they were taking a turn but because she was *hugging* him. Another first.

"You were afraid," she surmised, a note of wonder in that soft voice.

Sloane forced himself to blink. His eyes burned when he replied, "I don't feel fear."

"Who told you that?"

"My trainers," he answered, throat tight.

Cecilia was quiet for a moment. "Someone made you this way, didn't they? You were taught to be… what you are."

It's too soon, he thought, chest seizing. *She can't know yet. If she knows, she'll demand to leave.*

But his doe was smart. Of course she'd picked up on the fact that he wasn't normal, and that whatever he did for Patrol, he wasn't like all the other officers she might've encountered. He'd read her academic record, dug up all her papers on child psychology and behavioral development. Her putting the pieces together that he wasn't quite right was an inevitability.

Panic gripped him, but he was incapable of lying to her. "Yes."

"It's not normal elvish stuff," she guessed.

Defeat was another horrible, unfamiliar sensation. Sloane dipped his chin under the weight of it. "No."

A note he couldn't easily identify entered her voice when she asked, "You don't know how to do any of this, do you? Not just dating. I mean normal life stuff like conversation, having fun, touching. That's why you didn't know how to talk to me before. You were scared of… I don't know. Putting me off or frightening me. Or maybe even your own feelings. Am I right?"

"I needed to keep you safe," he insisted.

"And did keeping me safe from *you* play a part in that?"

It was a shrewd, ruthless question. Sloane swallowed hard but his throat wouldn't unclench no matter what he did. Barely able to get the words out, he rasped, "I would never hurt you. *Never.*"

"But you're a dangerous man. We both know that."

"Yes."

He couldn't exactly deny it, and wouldn't even if it were possible. He had one use in this world: to be a weapon. If he didn't fulfill that purpose for the safety of people like Cecilia, then there was no point in him at all.

He wasn't sure he had a heart to break until she pulled away from him. Sloane flinched when she climbed off the back of the bike, depriving him of her warmth. Watching her walk away from him was stomach curdling, so he didn't do it. He closed his eyes, waiting to hear her footsteps retreat into the house.

But they didn't.

Fabric rustled again as something was dropped onto the floor, and then a gentle hand touched his rigid forearm.

"Ease up," she instructed.

Sloane's eyes popped open. They widened at the sight of her there, her pink leather coat discarded and her hair wild from the wind. Without thinking, he let her unwind his fingers from the handle bar. It'd crumpled under his grip and would need to be replaced before he could ride again, but he didn't care.

Cecilia pushed against his shoulder, urging him to sit back a bit. Confused but relieved she hadn't left him, Sloane planted his boots on either side of the bike and shifted backward on the leather seat.

He thought he'd gotten pretty good at predicting her behavior over the past year. He was wrong.

The air escaped his lungs in a long, pitiful wheeze as his consort threw one long, thigh-high covered leg over the seat — facing him. Their size difference was enough that she didn't really straddle the bike so much as she straddled *him.*

Her thighs draped over his as she settled her weight on his lap. Without her jacket, she was left in small shorts and a skin-tight long-sleeved shirt. He'd seen her in far less, but something about this moment made the outfit somehow more erotic than the number of times he'd watched her in a towel or that distressingly small work uniform.

His skin heated in a flash as she hung her arms around his neck, pressing their torsos together until he could feel every perfect curve and padded inch of her.

Cecilia's fingertips found the tiny gap between the top of his collar and the accordion folds attached to the bottom of his helmet. When their skin touched, Sloane jumped like he'd been electrified.

"Is this okay?" she asked, dark brown eyes searching his visor.

Sloane's shoulders moved with the strength of his deep, desperate breaths. "Yes," he wheezed. "Your touch is… pleasurable."

She seemed to consider something very seriously for a moment before she asked, "Do you want to touch me?"

If his cock got any harder, he was fairly certain it'd snap off as easily as he'd taken that vampire's arm.

Making a pathetic sort of gurgling sound in his throat, Sloane answered, "I don't know how. I wasn't trained to handle soft things."

A small smile played at the corners of her lips. "Do you want to learn, champ?"

"Yes," he answered, short and sharp and sure. *I've never wanted anything more in my life.*

CHAPTER
NINETEEN

He watched in fascination as her cheeks turned a darker color. The urge to run his lips over them, to feel the heat of her blood as it settled beneath her silky skin, was a tearing thing in him.

"You're beautiful," he whispered.

Cecilia looked down. The long, curly wisps of her lashes hid her eyes from him as she skimmed her fingers down his arms to find his hands. Holding them between their bodies, she examined his gloves. "Do you have to wear these all the time?"

He peered at their hands. His looked monstrously large compared to hers, and tipped in the metal claw-caps, they couldn't have been more different. Sloane's jaw tightened.

He didn't want to be different from her. He didn't want to hold himself separate.

The helmet was a necessity, but the gloves… If the sovereign himself could defy convention and be rid of them, so could Sloane.

"I don't," he answered, offering her his hands in a pose very close to supplication. "You can take them off if that's your preference."

Cecilia traced the contour of one of his palms. Her fingertips trailed over the smooth, well-worn leather until she found the thick bar of his wrist. Slipping them under the edge of the glove, she silently began to strip it from his hand.

Pale purple flesh, callused from decades of hard training, was revealed by her careful work. Trails of fire were left in the wake of her touch, making the beds of his claws pulse and burn with the need to retract.

With his helmet on, his body hadn't been exposed to enough of her pheromones to completely start the biological cascade that would trigger things like that, but he felt it there, hovering just on the edge.

When she got to the ends of his fingers, the metal claw-caps slipped off his natural claws with a soft *shwick.* His right hand was left completely bare as she discarded the glove onto the garage floor.

"You have beautiful hands," she noted, cupping it in both of hers. Cecilia turned it over to look at his scarred knuckles and tips of his claws. "I don't think I've ever seen an elf's hands up close."

"Gloves are traditional," he explained, shoulders rounding as he unconsciously pressed closer to her.

"Why?"

Sloane watched his own fingers closely. The more she touched him, the more his nail beds burned, and as she pressed the pad of her thumb into the claw of his index finger, he caught the tiniest retraction.

So dangerous. So, so wanted.

"Because they hide our weakness," he murmured. "When we meet our mates, our claws retract. Gloves hide it."

"Oh." A shadow passed over her expression before a bright smile erased it. "Well, that's a fun fact most people probably don't know. And I guess it's a good thing that didn't happen with me, right? You should probably end up with an elf. I mean, who's ever heard of an arrant and an elf, anyway? That's crazy."

Something in him — pride, perhaps, or something more pitiful, like the childish need to be loved — roared with outrage at the thought.

"No," he hissed, bringing his visor very close to her face. "I will *not* end up with an elf. I'm *your* mate."

Cecilia's lips parted with an astonished breath. "But you just said—"

"You ask me why I won't take my helmet off. That's why. The air filter is protecting you. If I take it off or if it breaks again, I'll react to your pheromones and my claws will retract and I won't be able to give you a choice." His bare hand lifted to set his trembling fingers on the base of her throat, the most precious and private of places to an elf. In a raw voice she couldn't hear through the modulator, he confessed, "I want to be your choice. That's why I need you to teach me how to do this."

"Wait— Hold on." Cecilia sat back until her spine hit the dash. Fearlessly holding his helmet between her hands, she demanded, "Are you telling me I'm your *mate?* Like how orcs mate with the kohl and nests and whatall? Like… like—"

"We call them consorts," he told her.

For once, he managed to shock her into complete silence.

Cecilia stared at him, gobsmacked, until she let out a concerning bubble of laughter. It only lasted a moment before she started nodding her head. Eyes wide and hands still gripping the sides of his helmet, she breathed, "Oh. Oh, okay. Yeah. No. That makes a lot of this make more sense."

Tilting her head back, she unknowingly exposed the long line of her throat as she took several deep breaths. The urge to bite her, to pin her down with infinite care, made him clench his upper and lower fangs so hard they squeaked against each other, inadvertently sharpening themselves.

"Wow. Wow. Okay. *Wow.*" Cecilia laughed again, but this time it was a little less concerning. "So when you said you'd never hurt me, you meant that you're, like, *biologically* incapable of it."

"Yes," he answered, a mite defensive, "but even if I wasn't, I would have no reason to hurt you."

"Sorry, yeah, I get that. I'm just kinda… thinking aloud here. You know, processing the bomb you just dropped while also trying not to be quite as turned on as I am. Give a girl a second." She shook her head. "Man, it's been a weird few days. I can't seem to catch up."

Taking her rambling complaint as an order to be silent, Sloane occupied himself with counting the beats of her heart beneath his palm. He suspected it was a bit faster than normal, which was somewhat gratifying, but he couldn't know for certain until he had a vitals baseline for her.

Another task to add to the list.

"I have a mate. My stalker is my mate," she muttered, dropping her hands to his shoulders. Her blunt nails dug into the armored padding there, making it creak. "Or… I guess I *could* have a mate? If you took the helmet off?"

Sloane nodded.

Cecilia startled almost like she was finally understanding the situation. Her eyes widened in slow motion. "So you've just… decided that you're going to live with that thing on until I decide I want to keep you?"

He dared to brush his thumb over the tiny bit of her clavicle that was exposed by her shirt. It was as delicate as the bones of a bird's wing beneath his fingertip. "Yes."

She leaned closer again, until she was hardly an inch from his visor. "What if I don't?"

The muscles of his throat and jaw worked hard as he fought his instinctive response. "Then I'll keep it on so I can do my job."

Looking like she already knew the answer, she asked, "What's that?"

"Protecting you."

"You'd just… deny yourself a mate? Forever?" Cecilia's incredulous expression didn't sit right with him.

He knew what it was like to be denied free will. Sloane

couldn't claim to possess an abundance of moral fiber, but he would never do that to her.

"I would do what's necessary," he replied.

Cecilia touched the curve of his cheek, or what would've been his cheek if the visor wasn't in the way. In a voice full of wonder, she murmured, "Just when I think I'm starting to get a lock on you, you throw me for a loop."

Sloane didn't know what to say to that, so he simply closed his eyes and bowed his head, seeking out the touch he couldn't feel.

He sucked in a sharp breath as he felt her begin to strip his left hand of its glove. "I don't know whether I'm ready for a mate this second," she told him, "but I've always had a weakness for dangerous men. Maybe there's a reason for that."

He didn't dare open his eyes when he felt her settle his bare hands on the curve of her waist. A part of him worried that if he looked at her, the moment would evaporate, too good to exist both in his mind and reality at once.

And when she began drawing his hands up, guiding him to trace her shape in a slow stroke, he shuddered with a mix of lust and disbelief.

"Normally I'd end a good date with a kiss, but since the helmet is in the way..." Cecilia drew her legs up and around his waist, abandoning all pretense of sitting on the motorcycle. Sloane grunted as the shock of the position ricocheted through him. His hands tightened around her waist, drawing her into his body with an instinctive jerk.

She gasped, hands flying to his chest as she rocked forward. Her lashes fluttered. "Easy," she breathed, arching her back a little. "Just explore. Get comfortable with touching me. Find what you like."

Sloane turned his visor into the sweet curve of her neck. It was deeply unnatural to not be able to smell the sweetness of her skin or gently scrape his fangs against her pulse. Even someone as inexperienced as him knew that. But it was still gratifying when she didn't push him away from a place as vulnerable as her throat.

Cecilia tilted her head to the side, her hair falling in a dark wave over her shoulder, and cupped the back of his helmet. Instinct drew his right hand up to stroke the other side of her neck with greedy, ungloved fingers.

"I like everything about you," he breathed. "You're perfect."

Her fingers fluttered over the clasp at the neck of his armor. "Can I touch you, too? Or would that be too much?"

There was no stopping the rattling purr that erupted in his chest. Sloane nodded into her throat, incapable of speech.

"Just tell me if you need me to stop," she commanded him, flicking the clasp open. Cool air kissed the overheated skin of his throat.

Already on the brink of losing his mind, Sloane hissed, "I want to touch your skin."

He felt her breath hitch more than he heard it. "Then touch it."

He really, truly didn't mean to destroy her shirt. It just seemed like the most efficient method to get what he wanted.

Cecilia let out a squeak of surprise as his claws turned her clothing to ribbons. She didn't complain, though. Instead, she braced her elbows on the handlebars and thrust her chest toward him, one eyebrow cocked.

Sloane thought he knew what it was to be set aflame, considering it'd actually happened to him more than once. He was wrong.

Nothing compared to the sight of his consort lounging on his motorcycle, her legs wrapped around his waist and her breasts barely covered in a nearly transparent bra. Dark nipples hardened beneath the gossamer material, tightening with desire and beckoning him to touch.

He could barely comprehend the sight, let alone the smooth expanse of her stomach and the flush that suffused the skin of her chest.

It was a good thing he'd turned off all alerts in his helmet. If he hadn't, he was fairly certain every single medical warning would've filled his ears as he brought his trembling hands to cup the delicate architecture of her ribs. Sloane glided his palms up over the soft mounds of her breasts, his breaths shortening as he circled his thumbs over those silky nipples.

Cecilia's chest moved beneath his hands with every inhalation, but she was otherwise perfectly still as he explored her first through the thin material of her bra. When he couldn't stand even that barrier, he dragged the cups down, exposing her completely. He was so focused on stroking and gently rolling them between his fingers that it took him a moment to realize she was trembling.

Freezing, he glanced at her expression and expected to see revulsion or fear.

Instead, he found a desire that mirrored his own. It darkened her cheeks and forced her to suck her lower lip between her teeth, holding back a faint whimper whenever he scraped his thumb claws over her sensitive flesh.

"You like this," he marveled, pressing himself closer. "You like when I touch you."

Cecilia huffed. "That obvious, huh?"

"No," he answered, abandoning one breast to sneak his hand around her back. Pressing his palm against her tailbone, he rocked her forward again, recreating that singular, electric feeling of their hips meeting. Seeing the look of surprise and pleasure flicker across her flushed face was more thrilling than anything he'd ever experienced — even killing.

"Well, you're doing a good job," she assured him, voice thick.

"Tell me what to do next."

Cecilia's throat moved with a hard swallow. "I should probably stop you here."

Sloane's fingers curled, holding onto her possessively at even the suggestion that she might want to move from this perfect position. "Why?"

"Because this was our first date and this is new to you. We should go slow."

Head tilting, he pressed, "But do you *want* to go slow?"

Her tongue, small and pink and tempting, darted out to wet her lips. "No, I don't."

"What do you want, doe?"

Cecilia didn't say anything. Instead, she slipped her hands between their bodies and popped the little white button at the top of her tweed shorts. Eyes dark and needy, she told him, "I want you to make me come."

CHAPTER **TWENTY**

It was an absolutely terrible idea. Cecilia fully intended to do it anyway.

She didn't stop to think about all the reasons she shouldn't let Sloane slip his fingers inside her shorts. At some point between straddling his motorcycle and discovering that she was his mate, all good sense had been replaced by the desire she'd been failing to smother for days. Maybe even longer than that.

It seeped into every vein to burn away her reservations. Nothing mattered besides the heat and friction of his hands on her skin.

Her flushed reflection stared back at her in the smokey glass of his helmet as he dipped his fingers past the waistband of her panties. For a big, terrifying virgin, Sloane didn't appear to be in any rush. He moved slowly, every muscle tight with restraint. Her senses were so heightened with anticipation that she swore she could feel the whorls of his fingerprints dragging over the soft skin of her stomach and mons.

"You're so fragile," he said, in what she imagined was a murmur. "And warm. Warmer than I thought you'd be."

Cecilia bit her lip. Despite the fact that Sloane had exactly zero social graces to speak of, he had a devastating way with words. She wasn't sure if it was a good thing or not that she couldn't hear his real voice when he said things like that.

No, that's a lie, she swiftly corrected herself, *it's a very, very bad thing. I'm already straddling his dick. I might as well hear his voice while I'm at it.*

Trying not to squirm, she asked, "Sloane, is there a way for you to… turn off that filter thingy on your helmet? The voice one."

His downward path stalled. "I… believe so. Would it please you to deactivate the modulator?"

"Yeah," she answered thickly, "that would please me."

Sloane's left hand shot up to glide the tips of his claws below the curve of the helmet's jaw. He must've hit some hidden mechanism because there was a metallic click. A tiny pop of feedback preceded a bass voice asking, "Are you pleased?"

Cecilia's breath left her in an embarrassingly loud *whoosh.* "Yes," she wheezed, "I'm pleased."

Sloane dropped his left hand to her breast. Giving it a possessive squeeze, he rasped, "Good."

Cecilia bit back a groan. *Oh, good gods. I've unleashed a monster.*

She'd gotten a taste of his voice when she smashed his helmet, but it'd been layered with the modulator. Now she heard it with perfect clarity. Sloane had a deep, husky sort of voice that was far deadlier than his claws or his weapons. That single, delicious word rolled off his tongue in a way that made her insides *liquify.*

The part of her that was still somehow aware that this was a vulnerable time for him — and wasn't *that* a trip? — prompted her to tell him, "I like your voice, Sloane. I like it a lot."

He didn't preen like a normal man might've. He didn't immediately slide into dirty talk or even return the compliment. Instead, Sloane skimmed his left hand down to mold it to the curve of her waist and growled, "It's yours."

Cecilia jumped a little when his right hand finally continued on its mission. Sloane didn't go directly for the goods. Instead, he bent her backward over the motorcycle's handlebars and cupped her in that massive, deadly hand. Slick skin slipped against his palm when he gave her a proprietary squeeze that made her toes curl.

"I want to please you," he told her in that rough voice. "I want to earn you. I want to keep you."

Slowly, like he was afraid she'd stop him, two middle fingers parted her cunt to slide into the hot, wet cleft of her body. Her back arched over the handlebars, every one of her muscles tightening with that single touch.

"I'll do anything you ask of me," he promised her. Something in his tone made it feel more like a threat than a plea, which only heightened the painful desire throbbing between her parted thighs.

"Circle your fingers around my clit," she breathlessly instructed.

Gods bless him, Sloane did exactly as he was told. Cecilia's hips nearly lifted off the seat as he applied himself to the task.

"Slow circles," she breathed, rocking against his hand to help him find the best rhythm. "There, that's… that's good. Perfect, even."

Sloane tightened his hold on her waist as his fingers slid through the downright shameful wetness in her panties. His helmet tilted closer to her face, which probably gave him a great view of whatever expression she made when he experimented with gently pinching his fingers together to roll her flesh between them.

What he lacked in experience, he made up for in sheer determination to learn. With every swivel of her hips and breathy encouragement, he bore down on her with more intensity.

She'd never been the object of such perfect focus before. Most of the terrible men she tended to choose were often more concerned with their own pleasure than hers. If she wanted to get off, it was up to her to make it happen. With her specific…

quirks, she didn't often have trouble getting there, but that didn't mean she loved doing it all on her own.

That wasn't a problem with Sloane.

He was everywhere. He nearly smothered her with his bulk when he forced her to bend backward over the handlebars. The smooth glass of his visor slid against her sweaty throat as he pressed his face into the juncture of neck and shoulder. His fingers began to move quickly, occasionally dipping downward to explore the entrance of her body before he arrowed ruthlessly back to her clitoris.

Cecilia panted. Her breasts rubbed against the rough fabric of his armored uniform, sending a delicious thrill through her tight nipples. Desperate for more contact, she blindly pawed at his uniform until she got enough of a grip to yank his shirt… coat… breastplate thing out of his pants. When her hands snuck beneath it, she found miles and miles of hot, smooth skin.

Rigid muscle contracted sharply under her exploration. Sloane let out a tantalizing grunt. His fingers spasmed inside her panties, sending a shockwave of sensation up her spine.

Heart hammering, she breathed, "Are you okay?"

Sloane took a moment to answer. His chest, huge and deep and stronger than she could probably wrap her brain around, rose and fell with gulping breaths. "I am… experiencing intense sensation," he answered.

"Do you want to—"

Cecilia yelped when Sloane slid two fingers inside her. Using the position to grip her from *the inside,* he growled, "No. I don't want to stop."

Her core rippled around his fingers when he ground the heel of his palm down, firmly enough to feel a bit like a punishment. Sloane's chest rattled violently under her hands. A strange sound came through the speakers in his helmet, one she was beginning to recognize.

It was a purr of pure, animalistic pleasure.

"I love this feeling," he rumbled. "I love the way you look at me when I have my fingers inside you. No one's ever looked at me the way you do, Cece."

Hooking one hand around the back of his neck, she drew him against her naked chest. Her other hand trailed down over his pounding heart and heaving ribs to find the buckle of his utilitarian belt. It wasn't an elegant maneuver, unbuckling it with one hand, but she got the job done at about the same time he decided to test out rearranging her insides with his fingers.

The temptation to see him in all his purple glory was a wild thing in her, but she decided that would just have to wait for next time.

Because there's definitely gonna be a next time, she thought, dipping her greedy fingers past the waistband of his briefs. Burning skin met her fingertips.

The bar of Sloane's cock was hard and heavy in her grip when she gently extracted it from its prison. There wasn't a whole lot of space between their bodies, but she was nothing if not determined.

Her fingers tightened, sliding upward to give the damp head her own proprietary squeeze. Sloane's rhythm faltered. His fingers curled sharply inside her. Before she could even begin to worry about his claws, a blinding flash of pleasure made her clamp down hard on the digits. Cecilia muffled a moan by clamping her teeth on his armored shoulder.

Sloane shuddered. His hips began to roll in a jagged beat, shuttling his cock through her fingers. The bike rocked beneath them, but she didn't spare a single thought to the possibility of tipping over. He wouldn't let that happen.

And even if it did… Well, it wasn't like it would be the first time.

But any memories of other men and other times were too far away to reach her when Sloane stroked the inside of her cunt like that, as if he was hungry for every little ripple and slick glide.

The sounds of their bodies echoed in the concrete garage. Wet, sloppy noises and heavy breathing accompanied the creak of the bike beneath them. Everything she knew, everything she was, narrowed to the string of pleasure that pulled ever-more taut between them.

The pressure built and built until it threatened to explode out of her.

Determined to make this a good time for him, too, Cecilia twisted her wrist, stroking his cock with every bit of skill she'd developed over the years of bad decisions and worse hookups.

It must've done the trick, because not a moment later Sloane's massive body flexed in a fluid wave. His release spilled over her knuckles, hot and perfect, and when her name whispered through that damn helmet again and again…

Cecilia's back bowed. Her orgasm was as sweet and sharp and dangerous as the man who gave it to her. Tingles cascaded down her body as a rush of endorphins left her limp over the handlebars. Sloane had to support her back to stop her from sliding onto the garage floor to create a Cecilia-flavored puddle.

Threading her fingers into the tiny pale hairs that managed to escape the bottom of his helmet, she slurred, "You good, champ?"

Sloane wrapped his arm around her back. Dropping his helmet onto her shoulder, he wheezed, "Affirmative."

CHAPTER **TWENTY-ONE**

"WHERE DO YOU SLEEP?"

Cecilia leaned against the doorway. She'd showered and changed into her pajamas, a pair of soft pink flannel shorts and a button down shirt. It'd been good to take her time getting ready for bed, she thought, to give him a minute to process. To give her one, too.

Elves have mates. I'm his mate. If I want to be. What a trip.

It sure put a lot of things into perspective. She'd known folks who had mate drives and others who found themselves the fixation of them. Orcs, vampires, shifters, dragons — they all had their own special cocktails of urges that drove them absolutely batty for that one special person.

Sloane's behavior sure fit that description. He denied it, but for all she knew, stalking and murder was part of the mating instinct package elves were saddled with. If so, it would make their keeping it under wraps make a *lot* of sense.

She'd always suspected they were a bunch of kinky little weirdos. No one *that* repressed turned out normal.

The man stood in the hallway outside the bedroom, his shoulders back and hands tucked behind him in that military stance. She was pretty sure he'd changed into clean clothes, but it was honestly hard to tell since he seemed to own multiple versions of the same garments. The only evidence that he was affected at all by what they'd done was the lack of modulator disguising his voice when he replied, "In the armory."

Her brows drew together. "There's a bed in there?"

"No," he answered, "I rack out on the floor."

"You rack out on the— You *sleep* on the floor?" Cecilia pointed in the direction of the living room. "Sloane, there's a couch!"

He shook his head. "I can't sleep in an unsecured location. The Battery is safe, but there are still windows."

Understanding dawned. "You can't relax when you feel exposed."

"Correct."

She looked around with fresh eyes. The serial killer bunker sure made more sense now that she possessed that little tidbit of information. There was still so much she didn't know about him, but after tonight, Cecilia felt like she'd unlocked something essential.

Sloane was painfully, dangerously in love with her, and he was the single most vulnerable apex predator on the planet.

Guilt pierced her, though she knew it wasn't entirely fair to feel it. She didn't blame herself for being wary of him, seeing as he'd killed three men in front of her before he *drugged* and *kidnapped her*, but now that she knew him better, she didn't like the thought of him sleeping on the floor.

Scuffing her bare heel against the cool floor, she offered, "Well, if you want… you could share the bed with me."

Sloane made a funny half-step sort of motion, almost like he'd nearly lost his balance.

It was still thrilling to be able to hear his cautious tone when he said, "I would have to wear my helmet."

"I don't mind if you don't." Feeling weirdly embarrassed by her offer, she rocked back on her heels and looked away from that dark visor. "You know what? It's probably way too uncomfortable for you to do that. Forget I said anything. I wasn't thinking about what it would— I mean, I didn't consider the, uh, limitations. Sorry."

She didn't hear him approach. Sloane moved like a damn cat in those heavy-duty boots. Cecilia had no idea he was there until he slipped his fingers under her chin to tilt her head up.

"It would be the greatest honor of my life to guard you while you sleep," he rumbled. She'd never imagined there to be levity in his voice, or even insincerity, but to hear his seriousness completely unfiltered was a heady thing.

Sloane wasn't just saying things. He wasn't trying to charm her. If he said something that took her breath away, it was the raw, honest truth. She doubted he even knew how to lie to her, let alone *flirt.*

Insides turning to molten goo, she laid a hand on his chest. "Thanks, champ, but I don't just want you to guard me. I want you to rest, too."

"But—"

"Sloane, baby, are you really gonna tell me you won't wake up the *second* there's a weird sound in the house?"

"Of course I will," he answered, obviously offended.

"Then it's fine if you rest. There's no danger." Cecilia snagged his hand and began to pad backward, gently pulling him with her. "I trust you to protect me, but if this is gonna be anything between us, you've got to see me as something *more* than a target to protect, okay?"

Sloane let her tug him into the room with absolutely zero resistance. Sounding a touch uncertain, he argued, "You're not just a target. You're my consort."

She was much more used to words like mate, wife, or partner. *Consort* would've sounded deeply pretentious if it weren't for the reverence with which he used it.

"Right," she whispered, battling a tide of butterflies that had taken over her stomach. "Well, your consort wants you to sleep with her. Really sleep."

His head cocked. "Is that an order?"

The backs of her knees bumped the large mattress. Sitting down with a little bounce, she shrugged. "If it has to be."

"Understood."

Sloane sat stiffly beside her. He took a moment to rest his hands on his knees and take a deep breath before he began the oddly rehearsed process of stripping off his clothing. Scooting back until she could bring her legs up and cross them, Cecilia watched him unlace his boots and carefully align them beside the bed — almost like he wanted them in the perfect position to step in.

His black, armored shirt went next. She ogled him shamelessly as he revealed his naked torso to her, showing off slabs of hard muscle and so much deliciously lickable purple skin. Sloane wasn't built for vanity. His muscle was the thick kind that came from repeated motions and hard combat training.

It wasn't pretty. It was deadly.

Her mouth went dry as he stood up to quickly and efficiently unclasp his belt, roll it, and set it on the nightstand that once held the lamp she'd hit him with. He'd left his gloves in the garage, which meant she got to watch his deft fingers handle his button and fly completely unobstructed.

Gods have mercy on me, she thought, *if his hands are that hot, what is his face gonna do to me?*

And then he dropped his pants.

Cecilia choked on nothing when his tight backside came into view. Covered in plain black briefs, aggressively spherical and dimpled on the sides, it was the single most perfectly sculpted ass she'd ever beheld.

"Holy shit," she whispered, crawling forward to get a better look.

Sloane's head turned to peer over his shoulder. "What?"

"Have you ever considered becoming an underwear model?"

He took a moment to respond. "I have not."

"Well, you should," she told him, eyeing his strong thighs.

Sloane crouched down to pick up his pants. Folding them in a precise series of movements before setting them on the nightstand beside the sparkly urn that contained her dead cat, he gravely replied, "I will consider it."

Cecilia couldn't smother a giggle. It got even worse when he turned around to face her in nothing more than his skivvies and that sinister helmet.

Sloane's helmet tilted to one side. "You're amused. Why?"

Scooching backward, Cecilia tucked herself under the covers between bouts of giggles. "Has anyone ever told you that you're really cute, Sloane?"

"No."

"That's a shame." She patted the space beside her. "I'm pretty sure you're a sweetheart. You should be called cute at least once a week. Probably more."

Sloane crouched low to crawl onto the bed. It shifted sharply under his greater weight, but he still managed to move with all the grace of a big cat as he slipped under the covers. "I… don't know the appropriate response to that."

Cheeks cramping a little, she flopped back into the pillows. "That's okay. I don't mind if you don't always know the right thing to say to me. No one knows the right thing to say all the time, anyway."

Sloane's helmet settled on the pillow beside hers. In a quiet voice, he challenged, "You do."

Pulling the comforter up over her shoulder, she watched the way the twinkle lights gleamed off the curve of his helmet. He lay flat on his back, his hands folded on his middle and his legs perfectly straight. He looked a bit like an alien trying to fool her into believing he slept.

Despite the strangeness of it, she was comfortable. More than comfortable.

Sloane smelled like leather and musk and clean soap. His body heat immediately began to permeate the bedding, tantalizing her.

Aware that he was almost certainly not a cuddler, she resisted the urge to glue herself to his side and suck up his warmth like a little snuggle vampire.

"You think I'm pretty great, don't you?" she asked, not to fish for compliments but to hear his honest response.

"I do," he answered.

Cecilia's giddiness dimmed a little. Letting out a slow exhale, she dared to touch one corded bicep with the tips of her fingers. "I'm just a regular person, Sloane. I'm glad you think I'm special, but I don't think it's right to worship me." She shook her head against the pillow. "I'm kind of a mess, actually. Always have been. Even my own parents didn't think I was worth much. The only person who likes me even half as much as you is Dahlia."

Sloane didn't move when she touched him, but she was fascinated by the way the muscles of his arm twitched and shivered with even her slightest touch. She did it again, just to see, when she explained, "Not to get into the meat and potatoes of my trauma or anything, but my parents really hated each other. Don't ask me why they stayed married because I honestly don't know. But suffice it to say I spent most of my childhood trying to fix what was broken and failing. That meant my parents didn't really… well, they weren't very focused on me."

"Is this the reason you want to teach young?"

Cecilia shrugged. "Maybe. I like them. They're the best of us, and I know what it feels like to be an overlooked kid. Helping them be happy and healthy and prepared for the world is— I'm sure you get it."

She peered closely at his helmet. "Why did you decide to join Patrol?"

Sloane's big hand crawled across the mattress to find the curve of her waist. Settling it there like he worried she'd tell him no, he answered, "I did not."

"You didn't what?"

"I didn't choose," he clarified.

Mimicking her pose, Sloane turned on his side. Apparently

emboldened by the fact that she didn't push him away, he slipped his hand around her back to begin dragging her closer.

Her breath caught as he tucked her against him. His warmth blazed through the thin material of her pajamas, stoking that ever-burning fire of desire in her belly. Not being able to see his face squished on the pillow bothered her, but when she slung her arm over his middle to hug him back… It was all right. Maybe even more than all right.

Maybe it was even something awfully close to perfect.

In a softer voice, she asked, "What do you mean you didn't choose?"

"I was taken from my parents by the former sovereign when I was six years old and conscripted into service." Sloane played with the tips of her hair. He rubbed the strands between his fingers in a slow, repetitive way that made her heart ache. "My parents were killed when they rebelled and tried to take me back. This life is all I've ever known."

"Sloane…"

"I wasn't raised like you," he continued, like he had to get the words out before he lost courage. "I was trained to fight and kill and serve. We weren't given luxuries or comforts. All the good things in my life were taken from me or used as weapons against me. If *you* are a mess, then I'm something far worse. I'm Thaddeus's discarded weapon."

Cecilia's eyes stung. Blinking quickly, she tried to push down the horror of what he'd so casually shared with her in order to speak. "That's the saddest thing I've ever heard. I'm so sorry that happened to you. I…"

Kidnapped as a child. Too dangerous to be allowed to live a normal life. The strange uniforms and the pack mentality and the way he killed so easily.

She'd heard the stories. Everyone had. Sloane and his team were literally the stuff of nightmares — faceless tools Mad Thad had used to inspire fear in his people until his daughter lopped his head off and punted it into the ocean.

She was certain of the answer, but Cecilia still had to ask, "The sovereign— Does he order you to…"

"No," he grated. "We protect innocents now. We always did, as best we possibly could, but it was never enough. What we refused to do or got caught circumventing, the trainers and other shadow squads would finish for us. And if we disobeyed enough, then…"

Her skin crawled with horror. *A man with a moral compass like Sloane would lose a piece of himself every day he had to hurt innocent people.*

Maybe he'd been trained to no longer feel guilt. Maybe he'd even been trained out of feeling pain. But she was damn certain both were still there.

Petting his hair with shaking fingers, she forced herself to ask, "What did they control you with?"

"How—"

"There's no fucking way you would hurt people who didn't deserve it unless you had no other choice," she hissed. "So what did they do to you, Sloane, besides kidnap and torture you as a defenseless child?"

"Our families," he answered. "My parents were the example. They died… badly. Publicly. After that, they used everyone else's family as collateral and vice versa. Most of us came from prominent, openly rebellious families Thaddeus wanted to keep in line. And when it was finally over, we were so fucked up that they wouldn't even take us back. They're terrified of us."

It's my duty to protect you, he'd said.

Because if he didn't, he thought I'd be taken away from him just like his family, she realized. *Oh, gods. My poor elf.*

"Sloane," she choked out, digging her fingers into his dense muscle, "I'm so sorry."

"Cece—"

Pulling back to look him in the eye, she cut him off with a fierce hiss, "I'm *sorry* that happened to you, Sloane. I'm sorry about everything that's happened to you."

She could almost feel his gaze searching her expression with disbelief. "You don't… want to leave?"

"No," she answered, "I want to kill everyone who hurt you. *All* of you."

The old sovereign was a tyrant. She'd grown up hearing about him and living in a territory scarred by his desire for absolute control.

And yet she'd never truly hated him until then, when she imagined a terrified little boy being ripped from his parents and forced into a life of violence.

What did one say to an admission like that? There were no words to match the enormity of so much grief and pain, or even close to it. Her piddling little apology was nothing compared to what he'd been through.

In the end, she didn't say anything more. Cecilia draped one leg over his hip and hugged him close, until she could feel his heart beat against hers.

Sloane hunched a little, his much bigger body, curling over hers until the underside of his helmet brushed her hair.

"I'm bad, Cece," he whispered.

She exhaled slowly. "I don't think so. I think you're what you were made to be and what you've chosen to be in spite of that, just like everybody else."

"I am," he insisted. "I… I've done things that would give you nightmares. More things than I can even remember. And—" He cut himself off with a sharp growl.

She couldn't say she was particularly *shocked* to hear he'd done awful things. The man had squashed Duke's head like a teenager let loose on an over-ripe melon.

"What?" she asked, stroking his back. "And you like to stalk pretty waitresses? I know that already."

The sound of his swallow was loud in her ear. "I don't want to tell you."

"Why?"

"Because you won't want me anymore if I do. If I keep telling you horrible things, eventually it will scare you away," he answered.

A deep, painful lurch in her chest made her stop and take a breath. "Sloane… part of figuring this thing out between us is building trust. We can't have trust if you're always afraid I'm going to run."

With great reluctance, Sloane admitted, "I hunt people. Not for an assignment."

It took her a moment to comprehend exactly what he was and wasn't saying.

"Oh," she dragged out. "So you… go off book, so to speak."

Sloane held her like he thought she'd try to escape him at any moment. Helmet digging into the top of her head, he replied, "Patrol doesn't catch everything. They don't protect everyone — like you, and like the people who we— *I* was assigned to… I try to help the only way I know how."

Cecilia took a moment to let his confession sink in. Again, she couldn't say she was surprised. Thinking back to the night they met, it all seemed to click together. But it was one thing to suspect it and quite another to hear it plainly.

It felt a little dismissive of the seriousness of death for her to blurt out the first thing that came to her mind, but after several tense moments of silence, she decided that it was her true reaction.

Or rather, a lack of one.

Picking her words carefully, she began, "Listen, Sloane. I'm arrant. I'm not like you. I'm not strong or fast or magical. You said it yourself. I'm weak and defenseless. We're *prey.* We survive because we're adaptable and smart, but everyone knows how easily we could be gobbled up by elves or orcs or dragons or even vampires. We live with that knowledge from pretty much the moment we're born, and a lot of us… well, a lot of us learn to coexist with the fear that breathes down our necks every second of every day."

She stroked the tips of her fingers up his spine, tracing the strong muscles that bracketed either side, until she found the muscled wings of his shoulder blades. In a quieter voice, she admitted, "So… as long as you're protecting people, then I'm not going to condemn you. It's not pretty, but it's the truth."

She felt more than heard his sharp inhale. "You don't think I'm a monster?"

"I think that there are good monsters and there are bad monsters," she answered, eyes fluttering shut. "And I happen to know you're a good one."

"You're good, Cece," he murmured. "I'm glad you teach young. Children deserve goodness."

Heart breaking for him all over again, she told him, "So did you, Sloane."

"You're here now." He let out a long exhale, like a great weight had finally lifted from his chest. "That's all I need."

"I'm here," she repeated, arms tightening. "I'm here."

CHAPTER
TWENTY-TWO

Sloane slipped out from beneath his consort's arms and the warmth of the covers. It nearly killed him to do it, but he had no choice.

Standing by the bed, he leaned down to pull the blankets over her slim shoulders. He arranged them with painstaking care, delaying the inevitability of his exit, before he forced his feet to move. Grabbing his boots off the floor and his bundle of clothing, he left the bedroom without a sound. He only felt a small twinge of discomfort when he engaged the lock on the door.

It wasn't that he didn't trust her. He did. Mostly. But the lock would work to keep *out* anyone just as well as it worked to keep her *in*. That was a small amount of assurance for him and his raging instincts.

Very small.

It would have to be enough. He had work to do.

Sloane dressed quickly. Logically, he knew nothing had changed about his kit. It was identical to every other one he owned. And yet somehow it still felt different on his skin after what they'd done together. Maybe his skin was different. Maybe everything about him was different now that he knew what pleasure truly was — Cecilia's hands on him.

Whatever the case, it grated against the very fabric of his being to leave her sleeping in her— *their* bed, unprotected and unaware.

His stomach soured with every step he took toward the garage, and a cold sweat gathered beneath his helmet. Everything in him rebelled at the idea of leaving his mate. Sloane was well-trained in pushing aside any discomfort or pain to continue a mission, but this was worse than anything he'd experienced before.

It felt like it took hours for him to make it to one of his unmarked cars. It took longer for him to actually start the damn thing.

Nausea rolled through him, but he braced himself and hit the ignition. Protecting her came first. It came before his comfort, certainly, and definitely his own safety.

Sloane knew he was taking a risk when he drove back into San Francisco in the dead of night. He knew how to avoid the web of cameras and surveillance that blanketed the city, but his team *also* knew every trick he possessed. If they were hunting him, which they almost certainly were, then every system in place would be on alert for him specifically.

It was a risk he had to take.

Luckily The Lush was on the opposite end of the city from the barracks. Stepping into the alley where he'd seen Cecilia for the first time — and hundreds of times since — he didn't bother checking for cameras above the employee exit. With the kind of business Duke ran, they knew better than to have recording equipment around.

All it took was a sharp jerk of his gloved hand to break the lock on the door. The bar had closed for the final hours of the night, allowing vampires plenty of time to get home without being roasted and giving him the perfect opportunity for recon.

It wasn't the first time he'd broken in, but it was the only time he'd done so with a purpose beyond rifling around in Cecilia's locker.

Navigating the dark warren of employee spaces and private VIP rooms, Sloane found his way into what could only be the boss's office. Ignoring the ridiculous patent leather wall furnishings and chrome mini bar stocked with alcoholic synth, he made his way to the glass desk strewn with receipts, half-smoked cigarettes, and thankfully unused packets of condoms.

From all appearances, it didn't seem like The Lush was hurting without its boss. Going by the state of the desk, that was probably due to the competence of its managers and not anything Duke did before his death.

It was impossible to say whether anyone had noticed the man's absence yet, but Sloane intended to clean up any loose ends regardless.

It only took a few minutes to find a piece of paperwork in the desk with Duke's address on it. Tucking it into his pocket, he went back the way he came.

As he wound his way back through the employee corridors, he looked around and tried to imagine his doe wandering the halls every night. Since that time in her life had passed, Sloane made sure to make a pit stop at her locker to collect the twelve lip glosses, spare pair of shoes, and stain remover stick she kept in there.

It was a relief knowing Cecilia would never be back working among hungry vampires. Obviously it was better for her safety, but it was also because he knew it wasn't what she wanted to be doing. His consort should've been teaching young, not passing out synth in painful-looking shoes.

How can she do that if we go on the run?

Another problem to solve. Sloane ground his fangs together, sharpening their already deadly points, as he slipped out the alley door. Keeping to the shadows to avoid the traffic cameras that monitored the m-grid, he ducked into the driver's seat and set off for the bastard's townhouse.

It was a short drive to a trendy neighborhood full of gutted and grimly painted homes. Duke's home was all shades of gray, with ugly modern finishes that he was certain Cecilia would've sneered at. Figuring that the vampire would have at least half-decent security in place, he parked down the street and used a neighbor's unsecured backyard gate to access the narrow alley that ran behind the homes.

Leaping over the tall iron fence into Duke's backyard was as easy as breathing. So was bypassing the security on the back door. No alarm sounded when he strode into the vampire's unused kitchen. Whatever Duke did for the vampire syndicate, he wasn't high up enough to have his own private guards, either, making the entire process laughably easy.

The home was just as tacky on the inside as it was on the outside. If there was such a thing as the exact opposite of Cecilia's warmth and comfort, it was the chrome, cold light, and black granite of Duke's crime den.

Sloane doubted he would've noticed anything like that before, but Cecilia had changed more than just the chemical composition of his body. She'd made him see things he never would've before.

But his appreciation for soft carpet, warm light, and long dark hair tangled over his pillows didn't wipe out decades of training. It took only a matter of minutes to find the vampire's various caches of weapons, drugs, and cash. Accessing his various devices took only slightly longer.

Duke wasn't smart enough to turn off mirroring on his devices, which meant that once Sloane got past the password protection, he was able to see *everything.*

Multiple phones, multiple accounts, multiple illegal businesses. He found them all, alongside every other sordid secret the man saved in his digital spaces. A network of associates sprawled before him, each one a potential threat to the woman sleeping peacefully in his bed.

There were other things, too.

Sloane stared at the images on the screen for several long moments, considering the best course of action. He'd never had use for allies before, and he certainly didn't trade in favors, but he was adaptable.

Pulling his phone out of his pocket, he dialed the most recently called number.

A woman's voice came through the line in his helmet. "Cece? Girl, if you hang up on me again—"

"This isn't Cece," he said, claws drumming on the smudged glass of the desk. "This is her mate."

To her credit, Dahlia didn't immediately launch into questions. She paused for a beat before she drawled, "...You must be the friend she mentioned."

Hackles raising at the slight mocking edge in the woman's voice, he insisted, "Her *mate.*"

"No offense, weirdo, but until she tells me that with her own mouth, I'm still calling you a friend."

"Understood," he grated, "but irrelevant. I need to speak to your criminal mate."

"Excuse me?"

Growing impatient, he pressed, "Felix Amauri. Head of the Amauri crime family, responsible for underground gambling dens, arms trading, and illegal smuggling across territory borders. Sanctioned the hit that killed Yvanna Amauri—"

"Wow, can you *not* list a dozen things that might get my husband thrown in prison, please?" Dahlia's voice had lost what little good humor it possessed. Her tone sharpened with warning when she demanded, "Who the fuck are you?"

"I'm Cece's mate," he reminded her. "And I need to speak to Felix about a possible threat to you."

"What on—"

"I don't have time for this. I have information on Duke's associates who appear to be actively surveilling you and your family. Do you or do you not want this information?"

There was a brief pause. "Hold on."

Checking the time, Sloane ground his teeth. He needed to be out of the city before sunrise, and every minute that dragged by away from Cecilia made his physical discomfort worse. He imagined it was something like withdrawal. Despite his helmet's filter, he'd still been exposed to her pheromones enough that the Pull clawed at him, little by little, until there was no part of him untouched by desire.

And he just… *missed* her.

Just when he was beginning to debate giving up on helping Dahlia and her criminal, the sound of a door opening came through the line.

"Felix," Dahlia hissed, "we have a situation."

"What's wrong?" That was undoubtedly Felix.

Speaking closer to the phone, Dahlia informed him, "I'm putting you on speaker, *friend*. Felix, this is Cecilia's—"

"Mate," Sloane cut in, a deep, elvish growl in his voice. "I'm her mate."

"Yeah, I'm not sure about that one," she continued, apparently unbothered by the clear warning. "But he's claiming he has information on a threat and he wants to talk to you."

Felix's voice got closer. "You the guy that killed Duke?"

Sloane flexed his claws. "Yes."

"Did he die badly?"

A grim smile curled his lips. "Yes."

Felix chuckled. "Good work."

"I'm aware."

The vampire made a thoughtful sound. Speaking in a deceptively pleasant voice, he asked, "Do I get to know your name, killer? Since we're apparently family and all."

"We are not family," Sloane corrected him.

Dahlia snapped, "Listen, weirdo: if you're claiming you're my best friend's husband, then you better fucking believe we're family. Cece is the closest thing to a sister I have and I'll break every bone in your fucking body if you—"

"Cece already informed me of the consequences of harming

her," he broke in impatiently. "The only reason I'm calling is to protect her and by extension *you.* And the only reason I'm discussing this with a criminal is because you have ties to the threat and can more effectively eliminate them."

Felix's tone changed from pleasant to businesslike in an instant. "I'm listening."

Sloane clicked through the surveillance photos on the screen. "You're being watched by one of Duke's associates. He was dispatched from here to track Dahlia and await further orders. He appeared to be Duke's right hand man, but as of his last messages does not seem to know that his boss is missing."

"What happened with Cece?" Dahlia demanded. "If he sent someone to watch us and you felt the need to kill him, it must've been bad. Tell me what happened."

He didn't respond right away. Sloane had to weigh whether Cecilia would be upset or not before he eventually decided it was worth the risk.

"Duke and two other vampires followed her home, broke in, threatened her, and beat her. Duke claimed he was owed compensation for the death of his brother and that taking Cece's life was an even exchange. Obviously, I eliminated them, but I need to be sure that no one — this associate included — will seek retribution."

Two sharp intakes of air came through the line. Dahlia's voice seemed a little farther away when she breathed, "Oh gods, I'm gonna throw up. No wonder she didn't want to tell me. Felix—"

Muttering, her vampire soothed, "She's okay. You talked to her, remember?"

Some foreign thing in Sloane that felt suspiciously close to compassion compelled him to add, "She's safe with me now."

"You take care of Cece," Felix said, "and we'll handle Duke's man. Send me everything you have."

"There are others in United Washington who should be investigated," he pressed.

"Consider it done."

"Good." Sloane swallowed years of training and his own natural reticence with considerable difficulty. "And Dahlia…"

She let out an impatient sound that reminded him so much of Cecilia, it startled him. "Yes?"

Quickly extracting a memory card from the computer, he bit out, "My name is Sloane."

"Sloane, huh?" She huffed. "Well, Sloane, I'll be keeping an eye on you."

He stood up from the desk. "Heard. I'll keep you up to date with any developments that concern you."

"You're a military man, aren't you, killer?" Felix asked.

"No," he answered, tucking the memory card into his pocket. "I'm Cecilia's mate. That's all you need to know."

Mission accomplished, he ended the call. He'd barely taken a few steps into the hallway outside the office when the hair on the back of his neck stood on end.

CHAPTER TWENTY-THREE

SLOANE'S HEAD TURNED SLOWLY. THERE WAS NO SOUND IN THE house besides the normal city noise that filtered in through the walls, but he knew he wasn't alone. His steps were silent as he retraced his path back toward the main living space. The only illumination came from cars passing on the street, their headlights flashing across the shiny black floor.

He stood in the middle of the living room for a beat, his head turned toward the windows. Instinct bristled half a second before the glass shattered.

Two black-clad bodies burst through the windows in the same instant that another slammed him from behind.

The breath exploded out of him, but he didn't hit the ground. Tucking low and bending his knees, Sloane used his attacker's momentum to throw them over his shoulders and into the glass coffee table, which exploded into millions of pieces across the floor.

A fist just missed his helmet as he swept out one leg, aiming for another attacker's knees. Trying to get distance more than anything, Sloane threw himself backward. Movement was a blur around him as three powerful bodies came at him at once. He didn't have a moment to think, but he didn't need to.

His body moved on autopilot, matching every blow for blow, because he'd fought these people hundreds of times.

If they'd wanted to, they could've shot him. They all carried bolt guns and rifles. They all had their own special weapons of choice, as well as stun guns and more hidden on their bodies. But they didn't use them.

Because even Fracture had a code of honor for their teammates.

The moment he got his hands on the front of a dark uniform and lifted, he knew exactly who he was dealing with. Vesta sailed through the air with a grunt. Plaster and wood erupted from the hole she put in the wall, while a tacky framed print fell from its hook to crash onto the floor.

Mere moments after he let her fly, a lucky hit to his ribs nearly buckled him, giving one of his teammates an opportunity to wrench his right arm behind his back.

Pain radiated through his shoulder. Using the grip on his arm, Sloane was forced to kneel on the floor. Breathing hard, he let them hold him there for a moment as he got his bearings.

The living room was destroyed. A leather couch had been demolished, a television ripped off the wall, and glass scattered across nearly every surface. A pair of boots crunched the debris as they came to stand in front of him.

That raw nerve in his chest throbbed. There was no panic. There was no urgency.

Not returning to Cecilia wasn't an option. It was the only thing that mattered, and if he had to kill his teammates to do it…

Pain rippled through him, not from his various bruises and the very-nearly-dislocated shoulder currently being twisted out of its socket. It was a deeper, stranger feeling. It felt an awful lot like *reluctance.*

I… can't kill them. The thought worked its way through him in a great, internal earthquake. *I don't want to. Even now.*

But if he couldn't get back to Cecilia, what choice would he have? If he was forced to decide between destroying himself or living without her, he'd choose the former every time.

"You shouldn't have come back," a modulated voice informed him.

Sloane looked up at Arjun, a snarl lifting his lip behind his visor. He didn't need to smell him, see his face, or hear his real voice to know who he was talking to. They'd trained and fought beside each other for decades. He'd know Arjun by something as ephemeral as his shadow.

Arjun dropped into a crouch before him. His dark visor covered a familiar bearded face that no doubt oozed contempt when he said, "You fucked up, Fortuner."

Sloane didn't respond. The part of him that was more animal than man was in control, determined to get back to his mate, and that part of him turned his head to assess who it was that held his arm.

Cesare.

He breathed deep, pushing hard against the niggling reluctance to harm their youngest teammate. They had an unspoken rule that Cesare got special treatment, strictly enforced by Sloane himself. He was the last to be snatched from his family and the youngest of them by decades. Sloane had basically raised the boy.

He'd done his best, anyway. Not that it did any good. Cesare still ended up a killing machine just like the rest of them.

"Let me go," he bit out.

Both men froze. From somewhere deep in the wall, Vesta called out, "You've turned off your modulator?"

Cesare leaned more of his weight on Sloane's arm. Despite all emotion being scrubbed from his voice, the young elf still managed to sound wounded when he demanded, "Why would you do that? Why would you go AWOL? What are you doing, Sloane?"

Unable to face Cesare without feeling that uncomfortable, prickling pain in his chest, he turned his gaze back to Arjun, who was probably the unit's biggest asshole. "You've been assigned my capture, I assume."

"Not yet. The captain has given you a grace period of forty-eight hours to return without consequences. Mostly."

Surprise flickered through him. "What? Why?"

"Because as far as he knows, you haven't menaced the public yet."

"And Atria asked him to," Cesare added. Not even the modulator could completely scrub the boyish adoration in his voice.

The sound of Vesta peeling herself out of the destroyed wall drew his attention. She dusted plaster and drywall debris off her shoulders as she strode across the room. "It's against protocol, but she seems to believe you should be given a chance to come back."

"She's not a commanding officer," he pointed out, too dumbfounded to feel grateful.

"Incorrect," Vesta replied. "She's the captain's consort. That means she commands him, which makes her his superior officer."

That he understood. Cecilia was in all ways *his* CO, so he could only imagine what it was like for Kazimier.

"So you're coming home," Cesare announced, grip tightening for a painful second before he shoved Sloane away. "And everything will be good again."

Whatever confused relief he might've felt knowing he could return mostly consequence-free evaporated in an instant.

Rising to his feet, he surveyed his teammates with a look of grim resignation. "I'm not coming back."

"You can't do that," Vesta insisted. "They'll kill you. They'll make *us* kill you."

Sloane rolled his shoulder. There'd be bruises tomorrow, but they would hopefully heal before his doe got another look at him shirtless. And if not... well, he'd figure out an excuse, because he wasn't turning down any chance to be touched by her again.

"You can't kill me," he informed them. *Just like I can't kill you. They'll have to send another squad to do it.*

Arjun stood up. Crossing his arms, he replied, "Depends on why you abandoned us."

"What were you doing here? We got intel that you'd left the city days ago." Vesta jabbed a dusty thumb at the tipped over drink cart that once was full of expensive alcoholic synth. "You hunting vampires or something?"

"He couldn't be hunting vampires. They're too easy. There's no way that would take him away from us," Cesare argued.

Vesta shook her helmeted head. Swiping a gloved hand over the visor, presumably so she could see through the dust that made a film over it, she replied, "Depends on the vampire. They can be creative. Of course, it'd still be embarrassing for him, but—"

"I'm not hunting fucking vampires," he hissed.

"Then what are you hunting?" Arjun stepped dangerously close to Sloane. Head tilting, he pressed, "*Who* are you hunting?"

His teammate couldn't see it, but Sloane flashed his fangs in a vicious snarl. "Back off."

"Why? What are you hiding?"

"I don't have to tell you anything," he growled.

Vesta scoffed. "You do if it'll get you killed, and you really do if we're going to be the ones given the order. Whatever hunt you're on, there's a very slim chance it's worth your life."

They had no idea just how wrong they were. The urge to tell them rested on the tip of his tongue, a desire to share the burden and proudly proclaim Cecilia as *his*. But he couldn't do that. He'd been given a small reprieve from consequences only because the true reason for his absence was unknown.

Before he could think of a response, Arjun moved. Sloane stepped back sharply, expecting a hit or a swipe of his claws, but neither came.

Arjun simply unlatched his helmet. The seal broke with a hiss as he lifted it over his head. Dark eyes narrowed as he leaned in close to a deep breath.

Sloane realized what he was doing half a second too late. By the time he'd reared back, arm swinging in the direction of Arjun's unprotected face, the damage was done.

"A woman?" Arjun wasn't exactly prone to showing emotion, but whatever scent clung to Sloane's skin and clothing made his mouth drop open in surprise. "He smells like a woman. And *sex*. Fresh sex."

Sloane didn't blush. Whatever heat rose to his face came from fury, not from any embarrassment over the fact that he hadn't wanted to scrub the scent of her off his skin and now his team *knew*.

And just like that, they all took their helmets off.

Swinging his fists and snarling didn't put them off. Vesta lunged for him at the same instant that Cesare threw himself onto his back.

"Fuck *off!*" he raged, bracing his legs to take their combined weight.

"Smells like strawberries," Cesare noted, his eyes as wide as saucers. White fangs flashed against dark iridescent skin when his lips pulled back in an incredulous grimace. "And sugar. And... pretty."

Leaping back to avoid a swipe of his claws, Vesta breathed, "It *is* a woman. That's why you left."

Cesare took a nasty kick to his knee before he stumbled away. Clearly baffled, he asked, "Why would he risk being executed for a woman? Why would you leave us?"

Sloane backed toward the door he'd come in through. His heart beat hard and fast in his chest. His foot lifted, preparing to flee, when the truth finally occurred to Arjun.

"The same reason the captain ran." Arjun watched Sloane with dark, inscrutable eyes. "Because he found his consort."

The glass trapped beneath his boots screeched across the

floor as Sloane sprinted for the door. Vesta's yell followed him, but he didn't stop. He didn't look back. He couldn't risk it.

They know. They know. They know.

Fear sluiced through his veins as he propelled himself over the fence and down the alleyway. The only time he'd ever moved faster was when he saw the vampires through Cecilia's window. Getting away, getting home, getting her — it was a matter of survival.

He couldn't live without her, and he couldn't kill them, no matter what he told himself. Running was the only option.

Sliding behind the wheel of his car, he peeled away from the curb as fast as he could. *If they keep their mouths shut, I have forty-eight hours to convince Cecilia to leave with me,* he realized, hands trembling on the wheel.

Gods, please let them keep their mouths shut.

CHAPTER
TWENTY-FOUR

FORTY-EIGHT HOURS.

It was a very short amount of time to make her love him, but Sloane was nothing if not determined — or desperate enough to fight until the bitter end.

They sat outside on the bluff overlooking the ocean, a blanket spread beneath them. Cecilia had picked out several of her revolting foods from the cupboard and spread them on one side. She'd then commanded him to sit behind her. He hadn't been a fan of that particular order until she climbed between his legs and made herself comfortable against his chest.

Cecilia arranged his limbs like she owned them. She wrapped his arms around her middle and tipped her head against his jaw.

The sunset blazed over the horizon, setting the ocean aflame. It lit her in gold and pink, softening the edges of her until she appeared to be the thing that glowed, not the sun.

Ignoring the twinge of his bruises, Sloane squeezed her tight against him. That raw nerve in his chest burned when she was so near, when he got to touch her, when she draped herself against him, when she was just… *Cecilia.* It wasn't the bad kind of burn. It was the good kind, like a growing pain or sore muscles after a hard mission. He never wanted it to go away.

We have to leave, he thought, arms tightening around his consort's middle. But how could he explain that to her without telling her everything else?

"What's with the shag rug?"

Sloane sucked in a deep breath through his helmet's filter. It took him a beat to figure out what she was referring to. "In the bedroom?"

"Yeah."

"It looked like yours," he explained.

"I figured, but why did you want your room to look like mine? You're not exactly a pink and sparkles kind of guy. I mean, look at the rest of the house. You don't even have pictures on the walls." She leaned her head back against his shoulder to look up at him. "We could make this place more homey, you know? But I wouldn't want it to just be *my* taste."

As often happened with Cecilia, Sloane experienced a mix of opposing emotions. It was a heady thing, knowing she wanted to make a home with him. A *real* home. Something he hadn't experienced since he was six years old and never thought he'd have again. But he couldn't give that to her. Not here. Not when they would have to run — *should* have run already.

Choosing his answer carefully, Sloane said, "I like your taste. Soft things are… rare in my life. Your apartment seemed comforting. I wanted that."

"Hm." She watched him closely, but he had no idea what thoughts ran through her tricky mind. He'd stopped trying to guess, since he was always wrong. Cecilia had an incredible ability to surprise him at every turn.

The bow of the ribbon she used as a headband brushed his helmet when she looked back at the ocean. Waves crashed against gritty rocks far below them. The air was cool, but the warmth of the sun still managed to touch their little bubble of peace.

Cecilia wore a soft lavender sweater over jeans and shiny white boots. Her cheeks were dark from the brisk, salty breeze and her eyes glittered with the reflected sunset. Sloane couldn't stop himself from cupping her jaw. Turning her head to face him again, he held her there with infinite care.

"What?" she breathed, a smile pulling at her lips.

He rubbed the pad of his thumb over the corner of her jaw, savoring the slight burn in the beds of his claws. All he wanted to do was look at her. It was all he'd ever wanted. To have so much more than that was still hard to process.

Sloane struggled with the tight, panicked feeling in his chest — a fear that at any moment she'd be stolen from him. His trainers used to give him precious things only to snatch them away, teaching him the value of deprivation. But he'd never had anything so precious as her.

To lose her now, when he was so close to being chosen, would be unendurable.

No wonder the doctor thought we couldn't handle this, he realized with dread. *We can't. We can't survive the loss of it.*

"I..." He trailed off, unsure what he meant to say. His throat constricted as his body fought conflicting instincts.

Finding a few words he knew were horribly inadequate, he said, "I enjoy this. You. I don't want anything to change."

Cecilia let out a soft breath. "I don't know... Some change can be good, don't you think?"

His jaw clenched. "Do you want to leave?"

"That's not what I meant," she assured him. "I'm talking about doing normal couple things. You did great last night, so I don't see why we couldn't go back to the city and—"

"It's too dangerous."

It did something explosive to his ego when she simply rolled her eyes, utterly unconcerned. "Listen, champ, I'm not worried about danger. I've got you. Who would dare hurt me when I've got a hunky elf boyfriend who can literally rip them limb from limb?"

Sloane let out an astonished breath. "I'm not your boyfriend."

"You're my mate," she corrected herself. Hearing it come from her lips sent an electric shock through his body.

"Yes," he whispered. "And you're mine."

Ever curious, his brilliant consort asked, "What does it feel like for you?"

He shook his head. "You're asking the wrong elf. I'm not good at describing feelings."

"Try," she insisted.

Sloane licked his lips as he attempted to boil down the most significant shift in his life, his biology, and his eternal landscape since his birth. "We call it the Pull. It feels… like a pull. Like we can't be separated from our consort or we'll die. It's wonderful. It's also awful."

Her dark brows drew together. "Will you? Die, I mean."

"If exposed to your pheromones for long enough, then cut off, yes. We often waste away until infirmity or madness sets in. Usually both." He shrugged. "There are worse deaths."

And I've participated in nearly all of them, he silently added.

Cecilia sat up, depriving him of all that delicious contact. "Wait, so if I decided I wanted to be with you forever, and then one day I changed my mind, it could kill you?"

He nodded. "Affirmative."

Cecilia stared at him with an emotion he knew well: horror. "No wonder you want to wait to take your helmet off," she whispered.

Sloane frowned. "That's not why I'm keeping it on. I'm not afraid of dying, Cece. I'm afraid of taking your choice from you. Because I *know* you wouldn't let me die. That's the problem."

She let out a slow, trembling breath. "You think I'd feel guilted into staying with you?"

"Yes," he answered, stomach tightening.

"You're a complicated man, Sloane. You don't have any problem kidnapping me and saying I can't leave, but you also won't force a matebond on me, which most people wouldn't think twice about." Cecilia gave the center of his visor a poke with her index finger. "I don't know why that appeals to me so much, but it does."

The breeze pushed her hair over her shoulders. It tickled his chest as he grabbed the hand that had poked him and twined their fingers together. "Do arrants feel a type of Pull?"

"Mm, not really," she answered, lips twisting from one side to the other. "We have a lot of stories about love at first sight, and instant attraction is definitely a thing, but I don't think it's anything like what you and orcs and shifters experience."

He wasn't surprised but he couldn't say he wasn't disappointed. "I see."

He couldn't be sure what Cecilia heard in his voice. Whatever it was, it made her expression soften. She leaned in close to cup the side of his helmet. "Hey… That doesn't mean I feel nothing. If anything, I think arrants have a gift to give people like you. When we stay, it's because we *want* to, not because of biology or magic. It's our choice to love you. One hundred percent."

"Could you love me, Cece?" Sloane didn't mean to sound so pathetic and desperate, but he did.

She was quiet for a beat. That was one of those nuances he never could've picked up through distant observation, the way she talked non-stop until she really had something to say. Then she took her time.

Before she could answer, he continued, "I'm a monster. More than you know. I've killed hundreds of people in my life, and I'm not— I was made into something that's not right. I can't be fixed, and even if I could be I don't know that I'd choose it. But I'd die for you, Cece. I'll give up everything that matters to me for you. Not just because you're my consort, but because you're *you.*"

Her breath hitched. "Sloane…"

He lowered his head to rest it on the curve of her shoulder. "I'm sorry."

A soft hand drifted up to cradle the back of his neck. Normally, instinct would've seen him strike out at anyone, even a teammate, for coming so close to that vulnerable spot, but there wasn't even a prickle of unease in him when she stroked the skin beneath his collar. She was the only one who was allowed so close to the most vulnerable part of him because he knew without a shadow of a doubt that she'd never harm him.

She was safe. She was soft. She was his.

"Don't apologize for saying how you feel," she gently scolded him. "I like that. Actually, I love it. I love how honest you are, baby. And in the spirit of honesty, lemme just say this: I'm not quite right in the head either. I don't know… maybe the ways that I'm a little messed up and the ways you're a lot messed up align, you know? I find you outrageously charming, and I know it's fucked to say I don't care about you killing people, but I kinda don't because I trust your judgement. I mean, a man who values consent as much as you do has to have a solid moral compass, right?"

She let out a slow breath. Voice lowering, she continued, "Or maybe that's just an excuse I tell myself to justify the fact that I find how dangerous you are to be so fucking sexy it makes it hard to function. I think you're funny and earnest and sweet. I want to help you live a good life, Sloane, and I want to be a part of it."

Sloane couldn't catch his breath. He couldn't think. He couldn't do anything besides cling to her like she was a life preserver in a turbulent ocean.

Her hand fell from the back of his neck. "I have an idea, but you've got to let me go."

Instantly, his arms banded around her middle. "No," he protested, burying his visor in her neck.

A soft chuckle shook her chest. "I meant let me sit up, not let me run away, you dork."

It still wasn't his preference. Sloane didn't want to release her for even a moment, but he reluctantly allowed her to arrange his limbs again. When she stood up, he tilted his head back to look up at her gilded image, perfect and windswept.

Cecilia motioned for him to stand. "Come on. Up you go."

He rose to his feet and watched, baffled, as she licked the tip of her index finger and held it in the air. He'd never been so jealous of a finger in his fucking life.

"Perfect," she announced, dropping her hand. Grabbing his forearms, she gently steered them in a circle, so his back was to the ocean and hers was to the Battery.

"What are you doing?" he asked, head tilting.

Cecilia curled her lips between her teeth for a moment, as she often did when she was building herself up to say something. Her cheeks were rosy, and those dark, doe eyes glittered when she let out a gusty exhale.

"I'm standing downwind," she explained, unhelpfully.

Sloane gave her a puzzle frown she couldn't see. "Affirmative. But why?"

She searched his visor so intently, it felt for a moment like she could actually see through it. "So you won't smell me."

It took him several tense seconds to catch onto what she was suggesting. "You want me to take my helmet off."

"If I'm gonna fall in love with a man, I want to look him in the eyes when I do it," she declared. "And if you're gonna fall in love with me, you shouldn't feel like you have to hide."

He'd crashed through floors before. He'd fallen off buildings and down stairs during fights. None of those experiences compared to the way the earth fell out from under him when Cecilia said *that*.

Heart racing so fast it felt like it might pop, he rasped, "It's dangerous. What if I—"

Cutting him off, she told him, "First of all, I trust you. Second, if it's too much, you can hold your breath until you get your helmet back on."

Nervous sweat accumulated beneath the accordion folds of his collar. "Cece, if I fuck up…"

She firmed her delicate chin. "Then that's that. But I'm not taking this any further without looking you in the eye, Sloane. And I don't think you should, either."

Her trust humbled him, but it was the vulnerability she asked of him that made him hesitate. His helmet had been a part of him for so long that he didn't know exactly who he was without it.

Who do I want to be?

Sloane had no idea who he wanted to be, but he did know that all possible answers began and ended with having her by his side.

His hands trembled as he lifted them to the latches on either side of his jaw.

Cecilia's steady gaze followed every movement of his fingers as he disengaged the seal. He lost sight of her briefly when he lifted the helmet over his head.

The cold breeze contrasted with the warm glow of the sunrise on his face. The light passed through the thin skin of his closed eyelids. Something kept him from opening them. Maybe it was fear, or perhaps it was reverence.

Either way, he couldn't look at Cecilia when she whispered, "You're *beautiful.*"

A shuddering exhale left his parted lips. He didn't dare breathe in yet, terrified that he'd ruin everything with one reckless gasp.

Cecilia's hands settled on his chest, but they didn't stay there. They followed an invisible path upward, over his shoulders and the cords of his neck, to cup his cheeks. Blood rushed to those lucky points of contact, making his skin tingle and desire sit heavily in his gut.

"Take a deep breath," she quietly commanded.

Following her orders instinctively, he tilted his head up to avoid any hint of her scent on the wind. "Why?"

Cecilia guided his head back down with those careful hands. "Because I'm going to kiss you, Sloane."

CHAPTER
TWENTY-FIVE

His eyes snapped open just in time to see her stretch onto her tiptoes. The length of her body pressed against his, sending a shockwave through him as she effortlessly guided him down to her. He was helpless. Utterly and completely helpless under her command.

Cecilia's kiss was a bomb blast.

It knocked him down to his foundations and leveled all that he thought he knew. Whatever that first gentle touch in the alley had done to him, it was nothing compared to a kiss freely given.

Cecilia handled him like he was made of glass. Her hands were gentle when they held his jaw, supporting him and guiding him to turn one way, then the other. Her lips were as smooth as silk. They glided over his, occasionally accompanied by the brush of a hot, wet tongue. It wasn't just lust that roared through the empty landscape left by her cataclysm but a tenderness so sharp it was agony.

Sloane clutched her waist and nearly lifted her off the ground. He pressed his mouth against hers again and again, increasingly desperate for more, for *everything*. His lungs burned as he fought the natural impulse to suck in deep breaths of her, but it wasn't enough to stop him.

Her fingers tangled in his hair, anchoring him to her as sweet kisses melted into a frenzy. A strangled, breathless purr shook his chest. When her lips parted, he didn't think twice about dipping his tongue inside.

Sweetness exploded on his tongue and instinct snapped its jaws around his throat.

Sloane didn't make the conscious decision to throw himself backward. It just happened. One moment he was snaking his tongue into the delicious well of her mouth and the next he crouched in the scrubby grass at the very edge of the cliff, his claws stuck deep in the earth and his chest heaving with frantic breaths.

Cecilia leaned against the Battery's wall of windows, her palms pressed into the glass. She was wide-eyed and panting, her knees pressed together in a way that made it seem like she had trouble standing.

For several taut moments, they simply stared at each other.

"Come back," she commanded, voice husky with what he realized was desire.

Desperate to get his bearings, he tried to focus on the call of seabirds and the crash of waves beneath him. "I almost lost control," he gasped.

Cecilia straightened against the glass. "But you didn't."

He shook his head in a vain attempt to clear it. "Kissing you is… overwhelming."

A look of concern flashed across her face when she asked, "In a bad way? We can stop."

"No," he barked, claws flexing in the sandy soil. "I don't want to stop. I don't want to ever, ever stop."

She squared her shoulders. Even from a distance, he could see the determined gleam in her eyes. Had he once thought she was made of cotton fluff and sugar? His consort was far, far bolder than him. Something in her was fearless — a warrior's spirit disguised by pink glitter and blunt claws.

"Then come back here," she ordered again. "Because I'm not done with you yet."

He'd always thought he was smart. At the very least, he was the best at what he'd been trained to do.

But Cecilia had made him into a fool. Every bit of training, every shred of restraint, and all good sense disappeared when she beckoned him near.

Sandy soil and bits of grass fell from his claws as he stood up from his crouch. Sloane's chest sawed as he took in ragged breaths. Every step was a struggle — not because he didn't want to be close to her but because all he wanted to do was cross the distance between them at a sprint.

It was a thing of his wildest dreams, seeing her open her arms to him in the glow of sunset.

"You're the most handsome man I've ever seen in my life," she whispered, fingers curling into his kit as soon as he was close enough. Tugging him against her, she continued, "Seriously, Sloane, it didn't even occur to me that you'd be— Good gods, no wonder you have to hide behind a helmet. You'd be swamped if you left the house without one."

Even with the strong breeze blowing her scent toward the Battery, he didn't dare risk opening his mouth to reply. Not that he would've known what to say to that. He was just glad his face appeared to please her. And it wasn't like she needed him to talk, anyway. Cecilia barely stopped to breathe before she started up again.

"Not that what you look like matters, obviously. I mean, I liked you before. I just didn't think you would be so… so… *this.*" Cecilia yanked his kit, urging him to bend so she could more closely examine his face. He imagined he saw stars sparkling in her big doe eyes when she traced his cheeks, jaw, and brow with the tips of her fingers.

In a voice he'd never heard before, she noted, "You have such a kind face, Sloane. And such sad, sad eyes."

No one had ever or *would* ever say something as absurd as

that to him except his Cece. That painful tenderness slid between his ribs as cleanly as the obsidian knife he'd given her — the very same one he'd used to execute his cruelest trainer when word reached them of Thaddeus's execution.

The wind buffeted his back as he swooped down on her like a bird of prey. Cecilia gasped into his lips when he pressed her back against the glass. Her arms draped over his shoulders and her fingers dove into his hair. They knotted the strands, tugging sharply as she gave as good as she got.

He had no idea what he was doing, but it didn't seem to matter. Cecilia made soft sounds of approval when he hoisted her up by her ass and squeezed himself between her legs. Her tongue snaked out to lap at his mouth, seeking a way in despite the threat of his fangs. Powerless to deny her anything, he parted his lips and braced himself for the taste of her.

He wasn't normally a fan of sweet things. Elves were carnivores, so even small amounts of sugar in drinks or flavored meats tended to be more than many could handle. Some, like Cesare, seemed to take masochistic pleasure in torturing themselves with foul desserts, but Sloane wasn't one of them.

Cecilia was the exception.

She was as sweet and complex as finely aged syrup. Every brush of her tongue against his brought new nuances of her taste to the forefront — strawberry, vanilla, and a hint of salt. He wanted to gorge himself on her. He *needed* to.

In the back of his mind, a tiny, weak voice reminded him that this was a terrible idea. Tasting her wasn't exactly far off from breathing her in. Bit by bit, the Pull was sinking its claws into him to drag him under.

But he couldn't stop. Even when his lungs began to burn, he couldn't drag himself away from her.

Somehow sensing his need for air, Cecilia did it for him. She yanked his head back with a rough pull of his hair. When he growled, elvish instincts rising in a vicious wave at her silent show of challenge, she did the worst possible thing.

Cecilia *bit* him.

Sloane's hips jerked reflexively into the soft cradle of her thighs when her blunt little teeth clamped down on his exposed neck.

"Fuck!" he snarled, pressing her hard against the glass and rutting against her. His head was drawn back so he could only see the blush colored sky as she licked the crescent-shaped indents in his throat. "Cece, you *can't—*"

"Why?" she asked, breathing hard into his damp skin.

His eyes nearly crossed when she switched to the other side. Her bite wasn't painful, since it would take far more than her dull teeth to get through his tough skin, but the symbolism of it made the beast that existed inside all elves roar with the need to claim.

Choking on instinct, he tried to explain, "Because elves— Necks are sensitive— *Because* it makes me want to fuck you, Cece."

Her teeth scraped down the taut cords of his neck, leaving a trail of fire in their wake. "Then fuck me, Sloane."

She was on her feet again in a flash. Cecilia staggered, arms reaching for him as she cried out in protest, but he didn't run away again. Sloane turned his head to suck in a large lungful of air even as he dropped to his knees before her.

She steadied herself with her hands on his shoulders when he raked his burning claws down her jeans. "You have *got* to stop destroying my clothes, champ," she breathed, widening her stance as he ripped the shredded remains of her pants away.

Sloane waited until he'd slit the sides of her panties to reply, "Heard."

Her pale purple thong fluttered to the ground between her white boots. Sloane hurriedly stuffed them in his pocket before he turned his head aside for another risky breath. The wind blew against his back at exactly the right moment, almost like a gift from the gods. Permission, maybe, to fuck her with his tongue until he passed out.

What he couldn't claim in experience, Sloane knew he could make up for in sheer enthusiasm. There'd never been a skill he couldn't master. Making Cecilia come on his tongue would be no different.

Her grip on his shoulders tightened when she croaked, "Sloane, maybe going down on me can wait until you don't have to hold your breath?"

"If I pass out, I pass out," he growled, lifting her supple thigh over his shoulder. Cecilia squeaked as she was forced onto her tiptoes to make up for the considerable height difference.

Her cunt bloomed before him, rosy and wet and luscious. His swollen lips parted as he watched a bead of moisture escape and ran down the length of her inner thigh, leaving a perfect trail for him to follow.

Before he lost any more of his precious air, Sloane caught the drop with the tip of his dark green tongue. Her skin was unbelievably soft, and the taste of her cunt was unlike anything he'd ever had before. Sweet like her tongue but with an undefinable tang that made his mouth water with hunger, it immediately rocketed up to the top of things he'd die to keep.

No one else is allowed to taste this, he decided as he ran his tongue along her inner thigh to follow the taste to its source. *No one else can have her. I don't care what I have to do. I won't live without this.*

Sloane flattened his tongue against the entrance of her body. He nearly came out of his skin when she fluttered against him, begging for his touch. Cecilia's fingers threaded through his hair again as he feathered the tip of his tongue around that slick opening.

She dripped down his throat, as sweet as nectar, and he was lost.

It wasn't skillful, the way he attacked her with his lips, teeth, and tongue, but it was effective. Still holding his breath, Sloane tried to remember everything she'd taught him after their date — all the ways she liked to be rubbed and stroked.

"Sl—Slo*ane,*" she moaned, rocking her hips into his greedy mouth. "You need to breathe, baby. Please—"

The idea of her telling him to stop for *his* sake made that raw, hungry nerve in his chest explode.

Sloane tightened his grip on her waist and thigh as he pressed his face closer. He ignored the fire in his lungs. It didn't matter. Nothing else mattered besides the way she began to make nonsense noises and how, when he sealed his lips around that tight little knot of nerves, she bowed her back and came on his lips.

Spots appeared in his vision just as he lapped up the last of her sweetness from the mess he'd made of her inner thighs.

Sloane stood up, weak-kneed and so hard it felt like his cock was going to burst inside his kit. Turning his upper body as far away from her as he could without taking a single step backward, he sucked in a desperate breath.

The scent of her, the *taste* of her, burst across his tongue and in his nose. The hair on the back of his neck stood on end as his claws burned for half a second before the scent blew away.

But Cecilia was unbuckling his belt, and when her soft hand took control of his rigid cock like that, his willpower to stop crumbled.

When her lips sealed over the leaking head, sucking hard as stroked him against that delicate palm, there were no more options. Only Cecilia herself could end what they'd started, and by the way she lapped at his lucky cock, he doubted that would happen.

Sloane stared down at his consort on her knees before him in awe. Fearing he'd fall over, he braced his palms on the glass and watched as she sucked his girth into her shiny pink mouth. Her hands looked terribly small as they stroked him and slipped deftly into his pants to give his sac a gentle squeeze.

He groaned, toes curling in his steel-toed boots. A steady pressure built in the base of his spine as she bobbed her head up and down, taking him deep into the warmth of her mouth within the shelter of the shadow he cast. Her tongue cradled the underside of his cock, stroking it in time with her pumping fist.

Above the sounds of gulls and crashing waves were sloppy wet noises that tantalized him almost as much as the way she worked to swallow him. It wouldn't happen. He was far too large to even fit halfway in her small mouth, but he couldn't imagine it being any better than it was.

He'd seen a lot of sex in his life. One didn't go about assassinating people without coming across the things that happened in every backroom, office, bedroom, kitchen, alleyway, or filthy bathroom. He'd seen just about everything the world had to offer and never once felt moved by any of it.

But the sight of his consort struggling but determined to fit his heavy purple cock into her mouth was a sight to behold.

Pleasure unlike anything he'd ever experienced made him rock on his heels. Pressure building, he fought the urge to thrust violently into her mouth. Sweating and on the verge of coming, he slid his dirty claws into her hair and grunted, "Up, doe. I don't want to come in your mouth."

Cecilia's swollen lips came off the tip of his cock with a lewd *pop*. Tilting her head back into his hand, she looked up at him through wet eyelashes. "Where do you want to come, champ?"

"In you," he growled, his mind stuck on the feeling of her soft pink cunt pressed against his tongue.

Cecilia licked her shiny lips. "You have the shot?"

"Yes," he answered. All the members of Fracture were required to take the contraceptive shot whether they were sexually active or not. The last thing the captain wanted to deal with was a bunch of unplanned babies running around the barracks.

She ran her hands up his rigid thighs. Leaning forward to press a soft kiss to the base of his cock, she murmured, "Are you sure you're ready for this, Sloane? We don't have to go all the way."

Forty-eight hours.

Urgency was a drumbeat in his mind, pounding, pounding,

pounding. As certain as he was that he'd do anything to keep her, Sloane knew that she could be taken from him at a moment's notice. Nothing good ever lasted for him. No treasure was safe. And those that mattered most were always, always ripped from him.

So he didn't hesitate. He didn't care that he'd have to hold his breath. He took the chance she offered him because it might be the only one he ever got.

Sloane stroked her hair back from her eyes. Her bow slid out and nearly fell to the ground, but he caught it just in time. Wrapping it around his fist, he told her, "I could die tomorrow. I'm not wasting today."

Cecilia pressed another loving kiss to the flat muscle above his cock before she rose. Wrapping her arms around his neck, she let him turn his head to take a deep breath of clean air before she hopped. He caught her instinctively. Flattening her against the glass, he lifted her high with one arm while the other slid under her thigh to grip his saliva-slicked cock.

Holding her gaze as well as his breath, he traced the blazing hot seam of her cunt with the head, savoring every tiny brush of skin on skin. Her thumbs stroked the back of his sweaty neck when she murmured, "I didn't answer your question."

His cockhead slid past the seam to notch at the dripping entrance of her body. He barely heard her over the roar in his ears, but he somehow found the will to pause and raise his eyebrows. He couldn't waste a single breath now.

Cecilia leaned in to hover her lips over his. "I could fall in love with you, Sloane."

His hips shot forward. Instinct, raw and furious, howled with triumph as he sheathed himself in the burning core of her body. Cecilia cried out, her walls rippling around him in a wave, as he slowly withdrew. Fire licked up his spine as he pressed forward again, slamming her into the glass with a *thump*.

She could love me. She could love me. She could love me.

The words blurred together in his mind as his hips shuttled

forward and back. His cockhead carved a path inside her, striking that soft, spongy spot on her front wall that made her dig her nails into his neck and scream.

He moved fast and hard, more desperate than elegant. The hand that held her bow snuck behind her head, shielding it from hitting the glass as he fucked her relentlessly, like it was the first and last time. When one of her hands dropped between their slapping bodies to stroke that hot little bud, her walls gripped him hard enough to make his spine lock.

Spots exploded in his eyes. His lungs compressed, expelling the tiny amount of oxygen he had left, as his release tore through him. His seed painted the inside of her cunt in thick ropes, as if his body were trying its damnedest to give her everything he had while he still could.

Cecilia, limp and soft in his arms, grabbed his head just as his breath ran out. She turned it sharply to the side and leaned as far as she could go while he was still buried inside her.

When he took a ragged breath, she didn't hesitate to drag him close again. Speaking into his bitten neck, she whispered, "Gods, Sloane, you make it easy."

CHAPTER TWENTY-SIX

SHE HATED THAT FUCKING HELMET.

Cecilia stood in the doorway of their bedroom, a bowl of cereal in hand. It was just about all she'd eaten since she woke up from her drugged stupor because it was basically all he had in his kitchen. Going grocery shopping was on the list of things she intended to do that day, no matter what he said about dangerous vampires.

There were lots of things on that list, actually. Right near the top was seeing him without that damn helmet on again.

She spooned a mouthful of Fruity Crunchums past her lips and tried to chew as quietly as possible. It was the first time she'd seen her phantom sleep and she didn't want to wake him.

He lay sprawled across their mattress on his stomach, his powerful limbs spread. He'd worn an undershirt and briefs to bed, which she found a little strange after what they'd done, but she'd only slept with the guy twice, so what did she know?

Some tender place in her chest ached when she looked at him tangled in their sheets.

She'd only known him for a harrowing few days but she'd also known him for a year. He'd been her kidnapper but he'd also been her devoted servant. He'd been the most terrifying being on the planet but he'd also been… Sloane.

She didn't know what to do with all that. A storm of feeling churned inside her, never quite settling.

All she knew for certain was that he was hers.

Her spoon dipped back into the bowl. A part of her kept waiting for the calm that had come to her during their date to disappear, revealing her true feelings of uncertainty and flickering attraction. It didn't. Sloane just made sense to her in a way she couldn't explain.

She barely knew anything about him and he only knew what he'd observed of her, but it didn't seem to matter. Their messed up puzzle pieces locked together seamlessly.

I could help him, she thought, already putting together a mental file of things and experiences she could introduce him to. Obviously, the man had been hideously mistreated and deprived of basic comforts in life. The thought of taking him to a carnival for the first time or watching him learn to find joy in little things everyone else took for granted filled her with a giddy sort of excitement.

He didn't know how to function in the world the same way she did. If anyone was suited to the task of showing him the softer side of life, it was her.

She loved to teach and Sloane appeared more than eager to learn.

But it wasn't all about helping him. That wasn't the basis for a healthy relationship, and neither was his near-worship of her very existence. Beneath those things there had to be a connection that ran to the core of themselves — a foundational sort of belonging she couldn't put a name to.

If she said yes, if she told him to take off his helmet and keep it off as she so desperately wanted to, there was no backing out. There would be no safe math teacher or corporate middleman who'd coach baseball on the weekends for her. She'd be locked in with Sloane — and every terrible, nightmarish bit of baggage he came with — for life.

Cecilia was far from stupid, and she liked to think she'd outgrown a lot of her impulsive decision-making that had gotten her in trouble during her youth. She was aware that if she signed up to be Sloane's mate, it wouldn't be an easy life. The man smashed people's faces into brick walls and ripped off limbs without a thought. He was an elvish killing machine who appeared to act almost entirely without supervision.

He wouldn't be an easy partner. He wouldn't even be a run of the mill bad boy. He was a walking, talking disaster.

It didn't scare her like it should've. The calm didn't evaporate. The knowledge that she was dangerously close to rushing headlong into the most important decision of her life didn't worry her.

It was simply… a tactical consideration, as she imagined Sloane would say.

Cecilia finished her cereal. Padding back into the kitchen, she quietly washed her bowl and spoon before she wandered toward the bedroom again. A ridiculous grin spread across her face when she passed the wall of windows, which now sported several tell-tale smudges.

Her muscles were definitely sore, but she couldn't wait to get her hands on him again.

When she walked back into the dark, windowless bedroom, she found that he hadn't moved. The shiny dome of his helmet, which *had* to be uncomfortable to sleep in, gleamed with the soft glow of the twinkle lights strung up on the door.

The ones he got for me, she remembered, horrifically smitten.

She crawled back into bed as delicately as she could. He seemed like a light sleeper, but he must've been completely tuckered out from their activities the previous day because he barely stirred when she cuddled close to him again. In fact, he didn't wake up at all until she got bold enough to lift up his arm so she could tuck herself under it.

He jerked a little, the muscles spasming under her grip. A strained sort of grunt left him.

"Oh," she gasped, rearing backward with alarm. "I'm sorry! Did I hurt you? I wasn't trying to wake you up."

Sloane rolled his shoulder a little before he snaked his arm around her middle to yank her into his side. "S'fine," he muttered. "Just sore."

Eyebrows raising, she asked, "Are you sore from yesterday?"

He threw one muscled thigh over her hip, effectively trapping her under his bulk. Instead of answering her question, he asked in that soft, sleepy voice, "What time is it?"

"You slept in," she smugly replied. "I really tired you out. Who needs a workout when you've got doin' it on a cliff, huh?"

Sloane's arm tightened around her middle. "I don't sleep in."

"You did today, Mr. I-Sleep-In-Two-Hour-Shifts."

Helmet lifting off the pillow, she imagined he gave her a baffled look. "What time is it?" he asked again.

"Four PM," she answered. "You should probably go eat somethi—"

Cecilia yelped when Sloane rocketed into an upright position. She sat up on her elbows to watch him throw his legs over the side of the bed. Even through his undershirt, she could make out every defined muscle of his back bunched with tension when he reached for his folded pants.

"Sloane?" Concerned by the urgency in his movements, she laid a hand on his spine. "Baby? What's wrong?"

"I didn't mean to sleep so late," he rasped, sounding more distressed than she'd heard before. "I've lost a whole day."

Really sitting up now, she crawled to his side of the bed to peer at his helmeted profile. "Lost a whole day to do what? I didn't realize we had a schedule."

Sloane's breathing seemed faster than normal. Placing his palms flat on his knees, he didn't say anything.

In the short time she'd been able to see his face, Cecilia had gotten used to just how expressive his eyes were. Not being able to see them now when he was clearly upset about something made her hate the damn thing even more.

"Hey," she murmured, covering his right hand with both of hers. "You can talk to me, champ. Whatever it is, we can work it out. If you're upset about yesterday, that's okay. It's overwhelming to lose your virginity."

Sloane's head whipped toward her. "I'm *not* upset about yesterday. It was the best day of my life."

A warm rush ran through her from the top of her head to the tip of her toes. One thing she loved about Sloane? The man didn't know how to play coy. He just said the earnest thing a normal person would've rather died than admit.

Giving his hand a squeeze, she asked, "Then what's wrong?"

He let out what sounded like a trembling breath. That, above anything else, alarmed her. "Sloane?"

"We need to leave," he quietly informed her. "Now."

Cecilia stared at his inscrutable profile with confusion. "Like... go out?"

"No. We can't stay in the Battery. We need to pack everything and leave."

"And go where?" she pressed, too baffled to really process the flat seriousness of his tone. "Back to my apartment? Because I know you probably don't mind the blood and guts, but I don't think I can sleep there again."

Sloane turned to her. Shoulders tense, he grated, "No. We have to leave the Elvish Protectorate."

Her lips parted. "Wha... What are you talking about? Why?"

In an instant, her heart leapt into her throat. Her hands tightened on his, clinging hard enough to hurt someone with thinner skin than her elf. Whispering like they might be overheard, she asked, "Is it because you killed Duke?"

His hand flexed in hers. The tension rippled up his forearm until it ran like a wave through his biceps and shoulders. "No. It's because I..."

She waited for him to continue. Her heart beat a little faster with every second that ticked by. The gods knew it wasn't the first time a boyfriend had asked her to run away with him when the heat turned up, but she'd never actually considered it before. And she'd certainly never dated anyone who she knew for a *fact* killed people. It was always just sorta… implied.

But Sloane had. He'd killed three men right in front of her.

Normal people, even Patrol officers, shouldn't have been able to just get away with murder. It made sense that something might've gone wrong, that he'd been caught somehow. Maybe the bodies turned up somewhere or any number of terrifying prospects that end with Sloane being punished.

Cecilia's whole body tensed. *The thought of him being put away for murder is scarier to me than the thought of him murdering. I really am sunk.*

In a quieter voice, he told her, "My leave is up, Cece."

She blinked. That didn't sound so bad. "Okay… Then you should go to work. That's not a big deal. I need to start looking for a part time job anyway while I wait for my teaching application to go through. If you're worried about me being safe, I can just stay here while you're on duty. No biggie."

Sloane made a heartbreaking sound in the back of his throat. Reaching over with his free hand, he cupped her cheek. "You'd really stay?"

Her throat tightened to an almost painful degree. Fighting to get the words out, she whispered, "Yeah, I would."

"Fuck." Sloane dropped his hand. Hunching his shoulders, he braced his elbows on his knees and lowered his head. "My leave is ending and I can't go back on duty, Cece. If I do… If I do, they'll separate us."

"What?" She made a face. "Why? I thought elves were allowed to have relationships with other people now."

"We are, but *we* — my team and me — aren't. It's strictly forbidden." His claws flexed between his spread knees. "That's another reason I didn't approach you. I knew that if I got too close, they'd take you away from me."

Her mind whirled. "Wait, your team— I didn't know you had a team."

Sloane made that strange, sad sound again. "There are seven of us. Eight if you count the former sovereign. All of us were conscripted into service when we were children. Protocol doesn't allow us to keep consorts."

There was too much to digest there. She could barely wrap her head around the idea of running away with him, let alone the fact that there were seven other people — including *Delilah Solbourne,* apparently — who'd been put through the horrors he had.

"But... *why?"* she asked, clinging to what seemed like the simplest and most absurd part of the story.

"We're too dangerous," he answered in a flat voice.

She sat with that for a moment, letting the truth settle into her. Fresh memories of blood splashing across her apartment's floor rushed to the forefront of her mind.

She couldn't downplay that. She couldn't pretend like Sloane *wasn't* incredibly dangerous. The higher-ups who made the call to keep him and his teammates from their partners no doubt knew exactly what they were doing.

But that didn't mean she thought it was right.

Taking a deep breath, Cecilia reached for his hand again. Holding it tightly, she didn't look at him when she asked, "Are you close with your team?"

His fingers squeezed hers. "Yes."

"And you'd give them up to run away with me?"

Sloane bent at the waist to lean his broad shoulder into hers, giving her just a little of his weight. "Would you give up being a teacher in the city for me?"

Her heart stopped.

All she'd ever wanted was to be a teacher. She *loved* kids. She loved watching their brilliant little minds work and change every day. And it'd been a dream to work in such an incredible city with a famously choosy education system. She wanted to be the best of the best so she could give her best, and she'd worked damn hard for the opportunity.

But when the heat of Sloane's hand radiated through hers, it seemed… less. Not less important. Not less possible. Just less urgent.

Less once in a lifetime.

This thing, the man holding her hand, who was willing to put himself through just about anything to make her happy and give her the chance to choose him, was a true once in a lifetime possibility.

Cecilia sucked in a deep breath.

"I don't believe either of us has to give what we love up," she argued, turning her head to look at him. "There has to be a way to fix this. We can petition the sovereign, or we can go all the way to the United Court if we have to."

Sloane stiffened. "Cece…"

Before he could continue, she gave his hand a sharp squeeze. "But right now I'm going to trust that you know what you're doing. If you say we can't stay here, then we can't stay here." Bringing his hand up for a gentle kiss, she announced, "So let's go on vacation, baby."

CHAPTER
TWENTY-SEVEN

EVERYTHING HE'D GRABBED FROM HER APARTMENT AND A SINGLE black duffle bag of his own went into the back of a small, nondescript car parked in the very back of the garage. The vehicle didn't look like much from the outside, but when she slid into the passenger's seat, she was confounded to realize it was fully modern and equipped with extras she was pretty sure were illegal.

Like the black tinted windows, for instance, and the windshield that projected a different image onto the inside of the car so no one could actually see who was driving it.

Bundled up in comfortable clothes, running shoes, and a pink puffy jacket, she sat calmly in her seat as her elf roared out of the long concrete tunnel. He'd been astonished by her apparently easy agreement to run away with him and kept checking in every few minutes to be sure she hadn't changed her mind. Cecilia suspected that he peeled out of the garage so fast because he half-expected her to bail as soon as her ass hit the seat.

But she wasn't bailing.

In her mind, there was no way the situation was as dire as he said it was. She just couldn't imagine a system so blatantly unfair to people who'd been victimized their entire lives. There had to be a workaround, a plea they could make, that would allow them to return quickly and go about their business like normal.

In the meantime, there was nothing wrong with a vacation. It wasn't like anyone expected her at work after she'd no-showed multiple days in a row, and her parents certainly weren't looking for her. The only person who would care that she left was Dahlia, and it just so happened that they were headed right for her.

Strangely, Dahlia hadn't sounded all that surprised when Cecilia called to ask if they could come stay for a while. But maybe nothing shocked her much anymore. Having a husband like Felix could do that to a woman.

She'd offered to send Genevieve, the Amauri-employed witch who could open m-gates in the fabric of space-time — presumably to do crimes — but Sloane flatly refused to travel that way. Cecilia wasn't exactly excited about the idea of being squeezed through and spat out a cosmic straw, so she agreed that the car was the best bet.

All in all, Sloane was far more tense than she was as they roared out of what she learned was Marin County. They were making a break for the border, which would take several hours. She didn't exactly expect to be chased or anything, so she settled in with a soft blanket and a pillow, one arm extended to rest on his thigh as he drove.

They were silent for a while. She tried her best to give him time to decompress a little, but in the end, she just wasn't the kind of person who could take quiet for that long.

"So… your team," she began in her best nonchalant tone as she gently rubbed his thigh. "Can you tell me about them?"

Sloane's chest rose with a deep breath. "Tell me what pertinent details interest you."

"Are you friends?"

"No," he answered, "we're part of the same unit."

"Okay, but you kind of grew up together, right? And you've

been *part of the same unit* for how many decades? You must at least *like* each other."

He adjusted his grip on the steering wheel. "Liking each other is irrelevant."

Smothering a chuckle, she gave his thigh a quick, playful squeeze. "You know, another thing I love about you is how you think you can get away with not answering by being, like, super literal or side-stepping the spirit of the question. It's cute."

Sloane's helmet briefly turned in her direction before it focused back on the road. "…You are the only one who thinks anything I do is cute, doe."

"Well, I'm the only opinion that matters," she stated, shrugging. Cecilia wiggled her eyebrows at him. "Unless you're friends with your teammates, in which case they *also* matter."

She couldn't be sure, but she thought he let out a very quiet, put-upon sigh. "We're not friends. We're… pack."

"Pack? Like… shifters?"

Sloane tilted his head in one direction, then the other. "Not quite. Our structure is unique. Elves naturally gravitate toward hierarchy, but it's normally slightly looser. Due to our training, a stricter and more tight-knit formation was prudent."

Oh, she thought, eyes widening. *Oh no.*

Bracing herself, she asked, "So… where do you fall in the pack hierarchy?"

"I'm the most senior member of the unit," he confirmed, "followed by Vesta. There was a gap between our capture and the others, so we were slightly older. Leadership naturally fell to us."

Horror clung to the back of her throat like bile. "Is she sort of like your sister, then? If you're taken as kids together and… and everything else."

"We would never compare our working relationships to siblings or a family unit," he replied, as blunt and nuanced as a brick.

"*You* wouldn't say it but that doesn't make it untrue," she argued. "Sloane… I think they're your family. You're the big brother, aren't you?"

His voice came out clipped when he insisted, "If you must assign it a familial title, it would be more accurate to say I'm co-alpha."

"Oh good gods, that's *worse!*" she cried, twisting in her seat to give him her complete attention. Nearly draping herself over the center console, she grabbed his bicep. "Sloane, am I taking you away from your pack? The pack that *needs* you?"

Peeling one hand off the wheel, he completely covered her knee with his palm. "You're my consort. You come above everything. Even them. They'd do the same."

"But you're the example, Sloane," she insisted. "You're the leader. Even if they'll survive losing you, don't you think it'd be better to show them that this is something they should have, too? That they shouldn't have to give up everything for?"

"Cece," he said, a strained note in his voice, "if they can't separate me from you, they have orders to terminate."

"I just think it's not fair to— What?" She couldn't have heard him correctly. Cecilia stared blankly at the side of his helmet. "Terminate? What do you mean?"

"Shoot on sight," he clarified. "I would be deemed an unacceptable risk to a civilian and the population. Standing orders are to put us down in the event that we can't be restrained."

"Oh," she breathed. Cecilia collapsed back into her padded seat, nausea churning in her belly. "Oh. Okay."

Hours dragged by. The silence was heavy between them as she digested what he'd told her. She tried to, anyway. She'd never done well with guilt. Her parents had wielded it against her at every opportunity, molding her into the grinning, recovering people pleaser that she was.

Dahlia liked to remind her that just because she felt guilty for something didn't mean it was her responsibility. Objectively, she knew that to be true. Sloane's relationship with his unit — pack, *family* — was not hers to maintain or destroy. That was entirely his decision.

But she couldn't help but feel like it *was* her responsibility, and not just because he was choosing her over them.

She didn't know Sloane well. Or more accurately, she didn't know him in *detail*. That would come later. What she knew now was that he couldn't truly appreciate the gravity of what he was risking.

Her elf had never known a world without his team. Not since he was a kid, anyway. He didn't know who he'd be without them, and it didn't sound like he'd put much thought into what that would mean. Not because he didn't care, but because it *hurt*.

And Cecilia didn't fucking like the thought of her elf hurting.

She couldn't stop picturing those sad eyes in that beautiful face. He'd looked at her like she was everything good in the world, like she'd make every evil thing that'd been done to him right again.

Cecilia couldn't do that, but she was damn determined to find a way to make *this* right.

She turned the problem over and over in her mind, trying to see it from every possible angle as they drove into dawn. The main problem she faced was her lack of functional knowledge of elvish culture and the inner workings of their hierarchy. She thought she had a pretty good grasp on EVP law, considering her past relationships, but obviously she didn't if someone, somewhere had the authority to just put a man like Sloane down for running off with a girl.

It was as they were approaching the border into Nevada that she thought to ask, "Why did you suddenly decide today that we had to go?"

Sloane took a moment to answer. "I knew we would likely have to leave quickly."

"Yeah," she dragged out, "but you didn't seem like you were in a hurry a couple days ago. What changed?"

"I… was informed that I had forty-eight hours to return to

service. During that time, my reason for failing to appear for duty became obvious."

Cecilia made a face at the dark road that stretched beyond their windshield. A touch of blue and pink had begun to limn the horizon beyond the craggy desert mountains, highlighting the stars that shone over their heads.

Trying to puzzle out when they hadn't been together in the last two days, she asked, "When did this happen?"

Again, Sloane took a minute to respond. "After our date."

"When after our date? We went to bed after— well, you know."

Adjusting his grip on the wheel, he haltingly explained, "After you fell asleep, I left to follow up on Duke's business associates. I wanted to be sure you weren't in any danger from past orders or unhappy business interests. While I was out, I was waylaid by three members of my unit."

"And you didn't tell me?"

She was surprised by the punch of hurt that struck her right in her solar plexus. It wasn't like they'd talked about things like that, and gods knew they'd been pretty busy doing more pleasurable things the past few days, but it still stung.

"I didn't want to concern you," he replied, quieter than before. "And if I only had forty-eight more hours with you, I didn't want to waste them."

Really working up a head of steam, she bit out, "I can appreciate that, Sloane, but what if something had happened to you? What if your team members dragged you back to the barracks or Patrol caught you or— or you fell down a fucking flight of stairs?"

Nonplussed, he argued, "I would not fall down a flight of stairs. I'm very capable."

"First of all, *everyone* can fall down a flight of stairs," she exclaimed, throwing her arms up. "And second, it's not about that! It's about the fact that if something had happened to you, I wouldn't have known. I have to know, Sloane!"

He seemed incapable of understanding the source of her ire. Sloane rolled his shoulders a mite stiffly when he assured her, "There's no need to worry. You were safe. I locked you in the bedroom."

For a split second, she actually lost her voice. That didn't happen very often. Cecilia *always* had something to say. But that confession smacked her gob so hard, it damn near flew into the back seat.

Stumbling over her words, she gasped, "You locked me in the *bedroom?* What if something had happened to you? Would I have just wasted away—"

"I would've informed my captain of your location and given him the code for your release," he soothed. "You were never in any danger."

"I— Sloane— Holy fuck, you absolute—" Cecilia made an inarticulate sound of outrage. Spying a glowing rest stop in the distance, she demanded, "Sloane, pull over."

"Cece, we shouldn't stop. We need to reach the Orclind—"

Leaning over the console to hiss into his helmet-covered ear, she informed him, "Sloane Fortuner, if you don't stop right now and let me buy some damn gummy bears to calm *the fuck* down, I am pulling out that knife you gave me."

"That… would be unwise," he said, apparently just catching on to the seriousness of her temper. "But we can stop. Briefly."

She crossed her arms and stewed as he pulled into the luminescent island that was a desert rest stop. A massive charging station sat at its heart, complete with a sparkling twenty-four hour convenience store, a few drive through restaurants, and a smattering of long-haul trucks pulled off for the night that had yet to get back on the road.

When Sloane reluctantly parked the car in the dirt lot as far from the glare of the convenience store as possible, she barely waited for him to hit the break before she cracked the door open and stormed out.

She wasn't sure why she was so mad, other than the obvious.

Sloane didn't think like her. She knew that, and she was prepared to accept it. If pushed to it, she'd even admit that she *liked* his weird brain.

But something about hearing that he'd gone off on his own, possibly into danger *for her,* and hadn't bothered to say anything, made her blood boil. Knowing he'd locked her inside the bedroom while he was at it was the cherry on top.

The hair rose on the back of her neck. She didn't need to turn around or hear his silent footsteps to know he was following her.

"No," she announced, throwing her index finger into the air. "You're *not* following me. I need a minute to work through this and then I'll be fine. But you've gotta give me space."

"Cece," he called out, obviously distressed and confused, "I don't understand."

Her heart clenched. Standing there in the cold desert between the cheerful fluorescence of the convenience store and the darkness of the dirt parking lot, her anger left her with all the grandeur of a popped balloon.

She rubbed her suddenly tired eyes. "I know you don't, champ. It's okay. I'll be right back. I just need a second to myself, all right?"

Twisting to give him a look over her shoulder, she softened even more at the sight of his stiff shoulders and clenching claws.

He doesn't know what I don't explain, she reminded herself. *That's teaching 101. And I already know where his line is. All he ever does is try to protect me. This is no different.*

Shoes crunching in the packed grit of the lot, she made her way back to him. Cecilia laid her hand on his chest and stretched onto her tiptoes to press a kiss to the side of his helmet.

"I'm gonna get us some snacks. You wait by the car. I'll be right back, okay?"

"I don't like this," he rasped, hunching over her like he could guard her with his bulk alone. "We should be driving."

"A snack never killed anybody — unless that snack was peanuts. Or something you could choke on." She patted his chest before stepping back. "Five minutes. I need to use the bathroom, too. You should probably do the same."

Even with his visor obscuring his expression, she knew he was making a very serious and unhappy face as she walked away.

But he didn't follow her, and she *did* need to pee.

Temper smothered, Cecilia tried to be fast. After using the facilities, she snagged a few bags of candy for her and jerky for him before walking quickly to the counter. Behind the plexiglass shield sat a disinterested young man in a blue uniform, a cap pulled low over his eyes and a wad of what she hoped was gum in his mouth. He was perched on a stool and slumped over the counter, a tablet in his hands.

"S'cuse me," she said, pushing her items through the hole in the barrier. "Can I get these?"

"Mm?" The young man looked up. Sleepy eyes took her in for a moment before they glanced down at her haul. She expected him to shrug and start ringing her up, but almost as soon as his attention settled on her gummy candy, it zoomed back to her face.

Wide eyes fixed her with an unnerving look as his lips popped open. "You're the woman," he slurred around whatever was he chewed on.

Cecilia gave him a clueless smile. "I'm *a* woman. A woman who wants gummy bears."

Shoving the wad of… something into his cheek, the boy swallowed hard and clumsily dropped his tablet on the counter. "No," he squeaked, fingers crawling under the counter. A click sounded. "You're *the* woman. The missing teacher from San Francisco!"

A stone, cold and heavy, dropped into the pit of her stomach.

"What?" A strained chuckle didn't do her empty smile any favors. "I'm not missing. I'd think I'd know if I was."

Pulling his hand out from under the counter, the boy spun

his tablet around. She glanced down and immediately regretted it.

There, plastered across the screen, was a territory-wide alert with her face on it. Her teacher's certification photo sat beside a dark, grainy picture of her bruised face talking to a tall, helmeted figure in the sitting area of a roadside burger joint.

KIDNAPPED: CECILIA MARCELLA WARREN. ARRANT. BLACK HAIR & BROWN EYES. 5'8". MID-30s. ABOUT 165 LBS. LAST SEEN IN CAPTIVITY. BELIEVED TO BE IN IMMEDIATE DANGER AND TAKEN ACROSS TERRITORY LINES. IF SEEN, CONTACT PATROL IMMEDIATELY. DO NOT ENGAGE KIDNAPPER AT ANY COST. MUST BE CONSIDERED ARMED AND LETHAL.

Cecilia abandoned her gummies.

An alarm began to whine as she turned and sprinted out of the store. She burst outside into the cold air, the young worker's yells for her to stop completely ignored. Her heart jammed into her mouth as she spotted Sloane far across the lot. He stood military-straight beside the passenger's side door, waiting for her return just as she'd asked him to.

Glad she'd decided on comfortable running shoes, Cecilia took off in his direction faster than she'd ever run before.

"Sloane!" she screamed. "Get in the damn car! We have to—"

The world exploded behind her.

Magic, hot and blinding, knocked her off her feet as an m-gate ripped a hole in space and time behind her. She careened forward into the dirt, barely catching herself on her palms, as a flood of black-clad elves in masks, rifles raised, turned everything to shit.

CHAPTER
TWENTY-EIGHT

SLOANE BLINKED BLOOD OUT OF HIS EYES. THE INTERROGATION ROOM in Solbourne Tower was familiar to him, but for reasons that were momentarily hard to pinpoint, nothing appeared quite as it had before.

That almost certainly had something to do with his head wound.

A dark green trickle of blood ran in sluggish rivulets from his forehead, where an overzealous Patrol officer had slammed the steel butt of his rifle into him. It was a blow that would've made a human's head explode but for Sloane it resulted in a slight concussion and a laceration that would have to be stitched or healed.

If they even bother, he thought, flexing his arms against the restraints they'd clapped on his wrists. His ankles were locked, too, and bolted to the floor. It was a set-up he'd seen and participated in many, many times in his life, though he'd never been on the shackled side of things before.

Not since he was a kid, anyway.

Sloane stared at the blank wall across from the steel interrogation table. A yawning sort of emptiness had hollowed him out. It left nothing behind — no worry or fear for what was to come.

He'd failed.

He'd failed the most important mission of his life, and now he would pay the consequences for it.

The white door to his left swung open on nearly soundless hinges. Sloane didn't look. He knew his captain by the feel of the air and the tread of his boots on the smooth floor.

The metal chair across from Sloane's was pulled back with a terrible screech. Kazimier's kohl-dark hand seemed huge against the metal seat.

The half orc sat down and laid his forearms on the table. "What the fuck?"

Gaze fixed on a midpoint over his captain's shoulder, Sloane demanded, "Where's Cece?"

"You don't get to ask questions right now," his captain growled. Snapping his fingers in Sloane's eye line, he forced his subordinate to turn his focus to him. "You're gonna explain to me exactly how and why you fucked up so bad, Fortuner, so I can decide what we're gonna do with you."

In the midst of the nothingness inside him, an echo of that raw, angry nerve pulsed in his chest. The last he'd seen of Cecilia was when two Patrol officers took her thrashing arms and dragged her kicking and screaming through the m-gate. She'd fought like the fierce little beast she was, but she didn't stand a chance against two fully grown and trained elves.

To not know where she was or whether she was unharmed was intolerable.

Sloane's upper lip lifted over his fangs. "You already know what you're going to do with me. Tell me where Cece is."

Kazimier scowled at him. His green face was made of an assemblage of sharp geometric shapes that possessed the unique ability to convey disapproval in the most efficient and painful way possible. "She's getting treatment for her injuries in a secure location. That's all you need to know."

He stared at his captain. An acidic feeling bubbled in his gut, searing all his vital organs in a slow ooze. "Who hurt her?"

"See, I was hoping you could tell me that," the captain replied. His bulky, leather-covered arms crossed in front of his chest as he leaned backward into his seat. "Because the Sloane I know would never lay his hands on a woman, let alone an arrant who can't defend herself."

Sloane's split lips parted with surprise. *They think I hurt her.*

He was a danger to her, certainly, by his very existence, but she was still his consort. It went against the building blocks of his biology to intentionally harm Cecilia, as it would for any elf.

As far as he was aware, the Starsbury Protocol wasn't in place to keep their consorts from physical harm. It was to keep the members of Fracture from going off the rails and harming *everyone else.*

Too disturbed and confused by the implication to say anything, he stayed silent. Kazimier's lips thinned.

"Cecilia Marcella Warren," the captain began, eyes narrowed. "Server at a local vampire bar. Arrant. No criminal record. Recently submitted an application to the Education Board for a teaching position. Bachelors and masters in education and psychology respectively. Nearly perfect GPA and no tickets, citations, or tax notices."

The captain paused. Sloane held very still, his expression on lockdown, as the orc examined his face for any sort of reaction. When he got none, he continued, "She's no one. So I'm *dying* to know why my most senior soldier decided to kidnap her and flee the territory."

Speaking through clenched teeth, Sloane replied, "She's not no one."

"Clearly," Kazimier drawled. "But who is she to *you,* Fortuner?"

They don't know.

Sloane was stunned. He'd thought at least one of his teammates would disclose what they'd learned. Maybe they'd wait until his forty-eight hours were up, adhering to their unique sense of fairness, but they'd definitely tell the captain.

Except he was beginning to suspect that they *hadn't.* Because Kazimier would've known better than to imply Sloane hurt his consort, and he wouldn't have had to ask *why* he'd been so desperate to escape the territory.

Mind whirling, he dared to ask, "How did you find us?"

"Miss Warren was reported missing by a bartender at The Lush when she missed two consecutive nights of work. Her missing person's file went into the system at the same time that a group of teenage shifters armed with cell phone photos walked into a Patrol station to report a suspicious encounter with a bruised woman and a masked elf."

Kazimier raised his dark eyebrows. "The pictures matched in the system. Obviously, your helmet was flagged. Then the cashier at the rest stop recognized Miss Warren and sent an automatic audio and visual alert."

He knew the date was a mistake. That didn't mean he regretted it. If all he got was one, he would cherish it for as long as they kept him alive.

Still, it did sting his pride a bit to have been caught by some teenagers, of all people.

"You're not this sloppy, Fortuner," the captain noted, disapproval thick in his bass voice. "You don't kidnap women. You don't get photographed. We both know what you get up to in your free time, but you've never once left a shred of evidence behind. So what's different?"

Sloane met his captain's gaze steadily. His heart raced and his palms had begun to sweat, but his mind was calm. He didn't have a plan. He only had instinct, and an offer he never thought he'd accept.

Lifting his bruised chin, he calmly announced, "I want to talk to Atria."

CHAPTER TWENTY-NINE

THEY TOOK HER BACK TO SAN FRANCISCO, AND SHE MADE SURE every second of the trip was miserable for each and every one of them.

Cecilia had screamed herself hoarse by the time the masked Patrol unit transferred her into a blacked out van. They'd been forced to restrain her. If they'd had the option, she was fairly certain they would've gagged her, too.

At least Sloane had the foresight to drug her first. The yahoos who came busting into the parking lot, bolt rifles blazing, had no idea how to handle her kicking the backs of their seats or threatening to call their mothers. She'd never been spitting mad before, and she'd always figured she was a bit too much of a coward to really fight someone, but when she saw a dozen armed men swarm her elf, she wanted to take them all on herself.

It was no wonder they looked at her like she'd lost her mind. Between bouts of screaming, kicking, insults, and attempts to jump on their backs, she got the impression that they believed they were saving a poor, defenseless arrant from some sort of monster.

What they got instead was a yowling, hissing, pissed off girlfriend who absolutely refused to answer any of their questions without a lawyer or her elf present.

So she wasn't entirely surprised when the Patrol squadron who *rescued* her washed their hands of her. They drove her in the blacked out van for a chaotic and loud half an hour before they came to a screeching halt.

She'd been shoved in the back behind a metal screen, so she watched the men hop out of the van through tiny holes. Sweaty, with her hair sticking to the back of her neck and her throat raw from hollering, Cecilia slumped against the grate.

Beneath the raging fire of her fury was a sickly swell of fear. It rose and fell in tidal waves, tossing her insides around until she swore she would be sick. At least throwing up would serve a purpose. The prick who smashed his gun into Sloane's head deserved a little puke in his face.

The fear was harder to handle. It was a helpless, awful kind of feeling. Seeing Sloane desperately try to make his way through the throng to get to her, like all the rifles pointed at him didn't matter, was an image that would cling to her for the rest of her life. It colored every thought and every fantasy of what he was going through at that very moment.

Is he being beaten? Did they hurt him so badly that he's in danger? Would they really kill him if they knew he'd found his mate? No, he said they'd only do that if we couldn't be separated. Right?

She cursed herself for not asking more questions, and she felt like the world's biggest asshole for dismissing Sloane's warning like she had. If she hadn't blown her top about him leaving her, they wouldn't have gone to the rest stop. They might've made it to the border.

If he dies, I'll never forgive myself, she realized, eyes stinging. Her throat felt swollen and lined with glass when she tried to swallow her tears.

Before the dam could break, the back doors of the van opened. Cecilia squinted into the glare of the midday sun, her exposed skin prickling as San Francisco's signature wet air rushed in, carrying the sharp, medicinal scent of eucalyptus. Standing in front of the open doors were two masked figures who made her hair stand on end.

It took her only a moment to realize why.

The differences were subtle, but they were there. The helmet shape was different. Their armored clothing was ever-so-slightly more severe. And when one of them pushed their side of the door open wider, she caught a glimpse of a dark, round symbol on their bicep.

Sloane hadn't worn his official uniform. His clothing was armored, yes, but nondescript. He looked like a member of Patrol, but there was no badge number, no unit symbol, or identification on it. Obviously, he would've been pretty reckless to wear his official uniform to stalk her, so she hadn't thought much of it.

But the helmet…

The helmet was exactly the same, and there was something indefinably familiar about how they held themselves as they stared her down.

Breathing hard, Cecilia squared her shoulders and demanded, "Take me to my boyfriend. *Now.*"

The masked figures shared a look. Unfortunately for them, Cecilia had recently come into a fair amount of experience interpreting stunted elvish soldiers' body language.

"Hey!" she snapped, banging her heel on the floor of the van. "You're gonna take me to see him or I'm going to be *such* a pain in your ass, there isn't a healer in the world who will be able to help you sit right!"

A flat, modulated voice came from the slightly taller figure to her right. "You are very loud, Cecilia Marcella Warren."

Blowing a sweaty lock of hair out of her eyes, she grunted, "Call me Cece."

"Cece," the figure to her left announced, "you are being remanded into our custody for questioning. It is in your best interest to come quietly."

Despite the fact that her hands were cuffed behind her back, she lunged fearlessly at the faceless elves with a snarl. "What are you gonna do to me, huh? I don't have to cooperate with you or anyone who thinks Sloane did a single fucking thing wrong!"

There was a pause. The figure on the right seemed to hesitate for a moment before they leaned slightly into the van. "If you come quietly, we won't have to handle you much, which means Sloane is less likely to pull our jugular veins out and turn them into a belt. Your assistance in this would be greatly appreciated."

Cecilia blinked. "Um…"

The one on the left reached for her arm. For the first time since everything went to shit, she didn't struggle. Together, the elves helped her out of the van and down onto a gravel lot. All around her were massive, creepy-looking trees strung with pale moss leaning down from a circle of hills, and nestled in the center of the natural bowl was a stark military-looking building.

Staggering a little as she got feeling back in her legs, she let the elves support her as they began walking her past the small group of Patrol officers who'd escorted her there.

"Transfer complete," one of her new friends announced, nodding toward the group. "You are dismissed."

The man in charge, who'd taken the brunt of her ire, cleared his throat. He wore a mask, too, but it was nearly see-through and didn't have the voice modulator. That made it easy to hear the relief in his voice when he answered, "Understood. And word of advice? Don't uncuff her."

Cecilia cast him her biggest, sunniest grin as they marched her toward the building.

CHAPTER THIRTY

She expected to be thrown into some sort of interrogation room, or at the very least be sat in some sort of Patrol office for questioning, but once they bypassed the intense security at the door, she was led into a… living room.

It was a weird one, to be sure. A bit sterile, and large enough to accommodate far more than the average family. It connected to a large, open-plan dining and kitchen space. The table was large and everything was impeccably clean. It seemed a bit like a club house, if the only members of the club had zero personalities and couldn't be trusted with cutlery unsupervised.

Nonplussed, she let her escorts guide her to the head of the long dining room table. She'd only just began to sit down in the chair they pulled out for her when more helmeted elves appeared like phantoms in the doorway that led to what she imagined was the communal torture chamber.

Settling her butt slowly into her chair, she looked around with growing unease. Raw human instinct buzzed in her veins, like some unused part of her brain recognized that she was now surrounded by predators who could strip her bones in a matter of seconds. It was something more primal than even her danger sense.

She imagined it was the feeling the first animal with a brainstem experienced when a shadow passed over them in the primeval ocean.

Swallowing hard, she lost most of her bravado as they gathered around her. No one spoke. No one touched her. They simply stood, arms locked behind their backs and feet spread, *observing* her.

That, if nothing else, told her all she needed to know.

Taking a deep breath, she hoarsely demanded, "Which one of you is Vesta?"

The slim figure to her right, one of her escorts, dipped her head. "I'm Vesta Kincaid."

"So you're Sloane's team," she said, gaze crawling over each of them in turn. "Cool. Can one of you *please* get these damn cuffs off me?"

A larger figure hopped into action immediately, like they'd been dying for something to do. Circling around her, they gently pushed her shoulders forward so they could disengage the lock on the cuffs. It was a sweet relief to have her arms free again.

Swinging them around to her front, she massaged her wrists with a muttered, "Thanks."

"You are… Sloane's consort." Vesta's tone was impossible to hear through the modulator, but her body language was as stiff as a board. "Have you allowed him to bond with you?"

Unwilling to give any information out until she knew exactly who she was dealing with and what their intentions toward Sloane were, she snapped, "No offense, but I'm sick to death of faceless elves demanding things of me today. You want answers? Take off your helmets and tell me what the fuck is going on."

A ripple of unease went through the room. She watched as their helmets turned toward each other. A wave of silent communication happened, a whole conversation spoken through the tiniest shifts of muscle and tilts of their heads.

After several tense seconds, they seemed to reach a conclusion.

It was Vesta who removed her helmet first. The others followed. That familiar hiss of air from the seal disengaging went around the room like a discordant song. An array of elves stood before her, their helmets tucked under their arms, and every last one of them had eyes like Sloane's — the saddest things she'd ever seen.

"Have you bonded with him yet?" Vesta asked again, in a much higher voice than one would expect from a highly trained military operative.

Cecilia looked around at the group, trying to memorize their faces and assign them to the scant information Sloane had given her. Instead of answering Vesta's question, she demanded, "Are you going to help Sloane?"

"If we can," a man standing farthest away from her answered. Rich magenta skin was accompanied by a dark beard and heavy eyebrows that made him look even more serious than the others. "That depends on your answer."

Gripping the arms of her chair until her nails bit into the wood, she cautiously replied, "He told me that he's not allowed to have a mate, and that if we were found out, they'd kill him."

"Not necessarily," a soft voice argued. It was the other escort, who'd revealed herself to have delicate features and a pixie cut. "The Starsbury Protocol states that when a member of the unit discovers their consort, they are to immediately separate themselves and report to a superior officer, with permanent separation the most likely outcome. Termination is only necessary in the event of a threat to the public."

"Why?" she cried, gaze darting between impassive, colorful faces. "Why would that be the right thing to do? Don't you all deserve to find love if you want it? Why—"

"Because we're too dangerous to the general population," the one with the pixie cut explained. "The chemical changes a bonded elf go through are extensive and dramatic. The fear is that should we suffer mental disruption during that process, or were our consorts to leave us, we could do a disproportionate amount of harm to ourselves and others."

"Sloane would *never* hurt me," she insisted.

"That is unlikely," pixie cut agreed, "but I can only assume that the people who caused your injuries were not so lucky."

Cecilia paled. "He was protecting me."

"Correct," Vesta interjected. "And that was when he wasn't bonded. Imagine the damage he could do if you were and someone threatened you."

"Well, then they'd fucking *deserve* it," she snapped. "Are you really saying that he'd be wrong for defending me? If it'd free him right now, I'd fight all of you!"

The elves shared a long look. One of them, a younger looking man with impossibly dark, iridescent skin, marveled, "She's very fierce."

"The officers who brought her here told us to leave her cuffs on," pixie cut replied, like Cecilia wasn't even in the room. "They were terrified of her."

Cecilia muttered, "Well, I don't know about *terrified...*"

"She'll make a good consort for Sloane," the bearded one sighed. "If they don't kill him."

"Why would they kill him for finding his mate? You just said—"

"They wouldn't kill him for that," the young one replied, all earnestness. "They'd kill him for assaulting and abducting a civilian with the intent to cross territory lines. And for abandonment of duty, of course."

Her mouth dropped open. In a high, squeaky voice, she exclaimed, "He didn't do *any* of that! I mean, not the way they think. He— he saved my life and then took me somewhere safe. The only reason he tried to leave the territory or abandoned his post was because he believed I'd be taken from him!"

Her breath shuddered as she looked around, desperate for her only potential allies to understand. "He didn't want to leave you. You're his family. He just didn't think he had another choice."

"Your story will be more believable if you don't look quite so awful," pixie cut noted. Holding out an ungloved hand, she offered, "I'm Johanna Titus, the healer assigned to this unit. With your permission, I can heal your wounds and lend you more credibility."

Elvish healers? Cecilia shook her head. That was something to think about later, when Sloane wasn't stuck in a cell and being accused of crimes he didn't even commit.

"Sure, fine," she replied, dropping her hand into Joanna's. A warm tingle rushed through her as a peculiar kind of magic permeated her very cells, knitting things back together and fading bruises like they were nothing. "And for your information, no, we haven't... bonded or whatever. He kept his helmet on."

The bearded one's eyebrows lifted. "Why would he do that?"

"To give me a choice," she answered, horrified to find her chin beginning to wobble.

Vesta caught her eye. In a low voice, she asked, "Is he *your* choice, Cece?"

Do I want to be with Sloane forever? She could hardly imagine what that even meant. She'd only known him — really known him, not just his shadow or a flicker on the roof — for a few days.

But something in her knew something in him, and when she tried to imagine leaving him to go about her life like it was before, she couldn't. She just couldn't.

Whatever their future looked like, she damn well intended to see it for herself.

"Yes," she answered, meeting Vesta's seafoam green eyes with a stubborn tilt of her chin, "he's my mate. I won't let anyone take him from me."

Johanna set her hand down on the arm of her chair. "Good. Then our plan might just work."

Cecilia slammed her hands on the table. "Plan? What plan?"

All at once, the elves seemed to lose some of the starch in their spines. They folded in around her, all liquid, catlike grace, to fall into the chairs closest to her.

The young one leaned his elbows on the table when he said, "I'm Cesare, by the way. I'm very excited to meet you."

"Nice to meet you too, Cesare," she replied, carefully pronouncing his name as *cheh-suh-ruh.* "Now please explain to me how I can get my man out of jail."

All excitement, he gushed, "The Starsbury Protocol is all about prevention, but there's no rules in place for what happens if the protocol fails because no one's gotten around it before. That means that there's no precedent in the event that a member of the unit is *already bonded* to their consort."

"Legally speaking, it's pretty cut and dry," Johanna butted in. "The sovereign didn't think to make a provision for us when he passed the new laws. Anyone who seeks to separate an elf from their bonded consort, elvish or Other, can be charged with attempted murder, and no institution or authority is exempt from the law."

"They never think to plan for us," Cesare whispered, like he was confiding a hilarious secret.

Cecilia eyed him warily. She wondered just what kind of crimes they got up to that an entire government *ought* to consider how each individual law might be used by seven individuals.

"If we can get you inside his cell, he can begin the process of fully bonding with you," the bearded man explained. "It won't necessarily absolve him of the crimes against him, but it will be illegal to separate you."

A soft breath escaped her. "You... want to break into wherever he's being held and sneak me in?"

"If you're willing," Vesta answered.

Cecilia gripped the edge of the table. It was one thing to take a lifelong mate on a whim, but it was another to break into what she could only assume was some sort of jail. If she did that and she got charged with something, her career as a teacher would be flushed before it ever even floated.

Throat constricting, she asked, "And you're willing to do this for him, too? You could get in serious trouble."

"He's one of us," Johanna replied.

"And we want consorts," the bearded one added, a grave note in his deep voice. "If he gets one, we all get one."

Something indescribably sad passed over Cesare's youthful face. "We don't want to feel like we have to run. We should be together. And we want Sloane back."

Reaching out instinctively to cover one of his gloved hands with her own, she rasped, "I don't know much about any of you yet, but I don't think you should be separated, either. You're a family. And family helps each other. If I can, I want to help you, too. But first we've got to get my man out of jail."

Eyes wide and white in his striking face, Cesare turned his hand over to hold hers with such a gentle grip, she wondered if he thought even the slightest pressure would break her bones. "You want to be part of Fracture?"

Fracture? God, whoever picked that name had a sick sense of humor.

She shrugged. "Are we about to do some crimes together?"

"Yes," they answered as one.

Cecilia let out a hoarse chuckle. "Then sure, I'm a member of Fracture. Why not? A family that crimes together stays together, right? That's how the Amauris do it, anyway."

Vesta stood up from her seat. "Understood. Do you require a weapon?"

A nervous laugh burst from her lips for all of a second before she remembered. "Um, no," she mumbled, pulling her hand back to pat the pocket of her puffy jacket. "They didn't frisk me, so… I brought my own."

CHAPTER **THIRTY-ONE**

"YOU HAVE TEN MINUTES."

Atria tossed her long hair over her shoulder. "Fifteen."

"Princess," Kazimier sighed, pinching the bridge of his nose. "I'm breaking so many rules already. Please."

Patting his chest, she gave him a sympathetic look as she walked toward the interrogation table. "Don't worry, big guy. We'll figure this all out. Now please shut the door and go get yourself a coffee. You didn't sleep at all last night."

The captain shot Sloane a glare. "And whose fault is *that?"*

It was probably his, Sloane decided, but the question sounded like one of the kind that Cecilia often threw at him which she didn't actually want an answer to, so he kept quiet.

The captain muttered something under his breath before he stepped out and shut the heavy metal door. Silence fell heavily over the room as Atria took her mate's seat.

Dressed in a flowy outfit and sandals, she looked entirely out of place in the stark interrogation room. No discomfort appeared on her face, however, as she folded her hands together on the table and met his eye.

There'd been some good humor in her when she spoke to the captain, but it seemed to have vanished completely in the time it took her to sit. Her brown eyes were cool and her expression entirely neutral when she said, "I don't appreciate how much stress you've put my mate through the last few days, Sloane. He's dealing with enough right now. He didn't need this."

Under normal circumstances, he wouldn't have felt even a twinge of guilt. But the circumstances, such as they were, hadn't been normal since he laid eyes on Cecilia. If he were in Atria's shoes…

Sloane supposed he wouldn't have been happy with him either.

"Any stress my actions caused was unintentional," he carefully replied.

"I bet you didn't even think about what this would mean for him, or the team." Atria's lips pursed with clear displeasure. In a clipped voice, she continued, "Not only was this *bad,* Sloane, it was also incredibly selfish. I thought you were a leader, huh? This isn't what a leader does."

Sloane didn't flinch. That involuntary response had been beaten out of him by the time he was ten years old. But that didn't mean he was immune to discomfort — and Atria's censure was very uncomfortable.

"I didn't have a choice," he explained, fighting the urge to squirm in his seat.

"Oh, didn't you? I seem to recall asking you a few days ago if you needed some help, but…" She gestured expansively to the room. "Here we are! You've been arrested for kidnapping, my mate hasn't slept in three days, and I'm pissed because all of this could've been avoided if you'd just *said* something."

Sloane gnashed his teeth. "I couldn't."

"Why?" In an uncanny mimicry of her mate, Atria sat back in her seat to cross her arms and raise her eyebrows. "Because you knew telling me you wanted to kidnap and abscond with a woman wouldn't fly with me? Sloane, what were you *thinking?*"

The urge to confess everything came up as strongly as the urge to vomit, but Sloane swallowed it back. Bending over the table as much as his shackles would allow, he whispered, "You said that I could tell you anything and you'd keep it a secret."

"That is *not* what I said," she challenged. "I said I'd only tell if whatever it was posed a risk to yourself or someone else. If you'd told me you were going to terrorize an innocent schoolteacher, I absolutely would've told Kaz."

Sloane raised his blood-crusted eyebrows. "And if I didn't?"

"What do you mean *if you didn't?*"

"If I didn't terrorize an innocent schoolteacher," he hissed. "If there was a very good reason for what I did."

Atria scowled. "Sloane, if you try to tell me that Miss Warren is secretly evil, I—"

He shook his head sharply. It didn't matter what anyone said or thought about him, but he refused to let Cecilia's name be dragged through the mud. Protectiveness roared inside him, demanding he defend her.

Vision swimming a little, he grated, "Cece is *good.* She's everything good!"

A familiar, strange sensation crawled over his skin. It was like static, but it filled the air with the faintest tang of blood. Normally he couldn't stand it, but in this moment, he sat rigidly, enduring the magical scrutiny.

Atria's mouth opened a little in surprise. "Sloane…"

He swallowed hard. "Please, Atria. I… need your help. I need you to talk to the captain for me. I need *you* to tell him that I—"

"Oh," she breathed, "Sloane, you're in *love.*"

CHAPTER THIRTY-TWO

The plan seemed simple enough, but something about breaking into a high security facility still didn't sit right with her.

Maybe it was all the guns. Maybe it was the fact that her conspirators were all extremely scary elves. Or maybe it was the fact that they had no plan to get her out.

Whatever it was, Cecilia's nerves jangled like a sack of forks and broken porcelain.

It was decided, with very little input from her, that Vesta and Arjun — who she'd learned was the bearded elf — would be her escorts. They drove her in a blacked out SUV across the city and over the gray expanse of the Bay Bridge. She'd crossed it dozens of times, but she'd never had a reason to take the heavily guarded exit onto Treasure Island.

Cold sweat gathered beneath the collar of her puffy jacket when they rolled up to the checkpoint. Two massive guards carrying bolt rifles stepped out of a small building by the gate to examine their vehicle. Waving a hand, they demanded the windows be rolled down.

Cecilia tried to act normal in the backseat, but that was a useless endeavor, because what even constituted normal under the circumstance?

They'd agreed that when asked, they'd say she was being brought in for questioning. Did that mean she ought to act worried? Relieved to have been rescued? Annoyed that she was being bothered by all this fanfare?

In the end, she settled on a mix of all of the above, which mostly involved sitting rigidly in her seat and looking exactly as nervous as she felt.

Vesta lowered her window to greet the guards. One of the guards peered closely at her while the other slowly circled the vehicle.

Nodding, the officer at the window demanded, "State your business, soldier."

"Witness transfer for questioning," she informed them in that flat robotic voice.

The guard tilted his head to peer into the backseat. Cecilia stiffened but still met the guard's eye. A dark purple elf in sunglasses stared back at her, his lips pressed into a grim line. After a brief pause, he asked, "Is this the arrant who kicked Stafford in the back of the head?"

Cecilia rolled her lips between her teeth.

"Yes," Vesta answered. "That's why we're here."

Apparently done with his car inspection, the other officer, a deep green woman in a matching pair of sunglasses, joined her partner at the window. "Is this the arrant who bit Dex?"

Vesta took a second to reply. "…Yes."

"Should she be unrestrained?" the blue guard asked, a brow arching over his sunglasses.

Cecilia glanced at the backs of Vesta and Arjun's helmets. A small part of her found it hilarious that *elves,* of all people, were worried about her attacking them, but a much larger part of her was completely horrified.

What kind of teacher has a rep like that?

Arjun canted his head toward the guards. "Are you afraid of an arrant, Gwon?"

"No." Gwon sniffed. Stepping back, he gestured sharply with the end of his rifle toward the gate. "Move along."

Vesta took her sweet time rolling the window back up. The gate lifted and she pulled forward slowly, as cool as a cucumber.

As they rolled down a long, guarded road toward Solbourne Tower, Arjun asked, "Did you bite someone?"

Cecilia coughed into her fist. "Might've."

Not that it did much good, she silently added. *You elvish motherfuckers have tough skin.*

The elves currently helping her commit some sort of crime were quiet for a moment. She wondered what impression she made on two hardened soldiers who'd probably taken more lives than she'd ever met.

Did she seem foolish to them? Her face flushed at the thought. She was used to not being taken seriously, but it was a different sort of discomfort to know a bunch of predators saw her as little more than a buzzing gnat.

Sloane called her his doe because he saw her as soft and harmless, which was true. As hard as she fought to get back to him, it hadn't made a damn difference. She would've had better luck fist-fighting a wall.

"Not many arrants would try to fight an elf," Vesta noted.

Cecilia shrugged stiffly. "Yeah, well, if I can hit Sloane in the head with a lamp, I can bite the sonuvabitch who thinks he can drag me into the back of a van."

Arjun swiveled in his seat to look at her. "You hit Fortuner with a lamp?"

Miming the whack she'd given her elf, she answered, "Cracked his helmet and everything."

Arjun sat back in his seat. "Excellent."

"Very impressive," Vesta concurred.

The other elf replied, "I understand his disappearance better now. I didn't know they made consorts like her."

Cecilia looked down at her hands in her lap. It didn't feel right to smile, but it was also… nice to feel accepted. She'd only ever gotten that kind of easy camaraderie from Dahlia and the students she'd taught during her courses. To be so readily accepted by these fearsome people was special in its own right not just because they were Sloane's family but because they were hers now, too.

It was a warm shot of comfort she desperately needed as they pulled into an underground garage beneath the Tower.

Vesta drove past rows and rows of expensive vehicles, through another gate, and down a dark tunnel. Whatever normalcy was found in what could've been any other underground garage in a rich neighborhood vanished as they entered what could only be Patrol's territory.

The hair rose on the back of her sweaty neck as they passed lines of parked Patrol and military-looking vehicles. Vesta parked in an empty spot near a heavily armored and brightly lit entrance in the concrete wall, and almost as soon as the engine cut, both elves were out of the SUV.

Arjun opened Cecilia's door. Taking a deep breath of cool air, she prayed her legs would hold her weight as she slid out.

Dipping his head, he explained, "You don't need to do anything. Just walk and do as we say."

She swallowed hard. "Heard."

Adrenaline pumped through her veins like liquid lightning with every step they took. A buzz filled her ears, and the world became a narrow pinprick focused on Vesta's back as she escorted Cecilia through the armored doors and into a maze of underground tunnels.

She'd heard of the tunnels beneath Solbourne Tower. Everyone had. That was where Mad Thad took his enemies and his political prisoners and anyone who happened to look at him wrong. Myths and harrowing true stories about what went on in those tunnels still traveled through the EVP.

It hadn't occurred to her to be afraid before, but as she walked down those bare, white halls, a chill permeated her bones — like the shadow of a beast loomed over her, blocking out the sun.

Doesn't matter, she thought, clenching her jaw. *Sloane's here. He busted through a window to get to me. I'll walk through this nightmare fuel to get to him.*

Every time they passed a group of officers or soldiers, she tensed. But no one stopped them. If anything, they gave Vesta and Arjun a wide berth.

It all felt too easy, but she didn't dare question it. She barely breathed, afraid that any small noise or movement would ruin it. She was so focused that she was almost separate from herself, from the cool air on her skin and the sounds echoing off the bare walls.

She nearly came out of her skin when Arjun leaned close to her back to murmur, "Almost there."

All at once, she was back in her body, in the terrifying hallway, with an elf at her back. Trying to speak without moving her lips, she breathed, "Is he in a cell?"

"We received a report that he's in interrogation room three," he answered.

Her stomach dropped. "He's being interrogated? Is he— Are they torturing him?"

"Unlikely."

But not impossible, she realized, blood curdling.

"Get me there," she ordered. "Get me there *now,* guys."

Vesta's helmet tilted ever-so-slightly in her direction. "Heard."

Their pace increased just enough to make her feel like they were really moving. Her cold fingers curled and uncurled reflexively by her sides as they approached a corner. Somewhere up ahead around the blind corner, the sound of a heavy door opening and closing echoed off the walls.

Cecilia just caught a fluttering of soft green fabric disappearing into a stairwell as they stepped into a hallway lined with reinforced metal doors.

She'd never seen an interrogation room before, but she didn't need to. Cecilia knew exactly what she was looking at. The air in the hallway was different. The shapes of the doors were different. The glare of the lights was different.

It was *sinister.* And she would be damned if she left Sloane by himself in a place like that.

It wasn't necessary for one of her escort to point out what room he was in. The two guards stationed in front of it were a neon sign.

Her heartbeat slowed. Her fear eased. Even the armed guards standing outside the door didn't worry her. They were just obstacles to getting what she wanted, and if she had to get through them, she would.

One way or another, she would.

CHAPTER THIRTY-THREE

VESTA STOPPED IN FRONT OF THE GUARDS. "CAPTAIN LE ROY ordered Miss Warren be delivered to interrogation room three."

One of the guards gave Cecilia a disinterested look. "We didn't receive that order."

"You're not Fracture," Vesta replied, robotic and yet somehow cutting.

There was a moment of silence. The guards shared a long look before they stepped aside. Vesta lifted her chin in what Cecilia supposed was a silent thank you and punched a complicated geometric code in the door's locking mechanism.

A familiar hiss and thud brought her back to Sloane's bedroom. Her heart jammed into her throat when Vesta grasped the handle and opened the door for her.

It took everything in her to stop herself from sprinting into the room. Keenly aware of the guards' eyes on her, she moved stiffly, one foot in front of the other, toward her forever.

She didn't hear the door slamming shut behind her, or the locks reengaging. Cecilia's steps stuttered. She threw herself at the bloodied elf chained to the floor with a wordless cry.

Sloane's head whipped toward her. Without his helmet,

smeared with dark blue blood and a patchwork of bruises, he looked almost unrecognizable in that awful metal chair.

Except for his sad eyes that came to life the moment they caught sight of hers. Those she'd know *anywhere.*

"Cece," he breathed. His pale brows bunched as a look like pain crossed his face. Chains clattered against his chair and the concrete floor with the force of his instinctive twist in her direction. *"Cece?"*

She nearly tripped on her own two feet in her haste to get to him. "Sloane, I'm so—"

In an instant, his expression dropped. "Cece, *stop!"*

She skidded to a stop a few feet away from him. His expression morphed into one of horror as he wrenched himself as far backward as he could. "Get out," he hissed through his clenched teeth. "They took my helmet! Get out now, Cece!"

"I know," she choked.

Sloane's dark purple eyes looked like cut amethyst in the harsh light of the interrogation room. They were so bright that she could clearly make out the way his slit pupils expanded to swallow all that rich color.

His breathing stopped, so he didn't say anything more. Instead, he shook his head vehemently and jerked his chin toward the door.

Please, his expression pleaded. *Please go.*

Her hands trembled violently by her sides. For a moment, she worried that she'd made an awful mistake. But that moment was fleeting.

Meeting his frantic gaze, she calmly informed him, "I'm not going anywhere, baby."

She took a step. Then she took another one.

Sloane watched her like he couldn't decide whether she was a calamity or a savior. The cords of his neck strained against his high collar, and despite the way he'd shifted as far back as he could, his shoulders curved toward her like something in him was desperate to reach her.

"It's okay," she soothed, coming to stand beside his chair. Her heart broke when he stared up at her with a look of defeat in that proud face.

Gently stroking an undamaged part of his cheek, she leaned down to whisper, "I chose this the minute I decided to run away with you, Sloane. And I'm choosing you again now."

"Because you have to," he gritted out.

Gripping his chin, she growled, "Because you're my mate, and I'm gonna fight for you. Understood?"

Dark, glossy eyes stared up at her. Long, pale eyelashes turned spiky with tears she wondered if he'd ever been allowed to shed before. "Doe…"

She leaned down to press feather-soft kisses to his brow, cheeks, eyelids, and nose. "You chose me. I choose you."

Cecilia didn't think he had much room to move, but she was wrong. Or at least, she was wrong about his motivation. The sound of chains straining and metal creaking accompanied his sudden lunge upward.

She gasped, hands curling into his shoulders, as he slammed his split lips into hers. He kissed her with everything he had — lips, teeth, tongue, and soul.

Cecilia dug her nails into his dirty shirt, clinging to him as she gave as good as she got. His tongue swept past her lips. He tasted her without reservation, like it was the first and last time he'd get the chance.

It's just the beginning, she silently promised him, one kiss at a time.

His shoulders vibrated under her hands with an almost violent purr. A bubble of laughter left her and pressed itself into him, slowing his frenzied pace down bit by bit.

"Breathe, baby," she whispered between kisses, a grin pulling at the corners of her lips. "Breathe for me now."

Sloane nudged her cheek with the tip of his nose. Pulling back a little, she found him looking up at her with an expression so fierce, it made her danger sense tingle. She watched closely as he took one deep breath. Then another. And another.

In a rough voice, he said, "My gloves. Take them off. Please."

Cecilia let out a soft noise of understanding. Kneeling quickly, she reached around the back of his chair to where his bound hands stuck out the back. There was no chance of picking the evil-looking, super advanced lock on his cuffs, but she was able to wiggle and slide and pick at his gloves until they peeled away from the tips of his claws.

And before her eyes, the deadly tips retracted.

"It happened!" she cried, crouching low to press kisses to those strange claws.

Popping back up, she was astonished to find Sloane was *smiling.* A true, huge, fanged grin made his cheeks round and his eyes sparkle. He looked *young.* So much younger than the hardened soldier she'd only gotten to see once.

He looked happy. Truly, really happy.

"Oh," she breathed, nose stinging. Cecilia squeezed herself between the table and the chair to plant herself on his lap. Cupping his jaw with both hands, she told him, "Yeah, you make loving you easy, Sloane. All you have to do is keep looking at me like that."

Unable to wrap his arms around her, he seemed to settle for burying his face in her throat. The feeling of razor-sharp fangs gently pressing into the fragile skin of her neck was a shock that made her shiver. He held her there for several seconds, that earth-shaking purr rattling his chest against hers, before he dragged those fangs over her skin in a deadly caress.

Whispering into her pounding pulse, he asked, "How did you get in here?"

"Your family helped me. They came up with the plan, and Vesta and Arjun got me inside."

Sloane was silent for a beat. In a strange, halting voice, he said, "My family?"

"Your family," she murmured. "Who love you. Who aren't

gonna let you leave them or let themselves be taken from you. Who aren't gonna make you choose. *That* family."

"My family always dies," he choked out.

Cecilia stroked his skin. It was to comfort him as much as it was to comfort herself. "Not this time, and never again. I promise."

He nodded shakily into her neck. "Are you injured?"

She stroked the back of his neck with the tips of her fingers before taking the opportunity to explore his nearly white, corn-silk soft hair. "I'm totally fine. Might've busted a toe or two kicking some elves, but otherwise I'm fit as a fiddle."

A husky laugh tickled her skin. "You kicked someone?"

"Amongst other things."

"Why? They were rescuing you."

She gave the tip of his pointed ear a tiny pinch. "They were beating up my man. And it was twelve on fucking *one!* That isn't fair," she argued. "Look at you! How could I just sit and do nothing when they were doing *this* to you?"

Sloane drew in a deep and painful-sounding breath. She was no doctor, but she did *not* like the sound his lungs made. "I am… very proud to be your man."

"And I'm proud to be your consort," she replied, hugging him as close as she dared.

Resting his head on her shoulder, he whispered, "Cece…"

Hiss. Thud. Thud.

Eyes stinging, adrenaline surging, and rage searing her veins, Cecilia leapt up from Sloane's lap.

Teeth bared, she put herself in front of him and yanked the knife out of her pocket. Her elf said something, some order she was too furious to hear, when she unsheathed the blade and held it with both hands before her — pointed directly at the big, green orc who made the terrible mistake of stepping into the room.

"You can't take him," she cried, a furious tear spiraling down her cheek.

The orc, dressed in a leather jacket and dark jeans, stopped short in the doorway. From behind him, a much smaller, golden-skinned woman poked her head out.

"Oh," the woman huffed, "you *must* be Cecilia."

Raising the knife, she barked, "My name is Cece and I'm Sloane's consort. It's too late. You can't take him away from me!"

The orc put his kohl-dark hands on his lean hips. Letting out a very put-upon sigh, he said to the woman, "This is what you wanted to talk about, isn't it?"

EPILOGUE

The sun streamed through the blinds, casting streaks of warm light across the plain white bedspread.

Cecilia watched the dawn light creep across Sloane's restful face. The glow followed the dips and curves of his sloping forehead, proud nose, and softened lips. It sparkled in the pale tips of his eyelashes and the barely there hint of stubble on his strong chin.

He was beautiful. Astonishingly, brutally beautiful. There hadn't been a moment to truly appreciate it before, so she took every soft second of his slumber into her hands and held fast.

His bruises and cuts had been healed. The dark circles under his eyes had faded. The tension around his mouth melted away. Even in sleep, he was that young, hopeful creature she met in the interrogation room. As soon as Captain Le Roy explained that they wouldn't be separated — after he calmly asked her to lower her knife — Sloane had been in something of a daze.

She understood that well enough. Cecilia was in something of a daze herself.

I have a mate, she thought for the thousandth time. *I have a mate and he's my phantom and he's broken and he's perfect because he's mine.*

Cecilia watched his eyelashes flutter, a smile tugging at her mouth. "Good morning," she whispered, tracing one pale brow with the tips of her fingers.

Sloane eyes opened slowly, revealing those sad eyes that haunted her. Except they didn't seem quite so sad anymore when they widened with surprise then crinkled with obvious pleasure.

"You're still here," he rasped. The arm draped over her middle tightened.

Trailing her fingers down over his cheek to brush his lips, she replied, "I'm still here, champ."

Sloane sucked in a deep, deep breath. It was a fascinating thing, watching his pupils expand up close. It was similar to how her cat Oyster looked when he gazed at her, too. All big, dark pupils and devotion.

Oyster would've loved you, she thought wistfully.

"I worried you might leave." He pressed his forehead against hers. "I thought you might change your mind."

"I'm pretty stubborn," she informed him, "and when I decide on something, I like to stick to it."

Sloane found her lips with his own. "Thank you for choosing me, doe."

"Thank you for choosing me first," she answered, smiling against his mouth. "And thank you for ruining all my dates."

For the first time, Cecilia had the privilege of hearing Sloane *laugh.*

It wasn't a belly laugh or even what most people would consider a chuckle, but it was real. It was a soft, husky thing — all smoke and bass. It was toe-curling and delicious and she needed to hear it again and again and again.

"They were threats," he insisted.

Heart lighter than it'd been in… she couldn't even remember how long, Cecilia teased, "To you, maybe."

Sloane nipped her lip. A bolt of electricity ran through her with that gentle punishment. "Correct."

They were supposed to report to Captain Le Roy at seven, which she was certain was rapidly approaching, but she didn't really care. The captain seemed fine enough, she supposed, but she'd reserve any respect for him until she was absolutely certain Sloane wouldn't be punished for what he'd done out of very justifiable fear. If they were a little late for their meeting, then so be it.

Officially, this was her first morning with a mate. She intended to savor it.

Cecilia threaded her fingers through his silken hair and deepened their kiss. Desire rose, soft and insistent, as their tongues tangled.

Her mate's hands were big and possessive as they roamed her back and down her thigh. Gently guiding him to drape himself over her, she spread her legs and welcomed him home.

Sloane's breath escaped him in a hot gasp as she trailed her hands down his bare back to dip her fingers into his briefs. A taut backside met her fingers. It flexed with her touch, just as the rest of his powerful body did when he rolled his hips into hers.

The heavy bar of his erection pressed into her, already wet at the tip and demanding her attention. When her fingers slid around the sharp edges of his hip bones, she found it straining for her touch.

A deep, rattling purr shook his chest as she stroked him with exploratory touches. It wasn't hurried. It was indulgent. She traced every silky ridge and thick vein, memorizing the topography of the heavy cock in her hand. It was a thing of beauty, just like the rest of him.

Sloane braced his elbows on either side of her. He bowed over her, hips rolling in slow waves into her hands. His eyes squeezed shut as his lips trailed over her cheek and jaw. "This is torture," he murmured into her damp skin. "I never want it to end."

Cecilia turned her head to the side, exposing more of her

neck to his exploratory kisses. "Did you ever dream of this when you were on that rooftop?"

He reached down to begin unbuttoning her pajama top. Fangs dragging over her pulse, his greedy fingers closed over her breast with a possessive squeeze. A hot pulse beat between her thighs when he answered, "Touching you is better than anything I dreamed of. Smelling you is better. Tasting you is better. It's *everything.*"

Sloane rolled her nipple between his thumb and forefinger with just enough pressure to make her back arch. The weight of him pressed her into the mattress again immediately, almost like he thought she was trying to get away. A sharp, terrifying growl reverberated through her as he pinned her down.

Her danger sense roared to life with a needy pulse.

There was a predator above her. There was a predator who needed her, wanted her, and would happily devour her.

The bone-deep knowledge of just how dangerous he truly was twined with the unshakable certainty that he was hers to command. Nothing had ever stoked her desire like that.

When his fangs closed over her throat, she moaned and dug her nails into his hips, begging him for more.

That small bite from her nails seemed to spur him on. Sloane's growl grew louder, sharper. He abandoned her breast to yank aside her sleep shorts like they'd personally offended him. Thick fingers drove through the slick mess she'd made to stroke her with ruthless, tight circles.

Cecilia's hips bucked involuntarily. Instantly, Sloane tightened his jaws on her throat. His free hand bunched in her hair, holding her still.

"Sloane," she breathed, sweat dewing on her chest.

Her orgasm built quickly from a deep ache to a taut string pulled through her spine, ready to snap. Just when she thought he'd let it happen, he pulled his hand away.

Cecilia gasped, bucking sharply beneath him in reflexive protest. Sloane ripped his razor-sharp fangs away from her throat and used his grip in her hair to firmly turn her head to face him.

"You're mine, Cece," he snarled, lining up the swollen head of his cock with her cunt. The stretch of him was intense. The fullness *burned,* but it was also the rightest anything had ever felt in her life.

"You're mine," he said again, a groan into her waiting mouth this time. He bottomed out with a wet, hungry sound of their bodies coming together. "I can't let you go."

"Don't," she gasped, lifting her hips. "Don't let me go."

His hips ground into hers, almost like he refused to put even an inch of space between them. Looping her arms under his, she anchored him to her, reminding him without words that she wasn't going anywhere.

Sloane exhaled shakily into her lips. Slowly, almost reluctantly, he drew his hips back. When he rolled forward, it was like two puzzle pieces slotting together — a perfect, tight fit.

Stroke by stroke, every stress of the last few days dissolved. Pleasure was thick and syrupy, as unhurried as his thrusts. They found a steady rhythm that ended as all things needed to: with them together, predator and prey.

When his free hand slipped between their bodies to stroke her in time with those languid strokes, her orgasm wasn't explosive. The string snapped. She fell, slow and soft, into him.

"That's it," she whispered, dragging his sweaty chest against hers. His rhythm picked up as her cunt clenched around him, holding him in a vice she refused to release. "Come for me, baby."

Sloane turned his face into her hair and breathed deep. His back flexed hard under her hands as he picked up his pace, his rhythm faltering with every increasingly desperate thrust. He locked them together, burying himself as deep as he could as he filled her up.

Cecilia turned her head as much as she could to press soft,

comforting kisses to the pulse hammering in his throat. "It's you and me for good," she whispered.

A softer purr vibrated his chest as he stirred his hips. "Promise?"

She laughed, soft and giddy. "Promise. I can't let you go now. What if I require assistance?"

"Then you'll have it," he sighed. "Always."

EPILOGUE II

CONFIDENTIAL

25 OCTOBER 2048

A memo on recent events and recommendations for the members of Fracture from Dr. M. Starsbury, M.D. submitted by request to the Sovereign's Office:

On 24 October, I was contacted by Captain Le Roy on behalf of the sovereigns for an emergency assessment of Sloane Fortuner and the Starsbury Protocol following the high profile abduction of Cecilia Warren.

After my session with SF, I'm confident that he poses no risk to Miss Warren. Indeed, he displayed marked improvements in engagement, hostility, and verbal communication. It is his belief that the discovery of his consort has had a stabilizing force on him rather than the feared violent upheaval.

This remains to be seen, and it will take more sessions with SF and his consort to determine the long-term effects of the mating bond on him and the unit as a whole.

However, I am tentatively hopeful that this change could positively impact not just SF, but the entire unit, particularly because Miss Warren has shown remarkable skill in communication and social guidance. Should this prove to be the case, it will require a reassessment of the Starsbury Protocol. Even should the results prove mixed, it will have to be adjusted simply due to the impression the events have left on the rest of the unit.

What one does, so too do the others — for better and worse.

Personnel Profile:

CECILIA MARCELLA WARREN

DOB: 2 April 2014

PARENTS: Chiara Alba and Leonard Warren

DESCRIPTION:

Arrant

Deep olive skin

Long black hair

5′8″

165 lbs

Brown eyes

BACKGROUND:

Childhood spent in a small town in the Sacramento delta with two parents who "hated each other and used [her] as a middleman." She never felt comfortable anywhere except with her best friend, Dahlia. While it was Dahlia's dream to move to the big city, it was her idea to work in a vampire bar. Her goal is to be a teacher and now to help Fracture "live a little."

RECORD:

No confirmed or unconfirmed kills. Notable record of violence during her rescue from what was considered to be an abduction but no reported injuries.

. . .

DISCIPLINARY ACTION:

N/A

PSYCHOLOGICAL REPORT:

Miss Warren struggles with her inherent need to please and her understanding that she is a whole person with confidence. This insecurity conflicts her fascination with fear, which stems from her desire to let go of that rigid need to make everyone happy all the time. She's a deeply nurturing person. When it comes to SF, she often struggles with her need to help him and the awareness that "he doesn't need to be fixed, just accepted." This stems from a deep love and appears to extend to the other members of the unit as well.

RECOMMENDATIONS:

Miss Warren is remarkably equipped for dealing with the unique issues the unit faces, as well as elves in general. Despite her physical limitations, she shows no fear — or rather, acts in spite of it — and displays an earnest desire to help where and when she can. I believe that she should be allowed full access and resources to do so, and barring her from this task would be both harmful and ultimately useless.

NOTES:

I highly recommend Miss Warren's application for a teaching position be considered. Keeping her close to Fracture and to elves stands to benefit everyone involved, as I believe she has tremendous value in teaching compassion and curiosity to our people. If possible, I recommend she be offered a position in the Solbourne Nursery.

EPILOGUE III

He was released under supervision. No assignments for three months. Mandatory therapy sessions with Dr. Starsbury once a week. And the worst punishment of all: forty-eight hours of service in the Solbourne Nursery.

Sloane had never been happier.

For the first time in his life, he didn't feel the urge to hunt. He didn't *want* to be on assignment. He didn't even mind nursery duty, especially now.

"You're *sure* they asked for me?"

"Affirmative," he answered for the third time. "The captain requested your presence at their insistence."

Cecilia picked at the purple tweed skirt she'd donned for the meeting. Neither of them had been informed about the subject of the meeting, but only one of them was worried about it.

Whatever happened, he was absolutely certain his doe would handle herself better than just about anyone else could.

Sloane rested one hand on her thigh as he pulled through the Treasure Island checkpoint. He'd learned that she enjoyed and expected his touch often, which was so astonishing he still found himself hesitating sometimes.

He'd seen the captain and Atria interact like that — with

small touches and twined fingers and a whisper of lips on cheeks or hair or knuckles. It just never occurred to him that anyone would want those things from him. Especially if they knew who and what he was.

But Cecilia did.

Even after his release from Patrol custody, a large part of him expected her to take back her acceptance. When the crisis died down, it made sense for her perspective to change. He waited for it to hit after their return to the barracks. He waited for it the next morning. He waited for it the week after, and then the week after that.

He waited, but it didn't come.

If anything, Cecilia became *more* comfortable with him. Despite the fact that he wasn't allowed to leave the barracks except for official business, she found ways for them to continue what they started in the Battery. Eventually they would be allowed to return to what she called their home, but until then they'd been moved into a larger room in the barracks, which Cecilia had decorated with gusto.

The barracks had never felt warm until her.

They did *date night* in front of the television he moved into his room and went for picnics around Stern Grove. She required his presence when she cooked, claiming it was important to hear about each other's days during that specific activity. When he came into their room after a brutal training session, it smelled like sweet strawberries and sex and *her.*

It was a life unlike anything he would've dared dream of.

Walking beside her, holding her matching purple bag, to guide her up to the sovereign's office, was the first moment in his life he felt *proud.* His consort, as beautiful and fierce as she was, stood tall beside him even when the other elves in the lobby gave him a wide berth.

And when she reached for his hand, seeking comfort, as they stood before the sovereign's door… it was a gift he knew he didn't deserve.

"This isn't a prank, right?" she whispered as they waited for the door to open.

"It's unlikely," he answered. "But not impossible."

A sharp elbow hit his side. Sloane flinched dramatically, as he'd been instructed to do in such situations. Cecilia rolled her eyes, but her smile was as wide and beautiful as it ever was.

He loved that look. It meant she found him *charming*.

She also thought he was funny. And cute. And gentle. And sweet. All the things Fracture was beaten and tortured into believing they couldn't be, she knew for certain that he was.

The sovereign's smooth voice came through the heavy wood door. "Come in."

Cecilia paled. Giving him a wide-eyed, panicked look, she whispered in a high-pitched voice, "Sloane, we could still run, right? Like grab a car and book it? No one thinks you kidnapped me anymore. It'd be totally fine."

"We could, but we shouldn't."

"Why?" she squeaked.

"Because you're brave." He tilted his helmeted head to one side. "And Dahlia said we're not allowed to cause another newsworthy incident or she'll kill us both."

"Damn her." Cecilia straightened her matching tweed jacket with her free hand. Swallowing nervously, she whispered, "Okay. Okay."

Giving her fingers a reassuring squeeze, he reluctantly released them to open the door for her. He stepped aside, allowing her to enter first.

He hadn't visited the office many times in his career, but it was familiar nonetheless. A wall of glass backed the massive twin desks at the far end of the bookshelf-lined room. Light poured in behind the sovereign couple, who watched their guests enter with keen eyes. The captain sat in a leather chair before them, incongruously casual in his usual jeans, beaten jacket, and boots.

And then there was his consort, who stood in the center of

the luxurious office dressed in a pastel miniskirt and jacket, her white boots shining and her nail polish glittering and so nervous he could practically feel it vibrating the air.

She outshone every fucking one of them.

Sloane stepped confidently into the room, her purse held in one hand and his other automatically falling to the small of her back. He didn't snap into the rigid military stance he'd been trained to do since he was six. He didn't stand before his sovereigns as a soldier.

He stood before them as Cecilia Warren's proud mate.

The captain rose. Gesturing to Cecilia and the sovereigns, he announced, "Cecilia, meet the sovereigns. Sovereigns, this is Cecilia Warren, Sloane's consort."

Theodore leaned back in his chair. Dark eyes narrowing, he drawled, "So this is the famous Cecilia."

"Um..." Cecilia sucked in a quick breath. He could almost see her putting on her shiny pink armor when she summoned a megawatt smile. In a voice he could only describe as *chipper,* she said, "It's, like, super nice to meet you."

Margot Goode arched her copper-colored eyebrows. "Is it true you punched Gibson?"

Cecilia's smile flickered for just a heartbeat before she answered in that sweet, fake voice, "What kind of arrant would punch an elf, ma'am? That'd be crazy."

Sloane's gaze flicked to the captain, who'd tipped his head back to look at the ceiling. To his credit, the orc had taken a lot in stride — helped significantly by Atria's heavy advocacy. Still, Cecilia's sudden fame amongst the ranks of Patrol and her subsequent hero worship within Fracture seemed to vex him on an existential level.

But for as exasperated as he was, Kazimier *liked* Cecilia. He was almost certain of it.

Sloane had discovered them deep in discussion about "compassionate positive incentives" and "no bullshit de-escalation techniques" more than once. Cecilia took the captain's taciturn nature in stride, just as she took everything else. It was impossible to *not* respect a woman who held herself so confidently in a room full of *them* and still managed to sparkle.

Theodore took a long look at the captain's exasperated expression and huffed. "I've heard a lot about you, Cecilia."

"That's kind of terrifying," she replied. "You know that, right? You've *got* to know that."

Margot covered her mouth, muffling a laugh. "She's right."

Theodore glanced sidelong at his consort. A dimple popped in his cheek when a slow smile crossed his face. "Fair enough. My apologies. I meant that I don't think I've ever heard an arrant's name whispered with so much awe in the halls of my tower. I like it."

"You do?"

"We do," Margot answered for him. "And we'd like to offer you a job."

Cecilia sent Sloane a frantic look. "Huh?"

Theodore rested his forearms on the desk. "Listen, with the… events of the past few weeks and the psychological assessment we've received from Dr. Starsbury, we — Captain Le Roy, my wife, and myself — have come to believe that your presence can be a stabilizing force within Fracture. You're trained. You're compassionate. More importantly, you're fearless. I don't think there's a member of Patrol in San Francisco who hasn't heard the story of the arrant who fought four elves with her bare hands to get back to her mate."

Sloane had to breathe deeply to lower his heart rate. He didn't want the bio alerts to go off in his helmet and make him miss this moment. If he could've, he would've engrained it into his memory forever. Every single word.

Cecilia gave the sovereigns and the captain a wide-eyed look of confusion. "You… want me to work for Fracture?"

"No," Margot answered.

Kazimier tucked a hand in his pocket and clarified, "We want you to *stay.*"

Margot folded her hands on top of her live edge desk. Offering Cecilia a warm smile, she said, "We personally reviewed your teaching application and passed it along to the Solbourne Nursery. If you're willing, the headmistress would like to interview you for a position."

"At the *elvish* nursery?" Cecilia blinked fast. "But… why? Don't only elves—"

"Nothing should be *only elves,*" Theodore cut in. "And it would be an honor to have you teach our young. We believe it would benefit everyone involved, and selfishly, we also think it will keep you close. We want to do everything we can to make your life with Fracture — and Sloane — a good one. For all our sakes."

"I…" She took a moment to gather herself. Looking down at the tips of her shiny boots, she pressed her lips together in a way he recognized meant she was working through something tricky. "That's… very kind, Sovereigns."

Margot gave Cecilia a searching look. "But?"

His consort glanced up from her boots. Her dark eyes glittered fiercely when she bit out, "No offense, but I don't need incentives to stay with Sloane or Fracture. I don't want special treatment, like they're some sort of burden you need to compensate for. They're *not.* They're people who deserve care. And friends. And love that isn't conditional. Respectfully."

The captain leaned his hip against the edge of Theodore's desk. Crossing his bulky arms over his chest, he grunted, "And that's why you're perfect for the job, Cece. Not because you deserve special treatment but because you are the best fucking fit for the first non-elvish teacher to work in the nursery."

"Our kids need you," Theodore pressed.

Margot tilted her head toward her husband. "We need you, Cece. We'd consider it a great favor if you'd put yourself on the line for us like this."

"You really don't pull punches, huh?" Cecilia dryly noted.

Margot wrinkled her pert nose. "Not really our style, I'm afraid."

"Yeah, well, mine either," she sighed. "I… will do the interview. But I'm serious about special treatment. If the headmistress doesn't think I'm a good fit—"

"Then you won't get the job," Theodore finished for her. "We understand, and believe me, *I* know you're serious."

Cecilia nodded. "Good. Thank you. And… thank you, I guess."

"You're welcome." Margot lifted her chin toward the door. "You can escape now. We won't hold it against you."

Cecilia tried hard not to look too relieved, but it came through loud and clear. Sloane's smile spread into a grin as he moved to guide her back out the door.

Ushering her out, he was stopped from following her by Theodore's low voice.

"Fortuner."

Sloane turned. "Yes, sir?"

The sovereign gave him a long look. The hair stood up on the back of Sloane's neck when the full weight of the sovereigns' combined authority pressed down on him. They watched him quietly, perfectly in sync, with the same solemn expressions — as if they were silently weighing his worth.

It was Margot who broke the heavy quiet. In her soft, terrifying healer's voice, she informed him, "You're the example, Sloane. Act like it."

He brushed his fingers down Cecilia's arm to blindly find her waiting fingers. "Yes, madam," he replied. "I will."

"You will," Cecilia whispered from the doorway. "I know it."

Accepting the sovereigns' nods, he followed his consort out the door — and anywhere she chose to lead him.

END

GRIM GAMES: THE NEW PROTECTORATE SYNDICATE: BOOK TWO

Tempting a vampire is a dangerous game.

He's there to settle a debt, not to be entangled in the seediest game United Washington's underground has to offer. But when the prize is a woman like Francesca Sinclair, Luis Amauri will do anything to win — even if that means he has to kill to do it.

She's offered herself up to a group of hungry vampires for a chance at a better life, but she's completely unprepared for the bloodshed she unleashes when the infamously depraved Amauri sets his sights on her. He'll do unimaginable things to sink his fangs into her, and he'll do even worse to keep her bound and sated in his bed forever.

His victory isn't the end of the nightmare. It's when the *real* game begins.

Pre-order Grim Games now!

ALSO BY ABIGAIL KELLY

Find all new releases, short fiction, comics, bonus chapters, and exclusive content on the Works by Abigail Patreon!

GRIM'S DELIGHT: THE NEW PROTECTORATE SYNDICATE: BOOK ONE

A bloody war nears its end.

Felix Amauri is the rightful heir to the most powerful vampire crime family on the continent. After years of taking out challengers to his claim, everything he's fought for is finally within reach — until one sloppy assassination threatens to ruin everything.

To be human is to be prey.

For years, the worst thing Dahlia McKnight could picture was becoming a vampire's toy. She never imagined that she'd witness a brutal assassination, let alone that she'd be turned in the process. One day she's a waitress, the next she's the sole heir to a vicious crime family embroiled in a war of succession and the target of an icy vampire prepared to do anything to take what he's owed.

He needs her for more than just her blood.

Learning to be a vampire is hard enough, but when it's discovered that she can carry another vampire's offspring, nothing will stop Felix from claiming her. If she wants to be more than just his plaything, it'll mean becoming the predator she was born to be.

Available in Kindle Unlimited, ebook, and paperback!

GLOSSARY

A full character directory and map can be found at Abigailkkelly.com

PLACES

United Territories and Allies: What we would consider the continental USA. A loose federation of sovereign states established after the Great War. The UTA capital is United Washington, in the Neutral Zone.

The Elvish Protectorate: Also known as the EVP. Stretches from Oregon to New Mexico. Capital city is San Francisco. Led by the elvish sovereign Theodore Thaddeus Solbourne and Margot Goode.

The Coven Collective: Also known as the Collective. Encompasses Washington state. Capital city is Seattle. Led by a large coalition of witch covens, with Sophie Goode acting as their leader.

The Orclind: Encompasses much of the Midwest. Led by the Iron Chain, a close-knit government made up of orcish clans and Queen Sigrid Seagrim. Capital city is Boulder.

Shifter Alliance: Takes up a section of the midwest and all of the south. (Unfortunately includes Florida.) Run by a very, very loose alliance of shifter packs from three capital cities — Minneapolis, Oklahoma City, and Atlanta. Unofficial leader is Lee Seymour.

The Draakonriik: Also known as the 'Riik. The second smallest territory, it takes up all of the Great Lakes region and stretches to New York. Led by Taevas Aždaja, the *Isand* (ee-zand) of the dragon clans. Pronounced: *dra-kon-reek*

The Neutral Zone: Also known as the New Zone. Technically it is held by a coalition government consisting of representatives from the UTA, but in reality it is run by a syndicate of feuding vampire families. It is a small strip of land squeezed between the Draakonriik and the Shifter Alliance.

GODS

Light & Darkness: The primordial gods who created all the others. Also known as The Lovers and First Union. Both are generally represented as female.

Loft: God of the sky and creator of flying beings. Twin sibling to Tempest. They know no gender. Also known as the Boundless One.

Tempest: God of the ocean and creator of all water beings. Also known as the Hungry God and the god of love.

Burden: God of the Earth, creator of all beings who live within it — most notably the orcs. Husband of Glory.

Glory: Goddess of sunlight, magic, and creator of elves. Worshipped by witches for giving the gift of magic to humanity.

Blight: God of forested places and disease. He works in partnership with his daughter Grim and shares her dominion over demons and all reviled creatures.

Grim: Goddess of death. Known as the Merciful One and the Brilliant Lady. She is widely beloved.

Craft: God of change, newness, and messengers. Creator of humanity and viewed warily by non-worshippers as the Chaos Maker. They change their gender frequently, but generally is referred to using he/him pronouns.

TERMS

Alpha: a broad term used by many communities generally associated with a leader — either of a small family group, a pack, or even a territory.

Anchor: a vampire's mate. Anchors are carefully chosen and usually longterm-to-permanent arrangements, as they take considerable energy to make/become. A vampire must inject their venom into a host many times before their blood chemistry adjusts such that they become unsuitable for consumption by another vampire and their sleep cycle switches to a nocturnal pattern. At this point, they can also produce/carry to term a vampiric child. Temporary anchors do exist, although they are relatively rare due to the intense withdrawal symptoms associated with ending the regular venom intake.

Arrant: someone born without m-paths, or the ability to channel and use magic.

Burnout: the colloquial name for the degenerative medical condition caused by excessive magic in humans. Over time magic can damage nerves and brain tissue, which will inevitably result in death if not treated with development of a witchbond.

Change: an elvish term for a sudden shift into adulthood. This is marked by 5-14 days of "madness", usually triggered by some stressful event around the age of 16-18. The elvish body is flushed with hormones to the point where sudden growth, overwhelming hunger, and aggression take over. Viewed as an incredibly vulnerable time, only immediate kin are charged with the care of their loved ones — which includes isolating them, preventing harm to themselves/others, and feeding them. The change marks the second phase of an elf's life, when they are no longer coddled children but young adults who can accept challenges and family responsibilities. Formal adulthood is attained at 30.

Changeling: a term first used to refer to fey children fostered out to non-fey homes, now more widely used to mean any person raised by people who are not the same beings. *Ex:* A dragon couple raising a human child.

Chosen: the formal term for a dragon's mate. The act of finding a mate is called *Choosing,* and is considered sacred.

Consort: an elvish mate. A term used exclusively by elves to refer to someone they are biologically compelled to pair up with. This usually involves intense sexual attraction, but can vary from person to person.

Demon: a being with horns or antlers, pointed ears, and symbiotic shadows. They are generally considered to be some of, if not *the* toughest beings in the world, as their shadows can make them almost indestructible. They are also naturally extremely strong and durable. Demon clans tend to be extremely close-knit, partially due to the fact that the world at large is not wholly accepting of them and their mythological connection to the god Blight. Identifying mating features are utter devotion, heightened protectiveness, and the sharing of shadows. This is when a mate is "given" a piece of the demon's symbiotic shadow, which will then live on that person for the rest of their life.

Dragon: a person with a dual form. In their bipedal form, they have claw-tipped wings, horns, and a tail. In their quadrupedal form, they are roughly the size of a standard SUV and can fly at extremely high altitudes for weeks at a time. They come in a variety of extremely saturated colors that shift with the time of day (light to dark). They breathe cold blue fire and can see the Earth's magnetic field. Identifying mating feature is marked change in behavior, including the overwhelming urge to nest.

Elemental: a being created by a spontaneous magical eruption. They often take on the attributes of whatever weather they happen to be born into, *i.e.* a lightning storm might produce a lightning elemental, or a blizzard might make a snow elemental.

Empath: a person with the ability to feel and manipulate the emotions of others.

Elf: someone born with jewel-toned skin, claws, pointed ears, and four fangs. Very secretive and considered apex predators who require a strict hierarchy to function. Average height of 6-7ft. Identifying mating feature is the retraction of claws.

Fever: shifter mating imperative triggered by the "animal's" choosing of a mate. Marked by a perpetual near-shift — elevated body temperature, increased aggression, build-up of magic, and the compulsion to mark. A shifter displays their readiness to find a mate by creating a den.

Fey: a person with nearly vestigial, insect-like wings, small fangs, and claws. Usually live in large groups. Identifying mating feature is bioluminescence.

Foresight: the ability to see multiple possible futures. The average number is between 2-4, with the likelihood mental instability increasing with each subsequent possible future.

Great War: a conflict between the territories of the North American continent that began in 1817 and ended in 1917 with the signing of the Peace Charter, which established the United Territories and Allies of modern times.

Halfling: the elvish term for an elf with mixed heritage.

Harpy: a being with bird-like wings and talons for feet. They live in family units called flocks and prefer to build nests high off the floor with access to open air. Culturally, they believe that aggression and competition are marks of a well-adjusted person. They are monogamous and fiercely possessive of their mates.

Healer: a person who possesses the ability to see into and heal bodies through touch.

Isand: the title of the leader of the Draakonriik. Pronounced *ee-zah-nd*

M- : M- is frequently used as shorthand to denote when something is infused or otherwise combined with a magical element.

Marriage Sigil: a custom symbol branded into the foreheads of spouses (pairs or multiples). Each one is unique and infused with a small amount of magic as a reminder of the power love holds. They are typically sought out by worshippers of Glory —

mainly witches and arrants. Elves, though worshippers, don't usually take a marriage sigil when they find their consorts or form a unions with other elves.

Mate: a catchall term for a significant other. Used by many cultures, it has varying degrees of weight. To shifters, orcs, and demons, the word mate is synonymous with family, monogamy, and dependence. It is much more loosely used within arrant society, as well as amongst elves, who generally prefer the term *consort.*

Merfolk: a catch-all term referring to sentient beings who live in the ocean, lakes, or rivers. Due to the nature of the ocean and its inhabitants, classifying all beings individually is almost impossible, so a much broader term is used to refer to both mammalian and non-mammalian beings than would be used for those on land.

Met: acronym for *magically enhanced tech.* A branded home assistant that can do everything your Alexa can, as well as small, low-level magic to help around the house.

Metallurgic Inoculation: a vaccine given to all elves within hours of birth to make them immune to iron poisoning.

M-siphon: a containment device used to imprison a magical being and siphon off their magic. Highly illegal.

M-lev: a play on *maglev,* meaning a high speed train that levitates using magnets. In this case, magnets *and* magic.

M-weather: magic weather. Very common, but can result in "clusters" or storms that wreak havoc if not properly contained. In rare circumstances, it can also produce a sapient being known as an *elemental.*

Nymph: a person who possesses a symbiotic mycelium that allows them to communicate with plants, hibernate beneath soil, and access the collective memories and experiences of those in their family line. Every nymph is part of a network known as a *hyphae,* and all hyphae are connected to the original.

Orc: a person with green, gray, russet, or blue skin, two fangs, and claws. Widely renowned for their strength and beautiful voices. Identifying mating feature is "the kohl", or altered, dark pigmentation of the hands and feet developed after meeting their mate.

Pixie: a small, winged creature with compound eyes with about the same level of intelligence as a rat. In the wild they live in trees and in burrows, but have adapted to living in walls, pipes, mailboxes, etc.

Pull: elvish mating imperative. A sudden hormonal shift caused by exposure to a compatible partner's pheromones, marked by the retraction of claws and volatile mood shifts. The pull is only "satisfied" when hormone binding occurs — the term for long term exposure to a mate, resulting in permanent biological dependence on their pheromones. This process increases fertility and often results in the conception of multiples. Lack of exposure to a mate can cause severe physical reactions (lack of appetite, muscle pain, headaches, insomnia) as well as the deterioration of mental stability.

R-siphon: also known as *reverse siphon.* New technology that redistributes magic away from the siphon instead of into it.

Shifter: a person who can shift into an animal form. They can partially shift (changing only parts of their bodies at will) and often take on characteristics of their other half. Famous for their strength and tenacity, as well as their dual-voiced "shifter purr" which many people find deeply attractive. Usually found in packs.

Sigil: a symbol used to channel magic. Western countries use the alchemical alphabet formally codified in the 1800's, though many, many variations are used all over the world.

Sovereign: the title of the ruler of the Elvish Protectorate. It is capitalized when used in place of a name.

Turbo Virgin (c): Theodore Thaddeus Solbourne, Sovereign of the Elvish Protectorate and Head of the Solbourne Family.

Union: an elvish marriage. Usually done for financial, political, or procreational benefit. The parties involved are not fated or biologically compelled to be with one another, and might have many lovers or even a consort outside of their union.

Vampire: a person who drinks blood to survive and cannot go out in sunlight. Vampirism can only be "caught" with the exchange of fresh blood, and as of 2045 is much more widely spread through procreation. Vampires can only breed with their *anchors.* Identifying mating feature is marked change in behavior, including overwhelming desire and need for total isolation.

Ward: a magical barrier with varying levels of protection. A ward can be something as simple as a proximity alert — "someone walked into my garden" — or as complex as full on defense — "someone crossed the threshold and has now burst into flames". The severity of the ward depends on the complexity of the sigils used to create them, and wards can have many layers, each one with a unique purpose. Personal wards can also be used, such as in clothing or embedded into jewelry, though they tend to be expensive and difficult to foolproof.

Were: a person infected with the were virus, a much mutated strain of the vampirism virus, resulting in altered physiology and magical ability. They can be identified by their heterochromia, or different colored eyes. They are the newest magical race and viewed warily by the general public for a variety of earned and unearned reasons. Identifying mating feature is marked change in behavior, including highly increased territorial instinct and the urge to nest. Pronounced *ware.*

Witch: Humans with the ability to use magic, which is passed down genetically. A person needs to be born with m-paths (a unique nervous system) to use it, however, humans were not initially adapted to use magic safely. Geneticists believe they acquired the ability through interbreeding with other beings. This interbreeding resulted in many unique qualities, such as the massive variety of abilities, power levels, and unique skills known to select families. However, it is also responsible for "burnout", which is the degenerative neurological condition a witch with mid-to-high level power will experience if they do not share their magical load with another being via witchbond. Witches are classified from least to most powerful — brightling, brilliant, and gloriana.

Witchbond: a magical bond formed between a witch and another being. Due to the nature of magic and humanity's much more recent adaptation to it, witches of *brilliant* and *gloriana* power must form a bond with another being usually beginning around 150-200 years old. This bond filters magic through the other being, neutralizing its damaging effects and reducing the chances of burnout to almost none. This bond also gives a power boost to the partner. A witchbond is permanent and can only be severed if one of the partners dies, at which point the surviving partner can form a new bond. Though commonly associated with a romantic partner, a witchbond is not inherently romantic and can be shared with a friend, sibling, or (ill-advised) an enemy.

Wraith: sentient shadow beings not dissimilar to elementals. They can affect the world around them in small ways, but can only speak to a very small number of demons. They lack physical forms but those that fully develop have complete sentience, personalities, and desires.

ABOUT THE AUTHOR

Abigail Kelly is a writer and illustrator of alternate histories, love stories, and women with drive. Her work is heavily influenced by both her modest family roots and her passion for history. Her favorite authors are Shirley Jackson, V. E. Schwab, Ursula K. Le Guin, Kresley Cole, Nalini Singh, and just about anyone who writes about the weird and wonderful.

She lives in San Francisco with her dog, Babs, who remains stubbornly illiterate.

CONTENT WARNINGS

Graphic violence, stalking, surveillance, toxic marriage (parents), blood, kidnapping, murder, captivity, virginity, vigilantism, needles, child abduction (past), family estrangement, military action, and explicit sexual content.

www.ingramcontent.com/pod-product-compliance
Lightning Source LLC
LaVergne TN
LVHW010642110826
845149LV00014B/2924

* 9 7 8 1 9 5 7 8 4 4 1 8 3 *